The Worst Generation

Generation

A Myopic Prosperity

T0095899

The Worst Generation

A Myopic Prosperity

Dan P. Greaney

Winchester, UK
Washington, USA

First published by Roundfire Books, 2016
Roundfire Books is an imprint of John Hunt Publishing Ltd., Laurel House, Station Approach,
Alresford, Hants, SO24 9JH, UK
office1@jhpbooks.net
www.johnhuntpublishing.com
www.roundfire-books.com

For distributor details and how to order please visit the Ordering section on our website.

Text copyright: Dan P. Greaney 2015

ISBN: 978 1 78535 466 3
Library of Congress Control Number: 2016935419

A CIP catalogue record for this book is available from the British Library.

Design: Stuart Davies

Printed and bound by CPI Group (UK) Ltd, Croydon, CR0 4YY, UK

We operate a distinctive and ethical publishing philosophy in all
areas of our business, from our global network of authors to
production and worldwide distribution.

For Yari and Wren, and all their generation

Introduction

Dear Dad,

The title of this book is incomplete. I began with a torrent of ideas: *Why I Loathe my Father. Why I Love my Father. Why I Can't Forgive my Father.* Those sorts of things. I'd finally settled on *Why I   my Father.* It seemed that readers could fill in the blank with almost any feeling and it would be true to my experience and possibly theirs, too.

My editor didn't like that, a title with a blank in it. So we argued around and I offered *The Worst Generation.* I didn't mean it as a damnation. Maybe it's just bad luck. But with all love, I thought and still think it's true.

Jennifer Alhouse

PS: You'll note that I've had to imagine many of these events and musings. My little fictions, I'd bet the farm, reveal the truth better than their omission would have.

Jen

But of course none of us has a farm, do we.

J

One

You were born Dennis Arlington Self in Pullup, North Dakota, in 1954, the fifth child of seven, and the second son. A sister, Margaret, died of the flu when you were five, and I know from my own experience that you often imagined her as a presence in your life. She was older, so you would have used her as a confidant. At age five you wouldn't have known her much in a conscious, memorable way, but you would have known that you were comfortable with her, that her presence meant a song or a game or a bedtime story. That she loved you and you loved her. No doubt you later embellished the relationship, put words and with them feelings to it. Certainly you would have had cause for such imaginings—your mother was no angel of comfort offering the vital sense of love. But embellished or not, I'm sure your sister was sweet to you. *That* you were old enough to know. When I asked—only when I asked—you described Margaret, "Maggie," as an angel, kind and good humored. So if you did later enhance her compassion, only imagining it as greater than that of the dogs on the farm, she was still an important character in your life. The dogs were your father's. Maggie was yours. Your family farmed wheat, durum wheat. And it was a family project, each of you with your chores, whether driving the tractor or baking the bread or gathering eggs. Your family, with a sprinkling of similar families from South Road to Crow, from Sioux to Buffalo, and then out beyond them, far, far in every direction, with just the houses and barns and silos poking up here and there, it was all wheat, waving heads that rippled like an ocean. Your brother Jake told you that durum was the amber waves of grain in the song.

But it was Maggie who sang the song with you, when she was alive and later in your memory, and it was she who made the barns and farmhouses into ships floating on those amber waves.

3

Maggie was the muse of your youth, and since she was dead you could shape her into whatever image you wanted. She sang, she wondered. She loved the black earth and the melting of snow and the croaking of the geese V'ing across the sky, and the spring chorus of frogs that roared from every channel of spring water as loud as hail on the roof; and so you loved them, too. But finally those important sentiments seemed to be shared only between you and her, which means, then, they were only in you. She was dead, and you alone could not sustain or deepen the vision. Her star faded, and school and television and the farm became your consciousness. You stopped noticing the frogs and the buntings, or seeing much beyond the colloquial games of adolescence and the work of growing wheat. You should have seen farther, surrounded there on the plains by life and death and hope and horror, but nobody brought you to tears over the buffalo. Maggie probably never knew about the Sioux, and nobody else told you their story, or that Crow didn't mean a bird. The words were empty, so how could they fill your soul?

Poor you, really. How could you weep for the Plains or against the poisons just then taking over the fields and the farmers, when the meaning of the words was kept so thin: DDT kills the bugs that eat the wheat; that was the limit of your understanding. That was the limit perpetrated on the farms and the nation. There was no cultural consciousness, much less childhood tearing, for the mother meadowlark feeding her babies poisoned bugs gathered from the wheatfields. *Silent Spring* came along, but it was not taught in the North Dakota high schools, and happened slowly enough that one person's life scarcely saw it. When other poisons replaced DDT—except for the canister in the barn that your dad still used for rats that made it into the attic, or mice in the kitchen drawers—the subject was considered closed. And neither was there a vision of the change from family farms to agribusiness. Maybe a kid like you never had a chance.

Every spring you planted with Uncle Jake and your father,

and every fall you harvested. That was the life you knew and came to love, and any reality that challenged that simple beauty had to be disregarded or denied. Life and living were too wonderful to allow that there might be ugly changes weaving into it, threatening it. That wonderful was losing its wonder.

What plainly could not be disregarded was your place as the second son.

"Now, Dennis," your father told you out in the barn one summer evening, "I want you to learn this business. But you have to know. I can't split the farm, it wouldn't pay. You understand? So when I'm gone, well if anything were to happen to Jake I'd be happy for you to take the place. So I hope you'll be ready. It's not an easy living, but it's a good one."

The rule was pragmatism, not poetry, and you didn't need to be told twice. You had no special ill will toward your brother, no Cain against Abel or Jacob against Esau. Jake was older and that was that. As for being ready, I'm sure you felt you knew how it operated, at least in the field if not in the bank; you lived there, after all. But an accident that would throw the farm to you? Jake was your big brother, invincible. With no shrug at all you tried to do well in the alternative to the family farm, school.

That was no easy undertaking. In schools today it is generally considered the job of the teacher to ensure the learning of the students. Back then, at least in North Dakota, it was considered the job of the students to learn. Not their parents' job, either. The students'. So you and your classmates, except for eldest sons, were on the hook.

That much I'm sure was an advantage. But you, Dennis, had a disadvantage, too. Your parents had probably never heard of "Dennis the Menace" when they named you. The comic strip only debuted in 1951, and probably hadn't reached Pullup by '54. But by the time you were in school you could not avoid the tag, and when you were in the intermediate grades several students had bulky green televisions in their homes and "Dennis" was a popular feature. Teachers no doubt tried to overlook the elementary stereotype, but there it was, waiting for you at every misstep.

One time in fifth grade—the teacher was even a Mrs. Wilson, wasn't she? Good thing for you it wasn't *Mr.*! You had to turn in a paper on the circulatory system, which to you and probably Mrs. Wilson, too, was an incomprehensible and queasily irksome maze of tubes and arrows in the school encyclopedia, with no known rhyme or reason. You gently plagiarized an attempt to show understanding, but arrived late to turn it in. It was spring and you were planting, so the tardiness was endured, albeit with a frown from Mrs. Wilson over her skinny little glasses, those blue-framed wingtips. She told you to turn in the paper "Late" there on the desk. You put it on the top of the pile, your pencil-scratching right over Virginia's paper that had a tidy diagram in red and blue on it; but your sleeve caught Mrs. Wilson's pen, she had it tilted forward, and it tipped the inkwell that she insisted on retaining as a protest against the modernization that her family had missed when her grandfather in Wisconsin had failed to invest in his friend George Parker's fountain pen. The whole stack of reports was drowned in ink. Totally ruined, a sopping mess, from your paper to Virginia's and on down, everything. After their initial gasps all your classmates were fine with the accident, although they still abused you for it, because Mrs. Wilson decreed that others shouldn't suffer for your clumsiness. Everyone else was excused from the assignment. You had to rewrite yours. Dennis the Menace got his due.

The list of your foibles grew. Anybody else might have an inkblot on his paper, or play hooky, or run his sister's bra up the flagpole, or throw up on the secretary's desk, but those offenses were overlooked or grimaced away. For you they were labeled, named like an animal in the Bible or a pop-culture meme, so people could notice them, confirm their prejudice, and just naturally identify you with Nuisance. It wasn't fair, but that's the way it was. Maybe it made you tough, or might have given you a sense of humor, I don't know. The name Dennis and being the second son both. They were things to overcome. You say that if it doesn't kill you it makes you stronger. I think you believed that from right back then.

There was plenty that made you stronger, only some of which threatened your life or limb. You might have gone into the hardware business. Fred Harkin owned the True Value Hardware in Pullup, and he must have been a neighborhood's dream. He taught you practical skills—how to drive a nail, or wax a sticky door, or just figure technical problems out—that gave you confidence when it came time to go out on your own. One time your mom wanted a ceiling fan, and it couldn't go in the kitchen because the ceiling was too low, but you could put it over the stairwell, just off the kitchen. Your dad gave that job to you and Jake. Well, you didn't know anything about wiring up a fan! You could have electrocuted yourselves and burned the whole house down! But Mr. Harkin talked you through it all. It took you a few hitches between home and the store to answer his questions—you knew where the fusebox was, but you couldn't agree on whether they were two-by-fours or two-by-sixes under the ceiling. Turned out they were fours. And I don't know if you could still do it all now, even by the rough standards you must have had then, but you had to learn: you had to shut down the power main and put in a new fuse—you didn't have circuit-breakers, did you—and you had to run the wires parallel to the framing boards, just so they'd look better; you could tack them up along the framing and they'd pretty much disappear. And Mr. Harkin showed you how to connect the wires at both ends, with caps and black tape, and how to build a frame to hold the fan—that had to be hard because you had to hold up the fan, over your head, while Jake attached it to the frame, and you didn't have power drills back then. No wonder you were muscled when Mom met you! And even if your construction wasn't up to modern standards, with a fan flush against a textured drywall ceiling, it fit with the older, rougher construction of your house growing up. Your parents could be proud of you, even if your mom wouldn't show it.

And Mr. Harkin kept it to just a pull-chain for the power, so you didn't have to run wires down to a wall switch, where you couldn't have hid them so well.

He helped his customers out. Good customer service, as you'd say now with hollow praise. He loaned your dad tools sometimes. When you hired a plumber once and he was wrenching something under our sink you told him about a pair of rusty old pipe wrenches that he loaned your dad. You thought they must have been at least four feet long, and your dad had to dig a whole crater to have room to turn them. You bet he loaned those out a hundred times, and never even thought to sell them. You kind of got quiet after saying that, and I know what you were thinking, that Mr. Harkin wasn't being a good businessman.

But he wasn't the only one who was a good neighbor to you. You were part of a small town, and everyone helped out. Butler's Grocery would take credit, just a tab, especially in the weeks before harvest. Everyone was on the Volunteer Fire Department. If anybody got sick, neighbors would bring food to the house, just to help out. You could always hitch into town and back; it was rare the first car by didn't pick you up. It was a small town. It was then. You liked it.

But you didn't stick with it. Of course you weren't immune to the larger world. It was North Dakota, but it was the '60s, too, and even in North Dakota you saw the national turbulence. Some of it you were insulated from; but some of it you just were.

When Kennedy was shot you felt invaded. Everybody liked Kennedy, even if they hadn't voted for him. Your dad hadn't, and did your mom ever vote? You had an old Admiral radio with a telescoping swivel antenna about two feet long and just two dials, one for power and volume, and one for tuning. You like that two-knob style much more than the stereos and MP3 players that we have now that still make you fuss and gripe, "You have to read a manual just to play a song!" You always left that old antenna up, and just rotated the radio around to get the best reception. You liked your dad liking it, thinking he'd made a good buy because it had a pop-up handle that made it easy to rotate even while he held a cup of coffee in the other hand. When Kennedy was shot you had the volume up, and your parents' faces turned stunned and gray. "What's the world coming to?' your mom said, shaking her head, as if no one had ever been assassinated before. But maybe no one had in her lifetime, not since McKinley, wasn't it? And then when Jack Ruby shot Lee Harvey Oswald, well at first that got them mad. Your dad clenched, "There goes America! No respect for the law, for due process!" But then later he latched onto the conspiracy theories, and until the day he died he believed that Ruby was covering up a Commie plot. Lots of people still believe that, don't they. I wonder what stupid things we believe. There's no guarantee against stupidity, is there.

You were only eight then, so your memories are sketchy. Vietnam and Civil Rights appeared, mostly as uncomfortable words. You got a TV in 1963, and you'd never seen a black person before, so you were just washing that down, wondering what it felt like to have black skin, was it cooler than white skin? You weren't really hearing about a Dream or anything. You couldn't get that then. You couldn't really get that there was a problem, and certainly couldn't get why there should be one. You were just a kid. They say it takes generations to rebuild from wrongs like slavery, and I'm sure that's true. To you back then, King Jr. had a sing-song in his voice that was different from your reverend's, and your dad kind of scowled, and so you kind of did, too. I understand that. It was later that you should have learned more of what mattered.

But the thing on the TV that hit you most back then was

Vietnam. Or not Vietnam but all the angry young people in college. It was all foreign to you. To you the police were the good guys, and when all those people, Americans not much older than you, were shouting at them, and holding signs and throwing rocks and getting arrested, it didn't seem right. What were they doing but breaking down the rules of a decent society? They seemed wrong. I think you still believe that. You resent government regulation, but you don't approve of street demonstrations, either. Changes should be properly made in the board room and the halls of Congress, not out in the streets.

You felt you were patriots, your town, the county, the state. At your school things were kept decorated with red, white, and blue bunting, and you pledged the flag every morning, right through high school. When anyone talked about it, it was how you could support your country. Your friend Phil Ostrander, the one you called Outlander, like all of you he registered for the draft. But then after graduation he drove up to Canada. "I don't want to go kill people," he told you. You said, "But they're commies, and your country's asking you to." It was after track practice. You were a sprinter, 10.9 in the hundred; he was a miler, under five minutes. Probably pretty good back then, both of you. Anyway, he had a car from his parents, his parents' car, and he always gave you a lift home after practice. He shook his head about the country asking him to fight. "Part of my country is. But it's the wrong part. Nobody's attacking us, Dennis. We're over there. And we're killing people." "You're chicken," you told him, but he shook his head again, "Nope. We're trying to force our way of life on them, and it's wrong. Even if our way of life was good it'd be wrong, but you know what our way of life is? It's money. We need those people to buy our products, that's why we're there. We did it in the Philippines and in Cuba, in Korea, wherever we could in South America—heck, we stole a piece off Colombia to create Panama when we wanted a canal to ship our goods. It's all so we can sell stuff. And we call it progress and enlightening the

10

backward heathens, but you know what? They've got to sell their own stuff, and we're just bullying ours at them. So we get rich and they get broke. We're red, white, and bully, that's what we are."

It was your turn to shake your head. "I don't know where you get your ideas, Outlander." But that was all you could say, because you didn't know anything. You liked Outlander. And you could excuse him some, because his parents had been to school somewhere. That was rare back then, it seemed.

Anyway, Outlander drove his parents' car into Canada, doubtlessly with their approval. And afterwards he came back. But you were gone by then.

You didn't really know what you were leaving. North Dakota. Sky as blue as Maggie's eyes, or Penny's, too, or Mom's. Penny was your high-school sweetheart. She was—well, you liked her! But you could see she was rooted in the prairie deep like the old sod, and I guess you weren't. She no doubt stayed and made somebody a good farmwife. Bore him lots of little blue-eyed babies, and dressed them up in overalls, and yellow frocks for the girls, all cute and clean. Baked apple pies with criss-cross tops and chaperoned at the school socials. Penny fit her time and place. Married a local boy, no doubt, probably someone you knew. Do you think he treated her right? Better or worse— different from how you treated Mom, don't you think?

Anyway. North Dakota. In winter, laundry on the line would freeze and then your pant legs would clunk together in the wind like those wooden chimes. But out past the laundry line and the garden there was space. *Wheat and sky, food for your eye.* No end to it, every direction. And spring was pretty as a meadowlark, and the ducks would find the potholes, and lay their eggs, and sometimes the coyotes and the kids'd steal 'em, but then you learned to hunt, and you learned how pretty the birds are, close up. Even the females, who are mostly smooth soft browns, while the males are colored like calliope heaven, with bronzes and burgundies, iridescent greens, blue wingpatches. Beautiful! Take-your-breath-away beautiful! There were lowlands nearby where you could find them nesting.

And winter'd do that, too, take your breath away. Winter'd sing to you, call to you like sin or the wilderness, as pretty as death or the Milky Way, out there in the cold and dark and lonesomeness. And sometimes you'd court her just a little, looking at her stars and emptiness, maybe with a bottle to help out. But as long as you didn't get stupid you'd get back inside before you wandered too long. Get inside, get a job, find a girl like Penny and build a house around her; that was the idea! In North Dakota you knew your place in the world: small. That's what you were, small in a big grand universe. But small didn't make you helpless. It made you important. You mattered to all those other small people with you. Your work mattered. And you valued the land, because it was beautiful and it was life, your livelihood. You breathed the air, and it was life, too, even if it stung your lungs with the cold. It was dry air, and that was right for the durum, so it was right for God and you, too, all the small people who mattered. Your English teacher Mrs. Aronsen said that North Dakota must be the most patriotic place at the ends of the day, because the wheat turned red, the clouds glowed white, and the sky held blue. And even if it didn't really do that all at once, you always saw it that way because she'd said it. And she told you you had to see things right in North Dakota, because as North Dakota went, so went America. And as America went, so went the world.

Not all your teachers were poets like Mrs. Aronsen, but there were other ways to be good. You chuckled over Mr. Falcoff. "Maybe you can imagine what we called him behind his back. We were immature, didn't mean anything by it, we actually liked him pretty much." Mr. Falcoff was your business teacher, and as old as the prairie, or at least as the farms cut into it. And he understood that not all of you were going into farming, but he tried to teach something more basic. The product, he said—durum or corn or typewriters—what the product was didn't matter. What mattered was that it was quality. He taught you about goods and services, and either one could be your product, whether it was threshing or banking or taxi-driving, all services, but just like the wheat they were a product. And what mattered, Mr. Falcoff said, was that your product was good. That it "did a right thing, and did it right." He said that there was a new idea out called 'planned obsolescence,' but don't buy into it. He said it's the idea that you make a trashy product so customers will have to come back and buy a new one from you. Don't buy into it, he said. It'll ruin America.

I know you don't think Mr. Falcoff was the smartest businessman around. He was pretty off the mark, in your view. But I also know you valued him because he treated you with respect, like you mattered, and it helped you grow up, even if it couldn't protect you from yourself and your chums.

But even back then, of course, not everyone was good. Your mom as you've pictured her was a nagging old biddy, the worst. "People always think they had the greatest mom in the world, that nobody could be as loving and hard-working and kind and understanding as their mom, even if maybe she didn't totally understand them. My mom was none of that." Oh, she was fine as long as times were fat, as long as you didn't listen to her too closely. But she was always running you down. Especially Trudy.

Trudy was the second oldest, right behind Jake. Of all of you, she was the slow one. She didn't quite catch things. Your mom was always on her. "No, you ironed the wrinkles in again!" She'd throw in that *again*. "Gertrude, you've spilled half the dinner on the stovetop, and the other half's burned! Get out of the kitchen! I don't know how I'm going to feed this family!" Or, "Who did the sweeping? It must have been Trudy, there are streaks all over the floor!" Or after the Christmas play, with all you kids there she thanked Mrs. Tollafsen for letting Trudy have a bit role that let her be a part of it without screwing it up. "Oh, don't thank me! Trudy's wonderful!" Mrs. Tollafsen gushed. "Don't you think I know better than that?" your mom replied. She was just mean. Poor Trudy did her best, but eventually she quit trying. She quit school after eighth grade and got a job caretaking a widow in town. She finally started doing OK there, away from Grandma, and eventually got married and had kids. Her husband beat her, though. And you blame the guy of course, but you blame your mom, too, for teaching Trudy "that she was crap."

Poor Aunt Trudy.

You explained, "You know, you can do some razzing, like I took it for being Dennis the Menace. But I was strong, and it wasn't coming from my mom from the time I was old enough to hear. I don't know if Mom saw Trudy, the oldest girl, as a threat. I mean, my dad was good, but I don't know what old history there was in Mom's family, so maybe she saw Trudy as a threat and she attacked it. I don't know. I never met her family and she didn't talk about them. 'They're all dead,' she said, and we didn't ask again. Or maybe Trudy was really just slow, but I can't tell that because I was younger, and also, you do start to see things the way you're told they are, and Trudy, well, you start to act things the way you're told you are, too. Trudy never had a chance."

Your mom was mean to everyone, it seems. Your poor dad. Every day he was up in the cold and dark and working steadily until it was cold and dark again. And every night at dinner she'd have something to dig at him for. "Your faucet's leaking again. You must not have fixed it right," or "The tomatoes don't have flavor; it's probly that manure you brought in last year," or "You smell! Can't you do something about that?" "You slurp your food like an animal! How can you stand yourself!" "This coffee's not good, but we can't afford better on what you bring home." Or often as not if he'd put on a radio show in the evening and close his eyes to listen she'd interrupt, "Didn't you hear that dog?

Something's out there. Go look!" And he'd maybe heave a sigh or maybe not, but hoist himself up and step outside. Once you snuck out back and watched him. The dog, Henrietta, stretched up from where she was curled quiet on the porch, and she licked his hand, and they went for a slow walk. Sometimes he'd stay out a good while, and I'm sure he loved that quiet dark sky, soothing as sleep. But eventually he'd come back in. Not because of the cold, although that had to have helped; but the responsibility he lived by, not like some men. He'd come in and go to bed so he could get up in the morning. And not because the bed would have had any special attraction, either. From what you say that must have been a pretty cold place, too, even before they were done making children. I think your mom was damaged, and she couldn't have fun right, and she couldn't handle others having fun without her. Even if they were people she wanted to care for.

In the late sixties your dad must have gotten some bad seed. Every winter, back to the time *his* father started using hybrid seed, he borrowed to buy the seed and pay for the crop duster. Every fall he'd sell the harvest and pay the bills. That year he just owed.

At dinner your mom plunked a bowl of soppy pasta on the table. No sauce or salad, although there was plenty in the garden that could have dressed it up, and the chickens were doing fine, too. "There's your dinner. Your father's not making any money this year." Nobody said anything, and your mom filled the silence. "He's got three hundred and twenty acres and can't bring in a bushel of wheat. Some men'd be ashamed to let their families starve. Not him. He just shrugs. Look at him there, not a word to say, just a lump of coal, worse than coal 'cause he won't give heat. Your father, I'm sorry." And your dad was looking down and if he'd felt stronger maybe he'd have said, "Martha," and maybe she'd have stopped, but he was down, that was when she'd kick him, and he just pushed back his chair—it slid quietly because he'd tied leather socks on all the chairs' feet so they wouldn't scratch the floorboards—and he stood up without looking at her or any of you and stepped outside. The door closed, but you could hear Henrietta scuffle to him.

So, yeah, your mom was a bully. A needy bully, like all the ones I've met. You got as far as, "Mom just didn't know how to be nice. She had a home and a garden and normal kids and a patient, decent husband, but she couldn't just accept good enough and maybe put a ribbon on it." *Accept good enough.* If I'm right, and she was hurt, maybe on the order of what you guessed around Trudy, at least she had an excuse. I don't see yours. In fact you made *accepting good enough* a weakness, a failure.

There was no reason for you to stick around in Pullup after high school. Your mom was insufferable, and Jake would take the farm. Several of your friends were leaving. Lots of them had older brothers and were just like you, young bucks off to make their way in the world. And the ones who were the older brothers, well they had their lives laid out for them, plain as stripes on the flag. The girls left, too, but not Penny Sorensen. She would stay; she wasn't cut out for what you were. Maybe if you'd been the older son that whole scene would have been different—you and Penny and the farm and North Dakota—and I, your daughter, would have been unconceived and inconceivable, a creature of an alternate universe only. But you did leave, and so shaped our universe for better or worse.

Outlander kind of got you going, too. Outlander, ahead of his time. He hadn't driven to Canada yet, but he wasn't high on the Mom, apple pie, and the girl-next-door idea, either. Even if his mom was at least decent. "I don't want to be part of the money machine," he said. "What is it? It's just take whatever you can. Doesn't matter if it ruins a country or a culture. It's not just the US, I know. People have done it ever since two tribes lived in the same valley, hell, ever since two brothers lived in the same valley, if you believe Cain and Abel. And in the US? Old Sam Adams was no patriot! He was a business failure who drummed up the Boston Massacre with his buddy Paul Revere, and after the Revolution when he'd made his gold he wanted to cut the rights of the common rabble. That's our hero! And the New World wanted cheap labor, so what did they do? They paid businessmen to kidnap people from Africa and they kept them as slaves, and bought and sold their children. And they wanted more land, so what did they do? They killed the Native Americans and took it. Hey, George, come here!" George was an Indian in your class. "George, tell him what happened to the Dakota people." George sighed, he was a quiet guy. "He knows what happened to the Dakota," he said. "Tell 'im," Outlander insisted. George stared at you flatly and said, "We got screwed." But that wasn't enough for Outlander. "Railroads and hunters— no more buffalo. Fort Laramie Treaty, 1851 – Three Tribes' land cut to twelve million acres. Homestead Act, 1910 – Three Tribes' land cut to 3 million acres. Then more cuts, under a million acres. Then Garrison Dam, 1953 – flood a fifth of what's left." He paused briefly. "And it wasn't just any acres that were flooded. It was the riverside soil, the richest. And flood control? Whose floods? The white and wealthy farmers downstream, that's whose! For the tribes there was no control about it." He snorted. "Sorry, George." George shrugged and turned away. He was a pretty solid guy, George, but you lost sight of him. What do you think he's doing now? Outlander continued. "And that's how it always goes, Menace! Next I'm sure we'll find gold or coal or oil on their land. That's how it always goes." He snorted. "And we went and carved US presidents into their sacred hills!" He shook his head. "I'm not saying, Dennis, that it's just the US. I'm sure the old Indians did their atrocities, too, and out in history Fidel and the commies and the black tribes in Africa. I'm sure they've all been bastards. So it's not just the US, it's Power. But we're the coming generation, we have the Power now! So what are we going to do with it? We can be bastards with it, like most of history is, or we can be decent. We can try to treat others with respect, and that's what I want to do. I don't need to go kill people in Vietnam or anywhere else. It doesn't work.'

"You're running away," you told him, but he said No, he was just trying to keep away from killing people. "Look at the great leaders," he said. "Gandhi, Jesus, the Buddha. They didn't go around killing people, or subjugating them at all. They taught peace, love, self-composure. Jesus died rather than fight! Listen, you remember Aronsen: Hamlet asked whether 'tis nobler to suffer the slings and arrows of outrageous fortune or to take arms and by opposing end them. Well these guys said *Suffer!* And you could argue against them if taking up arms really did end the slings and arrows, but it doesn't. It just does another round of them."

"You can say that," you told him. "But it doesn't work when the invader comes with his gun at you."

"And that's why I don't want to go to Vietnam," Outlander answered. "It's one of those *near occasions of sin.* You know, sin no more and avoid the near occasions of sin? If I went there I'd probably have to make an ugly choice. But I don't have to put myself in that situation."

So you weren't going to hang with Outlander, and the farm and with it Penny was gone, and Maggie was buried and forgotten; so you were bound to head out, too. Your dad and Jake both shook your hand, and when Grandpa looked you in the eye it felt good. He respected you and you respected him, you always had. He was a good, hard-working man. You hugged your mom goodbye, too, and there was feeling, in spite of yourselves. But some of those feelings get all tangled up, and you were not the guy to spend your time untying knots. So you said your goodbyes and left. You never looked back.

You were the newest entrepreneur, the newest member of the uprooted populace of our immigrant nation, our emigrant nation, unburdened by community, ready to shape the world. You headed down to the Big City, to Chicago, and got in on retail with Samson's. It was a small chain, later bought out by one of the pharmacies, maybe Woolworth's; but you understood how to help a customer and track inventory, too, so pretty soon your boss moved you to shift manager, and then he told you to go get a degree. So you applied to the university, and that opened your eyes and threw stars in them, or a glint of gold that you mistook for stars. Some of your studies seemed like a load of words that who cared about, but most of it struck home and taught you things that have carried you through your whole career, and I guess that means launched me on mine, too. It was the idea of the Free Market. Ever since the Depression, people had felt that government should regulate the market to prevent its erratic destructiveness, but the University of Chicago re-awakened belief in the market, the Invisible Hand that Adam Smith talked about, that guided the economy to function best without government interference, or almost none. You were, just by accident, at the cutting edge of the revived philosophy, which really was an economic and political worldview more than a business one, but it seemed to support business. So by the time Ronald Reagan said Government is the problem, that's what you in the Chicago business world had been struggling toward for years. And Clinton, even though he was a Democrat, kept it going, and of course the Bushes.

But now, Dad, with the Great Recession, the Free Market has floundered again, and people are talking Keynes and regulation again. You think it's a shame. "But it'll lose—it's losing already," you say.

But that is later. First you met Mom down in Florida.

Two

You and Mom met on spring break in Miami. Let me tell it as she might have:

Oh, yes, spring break! Don't raise your brows, dear. Back then it was all very innocent. We didn't have the kinds of problems you have today. Oh, we had weed, I suppose—I mean, I didn't, your father didn't, but it was there. But we didn't have, you know, the drugs and problems you do today. We didn't have people we knew losing their homes and people from good homes having children kidnapped from a bus stop; and so many people on welfare, or Mexican children coming over the border. And it goes on and on, doesn't it! A president you can't trust! I don't even remember who we had at the time. And you have AIDS, and what's that new one, Ebola. We didn't have those problems! Society was more...settled. Oh, the black people and hippies had raised a ruckus, but that died down after the sixties. We were beginning a time of calm, we could enjoy life.

And Miami was a nice place to enjoy it, I can tell you that! I wore a two-piece bathing suit. It was pink and white, a flower print I'm sorry to say. We hadn't learned to wear a solid color that would show off our tans. That came later. But I would have worn that well! I had a figure.

But it was an innocent time. My friends and I, there were four of us girls, high-school friends. We were all at Shipley, and now Vickie and Cathy were at Bryn Mawr, Jeanette was at Penn State, and I was the only one going to school out west. Vickie's father owned the beach-house in Miami, so we were in like Flynn.

I remember when I first saw your father. We were all suntanning, with the smell of Coppertone all over us, and I do tan pretty well, if I say so myself. He was jumping in the waves, kind of like the farmboy he was, but not awkward, either, just unfamiliar. He didn't have proper trunks though. He was wearing some ridiculous striped shorts, maroon and yellow. But they did that then. And in spite of it, out on the beach, honey, your father cut a pretty handsome figure. All those years lifting hay bales hadn't hurt him any. There wasn't a better-looking boy on the beach.

Well, and the girls and I weren't bad-looking ourselves. Vickie and I went down to play in the waves, she was a little pudgier than me, and when I was running from one I happened to nearly bump into your father.

So that was how we met. We were both in love right from the start. And the timing was so good, with us both getting ready to graduate!

I'm not going to tell you all the details. You are our daughter, after all! But we kept in close touch with letters every week or more, and he'd call sometimes. You know, long distance was expensive back then, not like your Facebook today.

And there were plenty of boys at school, but none that had your father's combination of self-reliance and good looks. I was majoring in sociology, so I could judge. And he had a North Dakota farm, too, although that never panned out, of course.

We both graduated and he moved out to California. I was at UCLA, did I mention? And with him coming I just stayed there, in L.A. My parents had flown out for graduation, of course. PanAm. I'd found a job with the county, Los Angeles County, and they got me set up in an apartment. And they bought me a car, which I needed. I hadn't needed it as a student because everything was on campus and friends had cars for anything else. But now I needed it, so it was a graduation present.

That's a bigger expense these days, dear, so I hope you appreciate it! Mine was a pale blue Chevrolet convertible. What would a car like that cost now, thirty thousand dollars? As much as a house back then!

What was I saying? So yes, a week later, after my parents left,

Dennis arrived, all graduated and cocky as a Vegas cardsharp. None of that maroon and yellow striping! He was dressed like the businessman he was, now with his degree. A button-up shirt, ecru, and short sleeved for the weather, and dark pants over brown leather shoes. Casual but professional. I hadn't told my parents about him except vaguely, but then I was wishing they were still there, especially my dad, because I knew they'd have liked him. But that just had to wait. He rented an apartment just down the street from mine, so he could walk back after taking me home in the evening. And we used our time, I can tell you! In the next seven months I think we must have eaten at every restaurant in Los Angeles County, and on weekends we drove every highway from the San Gabriels to Santa Monica, with the top down and the wind blowing. One time the wind blew my sunglasses off, and he insisted on buying me a new pair at the next drugstore. I think he started the stylish sunglasses craze, because he wanted to get me these awful ovals with tortoiseshell frames, and I didn't mind the frames but I wasn't going to wear those eggs, I wanted rounder lenses. So I picked out a pair. He bought both the eggs and the rounders—no, I wouldn't be caught dead in them now, but back then the styles were different! Then a few days later I saw some skinny ones that looked like Geordi's glasses in *Star Trek Next Generation*—oh, you don't know him?— well, skinny sunglasses that curved around, and I bought those for him. He thought they made him look like a Hollywood producer; Geordi wasn't around yet. Then he bought me some rose-colored ones, and I bought him some really dark ones, "so I'll always be in the black," he said. They really were too dark. He couldn't see out of them very well. But we bought lots of silly sunglasses—moon and star shapes, and pince-nez, and some with a Groucho nose and mustache. It was all just fun.

He got a job at the US First Savings and Loan, and not a teller job. He was a loan officer. That changed later, and don't ask me what it became, all sorts of things. I never did understand it all, and I still don't. But I know he didn't wear his goofy sunglasses at work, although he did see black, honey! Everything he touched turned to gold! Midas!

My job was hard, though. You know, they talk about single mothers. Honestly, it's always been that way dear, you haven't lost much. Fathers don't raise the children, mothers do. But the fathers still brought home a paycheck back in my parents' day, and that started falling apart with divorce becoming so popular about the time I started working. I can't imagine working once you and Stevie came along! But I did then.

Gloria was my supervisor. She was very nice, gray hair that she wore done up in a beehive, and pantsuits. Always meticulous, with cinnamon nails that she never let chip or grow out, and bittersweet lipstick that was always exact. I learned a lot from her, although I've never liked that hairstyle, for me I mean. Our office helped these women either track down their deadbeat husbands for child support or else get social security. Gloria said that it was a change in clientele; that she used to get pretty much just physical-abuse cases. Now it seemed the husbands just left, she said. "All we can do is find what's best for them and do that," she said. She'd been beaten herself, way back in her teens. That's how she got into social work.

It was a little depressing, but not that bad because without good public transportation our office wasn't easy for these women to get to, so we weren't that busy.

We both worked, but we saw each other all the time we weren't working, and I felt like he was working himself up to something, and I was ready, but Christmas came and went and it was a month later I could see something still on his mind.

"What're you thinking on, Dennis?" I asked him.

He'd developed a little bit of a swagger, a businessman's bluster, but he didn't show it then. He was sort of hang-dog, and he said, "The S&L wants me to move up to San Francisco."

"Oh."

"It's not a bad thing. That's the corporate office."

"Oh. Well they'll pay you more then."

"Oh! Maybe!"

"You hadn't thought of that?"

"No. I mean yes, but it's not what I was thinking about."

Then it dawned on me that he was worked up about us. Well, us being together almost went without saying; I hadn't stumbled over it at all, but I was raised in a more cosmopolitan world than Dennis was. The poor farmboy didn't understand that we could easily move together, that we were in the age of the automobile!

I played it coy. "Oh. Yes, I suppose you'll have to figure that out." Just to let him know that I understood his problem but wasn't presuming anything, even though I knew well enough where we were going that he hadn't figured out yet.

So he waited until Valentine's Day to propose. He was very sweet, you know. The pier in Santa Monica wasn't in its prime, then. The city was just figuring out how to rebuild it with the whole new amusement park, Pacific Park that came later. But still it was beautiful at sunset. We had dinner and then walked the shoreline, and there were just enough clouds to catch some golden fuchsia after the sun went down, and the softest breeze came off the sea. The waves were gentle rolls, just a soft smack on the sand, as gentle as your breathing when you were a babe in the crib. He didn't kneel to me. He stood with the ring in his hand and said he'd stand with me and for me as long as he lived; would I marry him. I love that he stood that way, as a man, not a beggar, and of course I said yes; and we kissed under that sunset, and I don't think there could have been a prettier sight in the whole world.

So I gave notice and we moved to San Francisco. Our wedding wasn't big. My family flew out, and my friend Vickie, and we both had a couple friends from our new offices, but we were new in the area. His brother Jake came and stood up for him, and Dennis really appreciated that, because in June the farm was busy, I guess. And his sisters Amanda and Nichole came out, too. Trudy wrote, but you know, she couldn't afford to travel.

We honeymooned in Napa Valley. Back then it really was a country drive there. Windy little roads, the vineyards spread almost like wheatfields, Dennis said, but they were green and instead of farmhouses it was the winery castles. Very romantic. And all that is still there! But the traffic now is worse than the Bay Bridge at rush hour, so it's not the same. More like Riverside, I suppose.

At first we rented an apartment in Pacific Heights, and pretty soon we bought a car. Dennis had sold his little Cricket in L.A. and took the Muny to work, he said it was easier. So I had the Eldorado.

Gloria helped me find work, and she intended well, but it wasn't much of a favor. The new office was down in the Mission District, so people who needed help had easy access. There was a safe parking garage, so I was glad of that. But every day we'd get a new batch of homeless and disoriented people—stinkers I called them, but not at work. Sometimes they were drug addicts. Sometimes the women were abused, sometimes pregnant, sometimes both. Sometimes they had children who needed placement, and sometimes their children had things wrong with them, fetal alcohol syndrome or something. Sometimes the mom felt bad about giving up the child but she wanted to because she knew she couldn't care for it. Sometimes they didn't care, just vacant. Sometimes they cared but you had to take the child for its own safety, and that was horrid, the sobbing and sometimes the screaming, the mother or the child or both of them. It was all horrid, I don't know which was the worst. Sometimes they just needed a job, but mostly they wouldn't be able to keep one. And then the gay people started coming in, and they weren't like now, the upper class with nothing better to do. No, they were as crazy and stinky and drugged-out as any of them.

Mellie was our supervisor, and she was amazing, maybe

crazy, always optimistic for these people, always trying to find another bed and another meal. But honestly, it was much more depressing than the L.A. job. L.A. is more spread out. In San Francisco everyone is scrunched together, so the squalor just slaps you in the face like a wronged woman.

Which was of course my purpose, you know. To serve those people, I mean. Mellie made that clear. She said, "Whatever hard choices we have to make, our guide is this: is it good for our people? That's always the question to answer." But it was hard still. Mellie never gave up on them, but after a couple months, a couple weeks even, I couldn't hold out much hope. Just too many, too needy. Even with unlimited resources, which was not our situation at all, we were always scraping for money—making carbon copies instead of using the Xerox machine, no long-distance phone calls allowed, Mellie always going to the director for money, and he'd go to the Board of Supervisors, and they'd say sorry, no; and our wages!—here we were, college graduates, and I don't think we were making three dollars an hour! Some of the girls weren't as ambitious as I was, but it didn't seem right to me.

Helen was a volunteer with us. She was an Irish girl, or at least inherited the accent, and there was a Catholic influence there, out of Mission Delores, you know, the Father Junipero Serra string of missions. It was Spanish country, almost, and we'd be speaking Mexican and going to Sunday Mass I suppose, if things had gone differently. But anyway, Mission Delores was started the same time as the United States, 1776, so we ended up speaking English and being Protestants. I mean, as a nation. You know I was born Catholic. But my parents didn't follow it closely, and I doubt I've been to church fifty times in my life, and not at all since we married. We were supposed to raise you Catholic, you know, but it didn't really make sense. But Helen was a good Catholic girl, and she'd get down low with the children and make friends with them somehow, and they'd trust her and stop wailing. Mellie had her work with the children going into foster care. It was another way we saved money, using volunteers. And Helen practically bled tears.

"Those poor babies," she said to me in her brogue. "They just need a home and someone to love them! It's not their fault they were born into drugs and no roof for their wee heads."

"Well, it's good you're working on that, Helen," I told her.

She shook her head. "It won't do. They're just babes, but they've already been passed around like sandwiches down a picnic table, and they're falling apart, and you can't pick up the delicates that fell in the sand and stuff them back in—it won't work."

"It's the best we can do, Helen."

"No it's not," she said. "We can give the parents the jobs and security and support so they won't be homeless and addicted! That may be the best we can do!"

I could only shake my head. "I don't think we can afford that, Helen."

"And what can we afford instead?" she asked. "Look around you, LC! What do we afford instead? We have skyscrapers and opera and cruises on the bay and flights all around the world! Flights to the moon! We have all that, but we can't afford to give people a job and help them do it well? We can't take these wee innocents into a decent world where they can be warm and fed and cared for?"

And you know, she almost guilted me into thinking we, your father and I, should adopt one of those children. I brought it up with him, how we had all these children at work who needed foster or adoptive parents.

He said, "Yeah, it's a hard thing, I'll bet. Back home that didn't happen. If a man got hurt and couldn't keep all his children, or a woman for that matter, there was always family or at least neighbors who could take the child. And kids weren't a liability like they are in town. They were an asset. They helped work the farm, and nothing less was expected by anyone. I hope that keeps up forever!"

"But what do we do about these city children?" I asked him.

Dennis shook his head. "Send them to the country, maybe?"

"Where? Napa Valley?"

He knew that wouldn't work. You couldn't expect vineyard owners to take in these kids, and there weren't enough owners anyway. And the workers were all Mexicans, even their own kids would scarcely go to school.

He said, "I don't know, LC, you're the sociologist. I think it'd be hard for a man to take in a stranger's child. There's something about flesh and blood, you know, or at least kith, as they say. I know I wouldn't want to do it."

"But what if a baby needed it?"

"There's always need, babe. If we all catered to the neediest where would we be? If the Roman soldiers were all home coddling the babies, they would never have conquered the Mediterranean. If Louis Pasteur was teaching the homeless under a bridge he never would have discovered polio, or whatever he discovered. If I quit my job and volunteered along with you we couldn't afford our place, and the S&L would lose profitability. There's always need."

I nodded and didn't push the subject, although I could hear Helen's brogue echoing him, *"And if Hitler had stayed home tending the neediest, there never would have been a World War II!"*

But your father was right. We're only human, we can't do everything. Even Jesus said *The poor will always be with us.* So we might as well enjoy life.

We did, too, dear. Those were the best years. Dennis was rising like a star in the bank, and after a year we bought a Nob Hill home with a view north toward the Golden Gate, and a second car so we could both drive to work. He bought season tickets to the Forty-niners, and we sometimes went to the Giants games, too. Of course that was all outside in the seats then. They didn't have the boxes available like they do now, and once I got sunburned and lots of times I froze, wrapped up in the red and gold blanket or not! But that was when I became a Forty-niner fan. It was the Bill Walsh era then, the start of it: Joe Montana, Dwight Clark, then Ronnie Lott, Fred Dean, Jerry Rice, Steve Young. You remember some of those later ones maybe, you were too young to remember them all. But that was the time.

We went to a couple Warriors basketball games, too, but I didn't enjoy that so much, so he went with work friends. All of it was good for business, Dennis said, and good for him in the business. It must have been working, because he started getting bigger bonuses and then he took me to Hawaii on a cruise. That was sweet, but he got seasick and pretty much lay on his back the whole trip. Later I would have hula'd without him, but that first time I stayed by him and missed most of the fun. We didn't do that again. When we took you we flew, remember? Every summer for a stretch there, didn't we? No, you were too young to remember those first trips. We had that beach house, and he golfed.

But that was after you were born, and then Stevie.

I didn't like the fog at all. San Francisco is a cold place. I'd liked that about L.A., it doesn't do cold. But even though my job didn't pay, Dennis's did, and our house was snug, and heat was cheap. It still is, in the grand scheme of things, isn't it?

And on nice days I liked to get outside. We had a small yard, front and back. Not enough for a lawn, there in the city, but a row of pathetic little roses. I decided to take a rose class, and that's how I got to know Annie. I'd already met her through Dennis. Her husband Paul also worked at US First. But we accidentally took the rose class together, four Saturdays in a row, and that was the beginning of a whole new way of living for me. Not the class! Oh, we learned how to prune the bushes in winter, and fertilizers and treatments to get the best flowers, and dead-heading that I already knew but didn't do, and, you know, recognizing aphids and other pests, and a little bit of varietals. That was all fun and part of it, but the whole idea was beyond just the roses, and Annie made it all make sense.

She was a hoot, as you know. She had grown up in the City and she became my guide. Not just a human guidebook— Fisherman's Wharf over here, can't miss Chinatown, the Golden Gate Park museums, and the Presidio if you have time, and of course the best restaurants, bars, and nightclubs, blah-blah-blah. She was good for all that, but she was so much more, she was good for *how* to travel, what to wear, what to order—how to *be!* We only brought Dennis and Paul with us at the beginning. Then we had Girls Night Out when the boys went to a Warriors game. Sometimes we bought them tickets to go. This was *our* time!

Where did we go, what did we do? Not that much, really, but how we did it, those are the things of life! She was my mentor, and she was assertive! It started with shopping. She'd buy anything she wanted! But not just because it was cachet. I mean, she did have good taste, and always liked the best things. She's still that way, I'm sure, wouldn't be any other. But she got things because she *wanted* them. Not because they were hot, or weren't, or on sale, or weren't. Not because the salesperson told her how nice they looked on her. *She* was the judge!

And at restaurants, whoo! She could be tough! But as she said, "It's my money and I'm buying their service, and if they don't want to accommodate me then I can go somewhere else! That's fine! I'm free and they're free!"

At a hole-in-the-wall Greek place on Fulton—it's not there anymore—she ordered a salad. It came with green olives. Now I'd have just shrugged and eaten them, back then. Dennis wouldn't have even known there was anything wrong! But Annie, very nicely, flagged down a waiter and asked him to bring a side of the Kalamata olives that should have been on the salad. She explained to me, "It's a Greek Salad, for Zeus' sake! It should have Kalamata olives, and I like them! But you don't want to send the plate back to the kitchen. At these second-tier eateries you don't know what some minimum-wage cook is going to add. I prefer my own saliva only, thank you."

Another time we were at a first-tier restaurant. We were both in formal dresses, she in classic black with a string of pearls and I in burgundy with a layered jade necklace. We were seated and had begun our salad when a neighboring table was given to a gaggle of young couples. These tables were not overly close, but in the group's chatter, convivial, one of the young gentlemen laughed with a high, loud whinny. The first time Annie and I just exchanged a look. The second time she frowned and flagged the waiter.

"We would like to be reseated," she told him.

"Yes, Ma'am, may I ask why?"

The fellow neighed again, and Annie just smiled and raised her eyebrows.

The waiter surveyed his options and informed us that, regrettably, there were no vacant tables.

"I believe the conference room is open," Annie told him.

"Ah, yes." He looked uncomfortable.

"We don't want to inconvenience you. We will finish our salads here and then move over."

"Yes, Ma'am, certainly."

After he had left she leaned to me. "There's rarely a true no. We can work through most things, don't you think?"

And she tipped generously, so that helped.

You know what she mostly taught me? That I could do whatever I wanted. Clothes, travel, purchases, tweaking the rules. Always polite but never a pushover. The only real rule was Be Myself, Extravagantly! Annie was my inspiration, my model!

That's when I started calling myself Elsie again. You know, forever I'd gone by *L.C.* I suppose I thought it was cool back in high school, and then things stick. But with Annie I was thinking about my life condition, and what I wanted. And I wanted to be more comfortable in my own skin, I wanted to be me, I wanted to be real. How could I do that if I didn't even have my own name right? How could I be a force at work, or a partner in a marriage, or anybody to anybody, if I wasn't a person on my own? So I went back to my name, the name my parents gave me, Elsie. I don't mean the last name, you know that. That was something I chose, too, your father's.

I even, at least for a little while, felt better about my work. You know, here I was with all the advantages of modern society and these poor indigents couldn't even keep their health or their homes or their children. I don't know what caused all their problems—whether they didn't work back in school, or got into drugs. I don't know, but they certainly weren't functioning human beings. So I had so much—I mean, not like the super rich, what you call the one percent. But I had whatever I wanted, at least that money can buy—and if money can't buy it you just may have to do without—so I felt I should help the less fortunate.

But I wasn't going to be like Helen. I wasn't going to get down on their level. I wasn't going to try to become their friend.

There was one young man who wanted help going to school. We had a program for that, so I helped him fill out the paperwork. He said he had kicked his drug habit and there was an auto-mechanic certification he wanted so he could get his life in order. He was a good-looking young man—thick curly red hair, but he had it trimmed, and he didn't have that bleached-out skin that some redheads have; and well-built, too. He had played high-school football, he said, a receiver, and I told him he might be the next Dwight Clark. Maybe he could have, too. I figured some girl would be happy to have him, if he could get himself together. So he got enrolled and I kept tabs on his progress. We weren't supposed to do things like this, but I met him for lunch a couple times, just to give him a boost. He said he was liking school, and his teacher had a couple job leads for him. He dressed all right and didn't stink. I paid for lunch, of course, because he didn't have anything.

And then the last time, I could tell things weren't right. He had a funny look in his eye, and a swagger I didn't like. And he was just rude to me. Oh, I don't know if it was rude or just hopeless. It was sneering. It was empty, and it hurt. He said, "Thanks for the lunches, lady! It's been a fun ride! But you know what? You've got yours all set—your big home, your rich husband, your nice car and good clothes—and so you're the Queen and you come down here to help us gutter lifes. But some of us are just gutter-lifers. There's nothing you can do, dropping your breadcrumbs on us. Hansel and Gretel got lost on bread-crumbs. I bet you didn't know I knew that, did you? How would a gutter-lifer like me know about Hansel and Gretel? Well, I went to school. The whole country had declared war, did you know that? War on Poverty! So I went to school. But it couldn't stick. I couldn't keep track of school, I lived too many places—my aunt's, my mom's boyfriends', one of them had a tent, I don't want to say where. Some of the places were fine, the neighbors weren't too loud. Usually they were crowded and smelly, though, 'cause lots of people shared, especially when it was cold, and there wasn't always hot water. Some had TV, so her boyfriends and I could watch it all night. Sometimes Mom would be there. Sometimes she worked. But she didn't have nothing. She was smart; she'd graduated and gone to some college, too, just like I'm trying. But her dad was some fatcat bastard, maybe like your King, hey Mrs.?, and she left home when she was sixteen. Sweet sixteen, but she'd been kissed, you can bet, 'cause she was only seventeen years older than I am. Can you believe that? So, she's like Hansel and Gretel, too. And breadcrumbs ain't enough. They ain't enough, know what I'm saying? So I'm still going to school, but I'm not going to pass, I know that. You got money for a tent? Nah, it's just another crumb. But you got money? Nah, I don't want it. 'Cause... You know, the first war the USA ever lost, that was Vietnam, you know, right? You know what the second one was? You don't know, do you? The War on Poverty. That's the second war the USA lost. So that's what I'm saying. You won the War on Poverty, Mrs., you've got yours. Me, I'm on the losing side, America. So thanks for the lunches. I'm gonna go flunk my test now."

And he got up and left, and I didn't feel good at all. I never saw that boy again. He didn't come back to the office, at least not while I was there.

So I learned I didn't want to try to make friends with those people. They couldn't handle it.

I worked there down in the Mission for two years. Then, my dear, you were coming along, and I knew it was time to bring my efforts closer to home.

Three

The sun rose on another L.A. morning, and the season didn't matter to you. Out in Santa Monica the sky was clear with the usual cooling breeze off the usual quiet ocean. The wives at home there, useful for keeping spotless windows and counters, and the town's commuters, the men accomplishing miles and millions without breaking a sweat, could all enjoy with casual appropriation the pristine feel of the state that spawned Hollywood and Beverly Hills. Those who sweat were unseen.

To the east, in Riverside, the air was drier and the season did matter. October oranges were swelling thirstily, still as green as the thick citrus leaves that nested them in undulating rows over the local hills, promising more green, cash, for the basin, all under a golden glow that only showed a brown smudge westward.

There, in Downtown, sunrise was a hazy red fireball that would by evening descant to a coal-red disk, as it had the evenings before and before, all through the long summer inversion. Air-quality regulations had not yet scrubbed the L.A. skies, and many people vaguely and quietly wished for the Santa Ana winds to rise and scour the city. But that was the least of Downtown's concerns, for air conditioning and tinted windows would solve, or at least mute, the outside ugliness, and everyone who mattered was embroiled in the grander pursuits of commerce.

For you, Dad, it was the Savings and Loan. US First was a small independent, but you were fresh from school and ambitious as a sunrise, no matter its race or creed. Clean-shaven, in a brown suit and tie, you rose and shook hands briskly.

"Hello, Mr. Sender. I'm Dennis. What can I do for you?"

Mr. Sender shifted his bulk in the broad customer chair. "You probably know that we were hit pretty hard with the frost last year."

"Yes, I looked over your statements." Hank Sender grew some of those oranges eastward.

"And I had no crop insurance that would cover that."

"That's got to be tough." You nodded sympathetically.

"So the fruit this year is shaping up nicely. We had a bumper load of blossoms last spring, you could hear the bees all the way in the house, and now the trees are full of the most promising crop I've ever seen."

"That's good to hear."

"My problem is that I got another bill from the bank, from you. And I can't pay it, not until after the harvest."

"Which will be past due."

"Right. Now I want to treat you guys right, I know you've got to make a buck, too, but I can't give you what I don't have."

"No, I don't suppose you can."

"So, can I delay payments?"

You clicked your pen. "Well, that loan is already renegotiated from last year. There are a few ways we could go from here. The bank could offer a lien on your crop in exchange for a fifteen percent late-payment penalty."

"*Offer* me a lien? You'll take my crop in exchange for me paying you extra?"

"In exchange for you paying late. And it's a lien, not a taking."

"Fifteen percent is too much, it would put me under. What about four percent? You'll still make a profit, and I can survive."

"It's a delayed profit, Mr. Sender, and once again we won't have that money to lend for the duration of the delay. That's a real cost to us."

"But it makes no sense to ask me to pay before harvest time!"

"You should have thought of that before you signed for this extension you're in."

"How old are you, kid? What are you—twenty? Where's Max, Max Miller? I've always worked with him in the past."

"Max is retired. He set this contract up with you?"

"Yes. He did."

"I'm sorry, Mr. Sender."

"Sure you are. And that's all you've got?"

The pen clicked twice. "The bank really doesn't want your oranges. The lien is just protection for us."

"And the fifteen percent is bankruptcy for me!"

"I am sorry."

Hank Sender snorted and shot his gaze side to side. He'd been a gravel-hard worker all his life, and a hard-nosed businessman, too. *But I never tried to bury my customers!* he thought. "What are your rates on a second mortgage?" he asked.

"I think we could get you in under nine percent. There'd be some points with that."

Hank stared at you, pursing his lips to curb his tongue. He rose. "All right," he muttered, and turned and left the bank.

You smiled quickly and pulled up another file you had found—James Rose. You dialed Mr. Rose's number. A woman's voice greeted you.

"Hello, this is Dennis Self at US First Savings and Loan, is James available? No? That's all right. I've got an opportunity he might be interested in. Could you have him call me when he gets in? Thank you."

James Rose was another orange grower. He called back that afternoon and you arranged for him to come in the next Monday.

That weekend you and your girl LC drove out to Riverside, arcing south through Anaheim to avoid traffic. You didn't drive your car, the used Cricket. You'd just begun your working career, and from experience as a North Dakota farmboy you had an aversion to debt, so you still owned the Cricket. But LC's parents had given her an Eldorado convertible, and you both enjoyed touring in it with the top down. You loved the way LC's hair swirled forward in the wind, and she knew it.

You stopped for gas, and at the cash register you saw a pair of sunglasses with pink heart-shaped lenses. You picked them up and handed them to LC in the car. She immediately put them on.

"How do I look?"

"Sexy, Babe!"

She rode scootched next to you, your arm around her shoulders.

Urbanized L.A. yielded as you drove into suburban sprawl and orchards, mainly orange groves.

"Look at this, Dennis! You could be a farmer right here!"

"Not easily. I don't have the capital, so I'd always be in hock. Farming's good work, although I don't know about oranges. But the business of it is tough."

"Would you be interested if you had the capital?"

You took a breath considering that. "No, not here. When I said farming's good work I guess I was thinking of farming where I grew up, when I grew up. The job itself was good, a mixture of mind and muscle that suits most men pretty well, not like this desk-work we do nowadays. But the whole thing was more, too. It was a way of life, it was a community. Here it's none of those things. The muscle is farmed out to Mexicans and machines. The mind is business, not growing things; I can do business like that at the S&L. And community? You might know other farmers here, but it's pretty much just as farmers, just the business. The men know the men, and even then only their value. They don't know their kids, like they did back home. Maybe they've met the wives, but they don't know what they're like with each other, laughing or sober, foolhardy or stiff; or who's a good cook or how they treat their kids, or sometimes even what each other's kitchens look like. That was always a piece of it in Pullup, everybody knew everybody—at school, in town, the kids, 4H, everything. When a year was bad you could count on your neighbors to pull you through. When your kid was bad, you could count on your neighbors to pull him through. Here, there isn't that kind of sentiment. It's more sterile." You laughed. "Maybe that's why they grow navel oranges. They're sterile."

"That's why they don't have seeds!"

"That *is* them not having seeds."

"I like that, not having seeds. You can eat them without spitting out."

You nodded. "Yeah, even sterility has its advantages. And Riverside here is the navel-orange capital of the world!"

"Is it really?"

You shrugged. "Yeah. The original tree is still there. I'll show you, let's find it."

You drove into town and found the shrine at the corner of Arlington and Magnolia.

"Arlington! They named it for you!"

"Yeah," you laughed. Arlington was your middle name, but you thought you were named for the cemetery. A friend of your dad's had been buried there after the Korean War.

"But the other street is Magnolia! That's goofy! They could have named it Orange!"

"Or they could have named one street Orange and one street Navel," you said.

"Or just Belly and Button," she returned. She was still wearing her heart-shaped sunglasses, and you just laughed.

You parked and walked to the tree with the plaque.

"So it's the first one in California! Back in 1873!" she said.

"That's an old orange tree!"

"So it's the orange capital of California, not the world!"

"Some people think California is the world."

"Some people have small horizons," she humphed.

"Look at this tree! It's been doctored!" You were pointing at scars on its trunk.

"Well we all need a doctor sometimes."

"That's how it's still alive. This town is maintaining its history!"

"I think that's sweet."

"Yeah. So do I."

You left the orange tree hand in hand and stopped for a burger and fries. You had a Coke and she a Pepsi. Then you drove out north of town.

"There's a grove here I want to see," you said.

"Why?"

"Business. The grower is having financial difficulties."

"How sweet, you take me out on business." She pout-teased.

You laughed. "I thought you liked navel oranges."

"I do," she said. "That doesn't mean I like your business."

"You don't even know what my business is. It's making money. You don't like that?"

"I don't mind you doing it! And never mind." She fluttered her hands. "The hills are pretty. And they smell fresh even in the heat!"

"Do they? I can't smell them. I know what you mean, though. I sure smelled it back home, especially in the morning after a rain. If there's a heaven and it's got a smell, I think it's the smell of wheat after a rain. But you can have orange groves if you want."

You drove through grove after grove of the dark green, and finally crested a larger hill. You pulled over.

"Let's look at this fruit here."

You walked into the grove together and the smell of green oranges thickened. You bent over some and inhaled. "I can smell these now."

A trench of water contoured the uphill side of each row, and the trees were pruned into balls about eight feet in diameter.

"You see, these small trees make for easy picking," you said. "Of course, they're all like that."

"Look at the fruit." You pulled aside the thick citrus leaves to better show the turgid orbs. "This should be a good crop, don't you think?"

"Looks like it to me!" she agreed. "But I don't know these

things."

"Well, you know about as much as me when it comes to oranges. They look good, I can say that."

You studied the foliage. A very few leaves still carried the burnt yellow edges from last-season's frost, but warmer weather, lots of water, and time had brought the trees back to excellent vigor.

You returned to the car. She still wore her heart-shades, and you put on a pair of huge green bug-eye lenses that she had bought for you a week earlier. The two of you drove homeward, following the golden sun as it turned blood red.

Back at your desk on Monday morning, the Cricket parked invisibly outside, you again considered Hank Sender's grove, where you and LC had stopped. Sender was obviously a diligent and capable farmer. It really was too bad that his grove faced north, that his business sense had failed, and that he had no mortgage with US First. The S&L profited on the year-to-year loans, but when those payments could be tied to a stable long-term mortgage the situation was all the more favorable, you thought.

But Sender certainly didn't have kids at home at his age. He'd have grandkids out there in Riverside. He'd be all right.

At ten o'clock a balding man in gray coat and blue tie entered the bank, surveyed the desks, and approached you.

You stood. "Hello, is it Mr. Rose?"

"Jim, please." You and he shook hands.

"I'm Dennis. Thank you for coming in."

Jim smiled. "I'm happy to oblige."

"You've had a long string of very successful years with the orange grove."

"Yes, I have, thank you."

"And I stumbled on a growth opportunity for you."

"Yes, that's what you said."

"A grower may be looking to sell. He's got eighty acres of mature trees, irrigation all in and state-of-the-art, and what looks like a bumper crop on the trees right now."

"Why is he looking to sell?"

"I can't go into that. What I can do is offer you favorable terms on a thirty-year loan."

The man pursed his lips and leaned back, fingertips together. "Tell me about it."

You outlined the loan terms. You both knew what the grove should produce, and the numbers you offered would provide a tempting profit. Mr. Rose would sell oranges; the S&L would lock in a long-term mortgage. "Now the place isn't on the market yet, but would you like me to connect you with the realtor who will be working on it?"

"Yes, I would like that."

"I'll have him call you."

"Thank you."

You both rose and shook hands again.

After James Rose had left, you turned to the phone once more and dialed from your Rolodex file.

"John! Dennis here from US First. Yeah, thanks. Do you have a minute?"

John Burlison had contacted you shortly after you began at the S&L. He had offered that sometimes when a customer was in financial difficulty, particularly if he was older, it made more sense to sell some real estate rather than try to refinance a thing. He suggested that he would be able to facilitate such exchanges.

You explained the financial straits that Hank Sender was in, that Hank was not looking to sell and would likely be approaching other banks to find financing, but that there was an interested buyer. John took the information and said thanks.

That afternoon the branch had a management meeting. The home office in San Francisco had sent out new lending guidelines.

Bob Johnson, the branch manager, was short and round. He reminded you of a pumpkin, a sort of cherubic pumpkin with soft plump skin and thinning hair. He was wearing his usual expression of compliant weariness as he addressed his team of three loan officers.

"Basically," he said, "they want us to make more loans. They want to serve the short-term need that many customers experience. We'll be opening payday-anticipation loans. Someone with a regular paycheck wanting money in advance can buy that service.

"The service will initially sell for a flat rate of four percent of the loan plus half a percent daily. So if someone needs a thousand dollars a week before his paycheck will come, it will cost forty dollars plus seven days of half a percent of the principle, that's thirty-five, so seventy-five dollars. The loan is payable at any time, typically we'd expect payment when the paycheck arrives."

Chet Hodges, the oldest of the loan officers, groaned. "But if he doesn't pay it off then—and you know they won't—that's almost two hundred percent a year!"

Bob nodded. "The loans are for thirty days. They're designed as short-term only."

"Two hundred percent is not what we're about! A guy'll dig himself into an impossible hole with terms like that!" Chet rumbled angrily.

"So you of course will want to make sure that the terms are clear to the customer," said Bob.

"They don't hear that. You know they don't," Chet returned. "They all think they're going to be fine right after the next paycheck. But there's always something, the car needs tires, or the kid gets sick, or the wife needs some gewgaw. You know it's that way!"

"I'm with Chet," said Rick. He was an athletic middle-aged fellow, a winter skier and a summer surfer. "I think we would hurt our customers with these loans. Either they'd pay them off, and they're way too expensive, or they'd default."

"That's what bankruptcy's for," you said.

"But that's not good!" said Rick.

"A guy can come out of bankruptcy just fine," you replied.

Rick shook his head with exasperation. "But the community won't! People don't get paid! That's not good for commerce or employment or anyone!"

"Again," Bob interrupted, "that's why we would want to be sure the terms are clear. Listen, I don't want to require anyone to make these loans, but Headquarters wants us to offer them."

Rick continued, "You know who'd take them, the part-timers who are already failing to make ends meet. This would just drive them into default."

"I don't think so," you placated. "I think we'll find that professionals who can perfectly well understand the terms will be wanting these loans, and it will be a useful service to them."

"And they'll still default!" Chet retorted, his voice louder than Rick's and his neck bulging swarthier. "Professionals are no different from gutter-sweepers, they all think they're going to win the lottery, they're going to be on Easy Street if they can just get by this rough patch! They're all the same, and there are always new rough patches, and way too many of them will default! These loans are not a service!"

"That's for the customer to decide," you replied evenly.

"And the Savings and Loan, we won't do well if we have people defaulting left and right! Kiss our jobs goodbye!" Chet frowned.

Bob shook his head. "They're high-interest loans, Chet, and the home office calculates that as long as we keep selling them they will pay for themselves. We'll be making a profit."

"By gouging people!" Chet continued. "And on an impossible treadmill!"

"I can sell the loans," you volunteered. "I have no problem

with them. They are a service with a cost, and as long as we make the terms clear that's all they are."

Chet eyed you in negative appraisal, but Bob said, "Thank you, Dennis. I'll be eager to see how your customers do, and Headquarters will be, too."

The sign went on the front window, "Ask inside about Payday advances!" Within the week you had sold nine loans, and the word spread. The next week you sold thirty-eight, and the following week you sold twenty in a single day.

Your first customer, as you had imagined, was a professional, a young man dressed in a gray sportcoat, red and brown tie, and brown leather shoes. When he entered the bank, sunlight briefly streamed into the foyer and glinted off his wedding band, still too new to be burnished to a quieter luster. His thin auburn hair was combed flat. He stood a moment, his eyes adjusting to the cool lighting in the bank, and then proceeded to the first desk. Rick there leaned back, listened, and waved him on to your desk.

He waited for you to look up at him and said, "I was told you're the man to see about your payday advances."

"That's right. I'm Dennis." You rose and shook hands. "Please sit down."

"Thank you."

"Hot enough for you out there?"

"Yes, it's a...it's an oven."

"Cooler in here at least. So what's your name?"

"Ed Grande."

"Well hello, Ed. And what can I do for you today?"

"Well, I saw your sign out front. How does that work?"

"It's a new product for us, the payday advance. Basically we advance you an amount against your next paycheck. It's a little something to tide you through when you have pay coming. What do you want the advance for?"

Ed grimaced self-consciously. "It's our daughter's third

birthday. We want to give her a pony party. Well, it's my wife's idea. It's expensive, but she only turns three once."

You nodded appreciatively. "That's true, isn't it. Well, yes, we may be able to help. Where do you work, Ed?"

"I'm a department manager at Bullseye. Hardware Department."

"What does that pay you, Ed?"

"Three ninety-five an hour, so almost twice minimum wage."

"All right then. And how much do you want to advance?"

"The pony rental costs seventy-five. That includes the guy who helps the kids on the ride."

"And how about the cake? And beverages? Other presents? You want to get enough to cover your needs."

"Oh, my wife will make the cake."

"Good, good. She doesn't have a birthday coming up, does she?"

"No, no."

"All right, just trying to cover your bases, you know, sometimes sitting here we learn from our customers what they later wish they had thought about themselves."

"Thanks, I think we're OK. This is just something extra that we need the advance for."

You nodded. "So seventy-five for the pony, how much do you want the loan for, ninety, a hundred?"

"Well, how much does it cost?"

"It's four percent of the loan plus half a point per day up to thirty days, when the loan is due."

"So, how much is that?"

"Well, when's your next payday?"

"Just a week and a half. Her birthday is this Friday."

"So if you walked out with a hundred dollars in your pocket and paid it off in, say, ten days, when you get your paycheck, it'll cost you nine dollars. Not bad for a pony party!"

"No, no, that's not bad!"

"So a hundred dollars then?"

"Yeah, that sounds good."

"All right."

You had been filling in a form as you spoke. Now you turned it toward Ed. "This is the advance agreement. Here's your income and employer, the amount of the advance, and the conditions of repayment, which are printed in ahead because they're standard. Does that all look agreeable?"

Ed surveyed the form briefly. His ears reddened, because he knew he should take more time to study the agreement, but he didn't want to seem like a novice. "Yes, I think so," he said.

"All right then. If you'll sign here we can call to confirm your wages and you can walk out the door with cash in hand!"

"Just like that?" Ed asked.

"You couldn't do that for a home mortgage, but these payday advances, we want to make them simple and available. So here, if you can dial your employer and give permission for someone to confirm your pay we'll be all set. What's that number?"

"I don't know the office number, but here's the store," Ed said.

You dialed as Ed recited the number, and then handed the phone to him. Ed soon had HR on the line, and after a short identification process, the office confirmed Ed's salary to you.

"And there we are!" you said, hanging up the phone. "Would you like that cash in hand now?"

Ed nodded and you filled out a withdrawal slip. Ed signed for receipt and was out the door less than a half hour after he had entered, quick and easy as mercury.

Your next customer was a jewelry-store retailer who was paid on commission and needed a loan to meet rent after a slow month; then a woman recently divorced who wanted to afford school tuition; a road-construction laborer with medical bills for his eight-year-old; a furniture salesman who wanted to do up his house for Halloween. The next week a couple wanted to fly to Buffalo to visit her ailing mother, and an elderly man living on

Social Security wanted to buy his wife a ring for their fiftieth wedding anniversary. You and the S&L approved them all. When an excitable twenty-eight-year-old wanted cash to start a recycling business, you endorsed the loan against "anticipated earnings."

Most of those first loans were paid off before Thanksgiving. Some were paid by taking out a new loan. Some customers who paid off cleanly came back in December for a new "Christmas" loan.

Everyone in the bank, tellers to senior officers, was on a straight salary then, but the S&L often gave out small Christmas bonuses. That year you received a far larger bonus, nearly a full month's pay.

"Congratulations," Bob told him. "Headquarters is very pleased with your performance and supported this bonus."

You contemplated the extra cash. You knew what you wanted. Back in North Dakota your father had never developed a nest egg. He always owed the bank, and there was no reason to think your brother Jake would be any different. In hard years that debt was a source of stress and pain. You remembered your mother haranguing your dad over stuff they didn't have, and your father's good humor and vigor trounced down into steady but humorless duty. In good years she was less biting, and your dad would smile every now and then like the farmer philosopher he was. But he still had to pay the bank, just like his son's customers had to now, and it kept him from ever getting ahead so he wouldn't have to borrow. You didn't want to put yourself in that position, ever. But you knew everyone felt that way.

And you felt the desire to treat LC, your girl, and to buy her a ring at some point. You were already spending plenty on eating out and on little toys for her, with her, like those stupid sunglasses.

You decided not to tell LC about the bonus. You bought her a costume necklace for Christmas, and you knew it wasn't stinginess to tuck most of the bonus into savings. There would be bigger things to spend on later.

Four

Shortly after the New Year, Bob called you into his office, first thing in the morning, before the doors were open. He wanted to beat the day's after-Christmas rush for short-term loans.

"You're busy, Dennis!" he began, smiling like an out-of-season jack o' lantern.

"Yes, I am," you agreed. "You know, I'd always thought long-term loans were the way to go. Mortgages: steady income, stability. But I'm seeing that these short-termers develop repeat customers, and they're at way higher rates. This is a good business!"

"Yes." Bob pressed his lips together, a pumpkin pout. "I'll be straight with you, Dennis. I'm personally not thrilled with these loans. The default rate is way too high, and they're making enough to cover themselves for now, more than cover themselves, but only because the rates are outrageous. I come from a time when our purpose was to help our customers, and this..." He shook his head.

"But this is a new age," he continued, "and I'm not trying to second guess anyone. Truth is, as you know, the home office is very pleased with your work. Very pleased, to the point that they want you to move up to San Francisco. You're beating all their people in your sales volume."

"That's because I'm the only one in the branch selling them," you offered humbly.

Bob nodded thoughtfully. "Maybe I'll have to broaden the team so I can keep my staff."

"I haven't said I'll go yet!"

Bob's smile returned. "Well you're part of my staff!" His eyes narrowed. "But this is a big invitation, Dennis. I think you'd be a fool to pass on it."

You eyed your boss in appraisal. "I bet you're right. Is this an official offer?"

Bob shrugged. "It's real. But no, I don't have a contract. I'll let Headquarters know you're interested, and they'll give you a call."

You fidgeted in your seat, an awkward fidget because the chair was big and had no swivel or rocking capacity. For all your burgeoning self-confidence, you still sometimes felt like a seventh grader, wanting to be grown up but not quite making the grade. "Don't call them yet. I mean, I'll do it. But you know, I've got a girlfriend here, and we'll need to figure out what we're doing."

"That's easy!" Bob grinned. "Marry her!"

You shrugged with relict uncertainty.

"Dennis, how long have you known her?"

"Uh, we met... Last spring. It seems like longer ago."

"Do you like her?"

"Yes."

"Is she pretty?"

"Yes."

"Can she cook?"

"Yeah."

"Will she?"

"Yeah, she will."

"Then marry her! If she's been with you since spring, that's what she wants! She's wondering what's taking you so long!"

"Well, you're probably right. But I don't want to mess things up, commit myself to something before I'm ready."

"Oh, gawd, Dennis, you mess things up by watching the world go by! Come on, you're a go-getter! Go get her!!" He grinned at his pun.

"Do you have to get back to Headquarters right away?"

"No, I can put them off a while. But don't put them off too long, Dennis! Strike while the iron is hot!"

You then pictured your mother with the iron, smoothing the

wrinkles from your father's Sunday shirt, but not smoothing the sour I-do-all-this-work look from her face. What would LC look like? Would she want to iron his shirts? Would he expect her to? "Well, put it off, please. If you have to tell them something, then yes, I'm interested, very interested. Between you and me I'm thinking I'm sure I'll do it. But I need to arrange my personal life." You stopped, but then added, "But that won't interfere with work. You understand!"

"I understand, Dennis. I'll hold them off. But marriage and then raising kids, it's the best thing you'll do in your life. And you've got a lucrative career ahead of you, so that'll make it all the better! So you know what I think."

"Thanks, Bob." You stood and awkwardly extended your hand. The December pumpkin smiled and shook it.

January slipped by, and San Francisco did not call. You waffled. Sometimes with LC you almost broke down and proposed. Other times you remembered your father, not miserable but not jovial, either. Gradually your decision became clear. In the first week of February you bought a ring and told Bob that you would make the move to Headquarters. You received the call and then the contract the following week, and asked LC to marry you on Valentine's Day. You moved north together in time for you to begin the new job on March 1st. LC began planning for a summer wedding.

You had been told that it would be easier to get around San Francisco on the bus system than to try to park a car. Having no great love for the Cricket, you sold it to a high-school kid in Los Angeles, and moved north with just LC's Eldorado. You quickly found the ready Muny route to your new office in the Financial District. US First Savings and Loan occupied a section of the fourth floor of its highrise.

There you met, as expected, a very different tone from Bob's frumpy-but-affable office. This one was more in the style that you had studied under and adopted: the purpose and focus of a business was to make money. It had nothing to do with external-ities like quality of life.

Paul Anderson showed you around the office. Paul was dressed like you, in a conservative gray suit with a dark tie, and black leather shoes that were not over-shiny. He had a quiet demeanor of competence and a submerged humor that seemed ever-present but would only occasionally glint forth like sun on the rare ripple of a glassy sea.

"Restrooms are down the hall," he said. "But up here is where we design the crap." He exchanged an appraising glance with you. "What do you know of finance, Dennis?"

"I know its purpose," you replied.

A slow grin crossed Paul's face. "You'll do all right, then." He continued with an exaggerated drawl, "You ever hear of Michael Milken?"

"Yeah. Drexel."

"That's right. Do you understand what he's doing?"

These were more pointed questions than you had earlier received from Herm, the CEO, and you recognized that Paul was a force. "Yeah, it's pretty smart. He's underwriting loans on companies that are probably worthless—"

"We call them junk bonds," Paul interjected.

"With the loans the borrower is able to buy out a real company, then flip it. He can pay off the loans and pocket the profit."

"And how can that work?"

You shrugged. "We're coming out of the seventies. The energy crisis is over, it's a rising market. As long as the market keeps going up, it's a no-brainer. All you have to do is resell the company you bought and you make money!"

"This will be your desk," Paul said, indicating a heavy wooden bureau with a dark oak finish. On the desk were an electric typewriter, a black touchtone phone, a stapler, a plastic desk organizer holding pens and a notepad, and a magnetic paperclip dispenser. "Go ahead, sit down."

You sat, and the chair seemed to fit. You gently rolled, swiveled, and rocked, and looked over your desktop.

"How's it feel?" Paul asked.

You nodded. "Like I can move."

"What do you do for fun, Dennis?"

You grinned and shook your head. "Where I grew up we didn't do fun. We worked."

"We work here, too. But you should think about how you want to use your bonus, when the time comes." He continued, "Dennis, you're here because you recognize opportunity, and the company values that. You were just describing flipping companies in a rising market. Do you recognize that we aren't passive in that process? That feeding the process keeps the market rising?"

You nodded. "Yes."

"So, by making these sorts of loans we are creating the rising market, creating wealth, right out of thin air. Do you see what a service that is?"

"Yes, I do."

"And who it's a service for?"

"I do."

"Yes, I think you do. And you know what it takes to sustain it?"

"Well, anything that's going to grow needs to be fed," you offered.

Paul smiled. "You'll do all right, Dennis. And US First will reward you for it." He studied his new colleague and then abruptly sat in a desk-side chair, leaning forward. "You probably know that S&Ls and the Feds are like *this* now." He held up two fingers tight together. "Ten years ago we couldn't do anything. The industry was old school. Well, we're past *It's a Wonderful Life*. We're not owned by depositors any more, we don't have to tie our personal wealth to the company's. We can actually reward ourselves for moving the economy, like any business ought to be able to. And trust me, we will. You've come at a good time."

"I'm glad to be here, Paul."

"Good. Listen, the leadership team is going to meet at two this afternoon. We're considering making some loans to ourselves—you know, we'd create a subsidiary—and want to discuss how that could be profitable. You should join us in the conference room."

"Thanks, I will."

You were, no doubt, in a first-day haze, but you figured all eyes would be on you, the new guy, so you determined to stay sharp. You drank another cup of coffee before the meeting.

The conference room held an oblong table that could seat perhaps a dozen people in the black, upright leather chairs that lined it. Only half the seats filled for this meeting. Paul introduced you to Phil and Ken. Jackson you had already met, as well as the boss, Herm. The group clustered loosely toward the center of the oblong. You were surprised to feel comfortable. Like you, everyone there was dressed in a gray or brown suit; they all wore their hair short, although Jackson's curls formed a dense brown mat. They were all men, although that didn't even rise to your consciousness. They all talked with a quiet brashness.

"Dennis, nice to meet you," said Ken, extending his hand. He seemed to be the oldest of the group, perhaps fifty. "Welcome to US First!"

"No, he's been with us! He just transferred up from L.A.," Paul corrected.

"Ah! Welcome to San Francisco then," Ken amended.

"Thank you, on both counts. I haven't been with the company long," you replied.

"Good, good," said Ken absently, apparently following his own thoughts and oblivious of yours. "Welcome aboard!"

"Hi, Dennis," said Phil, raising a hand spread open wide and smiling a big empty smile. "Hey, Paul, I still have to pick the Raiders," he continued.

"You *are* a raider, Phil! What did you do to that construction company?" Paul jibed.

Phil shrugged innocently. "Hey, they bit off more than they could chew! I just offered options!"

Herm interrupted, "All right, let's get going. You've all met Dennis? Dennis comes to us from the L.A. branch, which for us has been a sleepy little operation, but where he showed its potential with an impressive string of high-revenue loans. We're happy to have you aboard, Dennis."

You nodded appreciatively.

"Dennis the Menace?" quipped Phil.

You smiled blandly, hoping your new office-mates would recognize that it was an old line.

"That's good," said Herm. "Dennis the Menace, I like that! ... But listen, let's get to business. I've got a three o'clock. What we want to talk about today is forming a subsidiary that could receive loans and prove profitable. This is cutting edge. Paul, can you run through it for us?"

"Sure. You're all familiar with the part that isn't cutting edge. The subsidiary should qualify for tax breaks, so we could farm business to it and lose less to Uncle Sam; and maybe even get small business loans that we could leverage into more lucrative operations—loans out at higher interest rates."

Herm interrupted, "Paul would be its president, so he'd get a title, and he would take one of you along as an employee. Of course everyone would continue to be an US First employee."

"Right. Or at least there'd be no difference in pay from the S&L to the subsidiary," resumed Paul. "The part that is cutting edge is this: we could make our own loans to the subsidiary. The subsidiary could then make high-risk loans that are more profitable. Either those loan obligations are met, and we net the high return, or they're not met, but the loss is the subsidiary's, not

US First's."

Herm rubbed his palms. "And those losses would be insured. FSLIC."

"It looks failsafe," said Paul.

"Is it legal?" asked Jackson.

"It's becoming legal," replied Paul. "Our old governor is going to run for president again, and he'll win this time. And he understands the value of letting businesses control their own fate."

"It's genius!" Phil exclaimed. "Is there a signing bonus if I work for you, Paul?"

Paul smiled flatly. "Let's not get ahead of ourselves. I'd like you all to take a day to think of how this could go wrong. Then we'll meet tomorrow and start the ball rolling!"

"Brilliant!" Phil cried again. "And that's why you make the big bucks!" He pointed at Paul and Herm.

Herm looked at his watch and smiled. "Well done! There might even be time for a drink at the 19th first! All right, we'll follow up tomorrow!"

You returned to your desk thinking, *Well, well, this is an ambitious crew. They're ready to jump right quick, no doubt about that! And Paul is the key.*

The team found no objections to creating the S&L subsidiary, and Paul and Herm set up Western Freedom Savings & Loan, a wholly owned subsidiary of US First.

"I'd like you to be my employee," Paul told you. "Chief Loan Officer."

"Thanks, Paul. Why me? I'm new."

"You're not an airhead," Paul leveled. "And I'm hoping you're ambitious. Are you ambitious, Dennis?"

"My brother inherited the farm because he was older than I. I don't begrudge him. He'll be a good farmer. But here I can make my way by my own effort, not by birthright. Yeah, I'm ambitious."

"That's why you."

You took two days off for your wedding and honeymoon. When you returned Paul had had a wall installed cordoning off a prime section of office space for Western Freedom. Dennis Self, the Chief Loan Officer, got his own office with a window, although the view was of just another gray office fortress across a busy street where pigeons and waste swirled below in the city wind.

Western Freedom opened for business: "Bad credit? No credit? We'll work with you!" These were the loans that you processed, and you soon opened a ground-level office to accommodate the customers for these loans. You didn't mind the ground-floor office. It added people to the mix of pigeons and trash. The foot-traffic was excellent, and the clientele was lucrative. The financial-district buildings were crowded with men who were living or wanted to live beyond their means, and they were optimists willing to gamble on tomorrow's unlikely fortune. "They're Willy Lo-men," you told Paul, remembering the play from Mrs. Aronsen's class.

You found the process very similar to what you had found in L.A. The people were eager to take on frivolous debt they often couldn't afford. Now the loans were bigger, though. You weren't negotiating payday advances. These were fifteen-, twenty-, and thirty-year mortgages, taken on by men who wanted to impress their wives, or perhaps fool them; or who believed the housing market would only rise and wanted to get in on it as soon as possible; or who were already feeling the tug of the downward swirl of financial ruin and were desperately trying to escape it, to survive until the miracle of the Invisible Hand made them wealthy. These were men who did not understand what twelve- and fifteen-percent mortgage rates would do to them.

You churned the loans out furiously. You were funded by Paul's work. Paul received the loans from US First and shuffled them to you. Also, Paul was increasingly taking advantage of Michael Milken's leadership, creating loans to fund the purchase of junk bonds by eagle-beaked entrepreneurs. Western Freedom was on the rise!

"Dennis," Paul said. "I'm glad you came along!"

After three months Paul told you, "Listen, I think it's time you and I changed our pay structure. Herm's not watching what we do, he's just glad to see the dollars coming in. And we are a separate company, so I have the authority. What do you say we move from the old flat salary?"

"Well, if pay is supposed to reflect earnings, then..."

"Right. I think we want to keep a base salary just as insurance, but then we can take a percentage of earnings, too."

You nodded. "And a Christmas bonus commensurate..."

"Absolutely!"

"Do you have specifics in mind, Paul?"

"No. No, I think we should keep this flexible. We'll keep the current base pay and then be nimble with earned compensation. See what the market creates."

You nodded. "That seems fair."

"We're agreed then."

"We are. It's a dog-eat-dog world, so best be a wolf."

"Amen."

The next month you bought a car. You waited six months more before buying a house.

"You could have bought it sooner, you know," Paul chided.

You shook your head. "Rates are high. I didn't want a big principle at twelve percent. But rates're only going up, that's why I bought now."

"Dennis," Paul sighed. "Sometimes you're brilliant, and sometimes you're as blind as your clients. Dennis, you *make* the rates! You're a good risk, right? So you reasonably write yourself a lower-rate loan. It's that simple! No one's looking, Dennis!"

You nodded sheepishly, and refinanced yourself that

afternoon.

You and LC joined Paul and his wife Annie at a Forty-niners game, and then at another.

Paul shook his head as you all watched the team lose again. "They're dismal. This new coach, Walsh. They liked him down at Stanford, but I don't see him doing anything here. They're as bad as they were last year."

"He seems like a classy guy, though," you replied.

"Who cares? He's losing."

"Who cares? It's football!" Annie wisecracked, and LC giggled in agreement.

The team went two and fourteen that year. Paul was disgusted. Football's losses faded into basketball's, as the Warriors set about compiling their own doleful record. LC and Annie stopped going to the games. Paul watched and shook his head.

You commiserated, "They have to do something dramatic, don't they. They need a Wilt Chamberlain!"

"A Wilt's not easy to come by," Paul rejoined.

"I know. But I'm thinking they've been losing a while now, and they just keep doing the same piddle year after year. If they want to make a splash they have to run off the diving board, don't you think? They've got to take a chance and do something different!"

"Like win?" Paul jibed.

"Like draft some winners! Open up their play! Get a good coach, not like Attles or this Walsh that the Niners got! I don't know, I'm new and I'm not the coach, but I know you can't keep doing the same thing and hope to win!" You fidgeted in your seat, the junior partner working to articulate yourself. "It's like us, Paul. We've done well because we tried something new. We saw which way the wind was blowing, and we put up a sail." You dropped your shoulders and raised your left hand to your chin, propping your elbow on the seat arm. "Actually, there's something I've been thinking about. This junk-bond market. We don't have to just fund it, do we? We could purchase some companies ourselves—hold them a little, maybe strip out some losing departments, and flip them! You made the point yourself—it's a sure winner!"

"As long as the market keeps rising, it is."

"You think we should then!"

"I didn't say that."

"Are you worried about the legality, Paul? We're still a Savings and Loan, technically."

Paul chuckled. "You're right about the *technically*. As I've said before, and it's truer every day, no one's looking."

"Then why not take advantage of the easy pickings?"

Paul shook his head. "I'm pretty game, Dennis, but—"

"Look, successful entrepreneurs take chances. You know that!"

"So do a lot of unsuccessful ones. You just only hear about the successes. The magazines don't write stories about the losers."

"Oh, come on! Who ever heard any success say 'Hold back, be careful'?"

"Again, we only hear the success stories, the surfers riding at the crest of the big wave. But that's not the whole story."

You paused at that. "No, you're right. You're right. Aesop: *Be an ant, not a cricket.* Frost: *Provide, provide.* It's what I heard most of my life. From farmers and poets. But I heard it all from people who scraped by, not people who scored big."

"You don't think what we've got going is scoring big enough?" Paul queried.

"Is there any such thing as enough, Paul? I thought you wanted ambition!"

"I do, Dennis, but there's ambition and there's foolhardiness. The market can't keep going up forever. At some point these junk bonds, which, face it, only keep rising because of the Ponzi feed, are going to crash. Where we are now, the crash doesn't hurt us.

Any defaults, FSLIC will cover. We're good! It's the bond buyers who will suffer. Look, in a gold rush you don't want to be a miner, they boom and bust. You want to be the guy who sells stuff to the miners. It's far more lucrative and much more stable."

"More stable maybe, but not more lucrative," you grumbled in retreat.

"It's a pretty good set-up we've got, you have to admit," said Paul.

"Yeah, it is. In this market any dummy can be a millionaire."

"Right. But not every dummy. If we're going to be rich, somebody else has to be poor. That's the way it works when we're making money on defaults."

"All right, all right." You scratched your nose in irritation. "Like this basketball team—somebody's got to lose for them to win. Somebody's got to teach the Bay Area how to get some winners! I used to watch the Purple People Eaters! There was a team! These guys here are losers. Forty-niners: don't be a miner! And Warriors: the Indians lost a long time ago."

That spring, after the Warriors had struggled to a twenty-four and fifty-eight finish, you took up a new pastime. Jackson had invited his colleagues at US First to go kayaking with him, and you took him up on it.

"It's river kayaking," said Jackson. "That means you have to learn more than just lake kayaking. There's no current in a lake, but in a river it can kill you. You have to learn how to read it and use it. You have to learn how to Eskimo roll."

"I've been after a challenge!" you said.

On a Friday afternoon you left the office early and drove to Lake Berryessa with two kayaks on Jackson's roof. He taught you how to Eskimo roll. On land first he demonstrated and had you copy the motion for the roll, the twisting of the body, the broad flat paddlestroke, the snap of the hips. Then he had you jump in the water "just to acclimate" before climbing into the kayak.

Jackson stood in the water himself and held the bow of your kayak, the stern extending into deeper water. When you were ready he rolled you and let you try to right it. Twice Jackson himself righted the kayak and you, spluttering.

"I thought you were going to let me drown there!" you said.

"I won't let you drown," said Jackson. "It takes a few tries, just like anything new."

After the third attempt your coach told you, "You almost had it that time! Just pop it a little more."

"Yeah, I could feel it there," you nodded.

On the fourth attempt you successfully rolled up on your own.

"You're a quick learner!" Jackson exclaimed.

He continued to practice in the shallows with you until you rolled up five times in a row. Then you paddled together out farther into the lake and practiced some more. "And remember, at worst case, you can come out of the kayak," Jackson coached. "Just try to hang onto it then, and onto your paddle, too." He demonstrated the action. "In a river, having those things can be necessary. And at the least, losing them is a nuisance, because the current doesn't mind carrying them away from you. Your partner has to go paddle after them then, and that's not always feasible."

You decided to drive on up to the American River that night to be ready for an early start the next morning. Jackson chose a quiet stretch, not far above Folsom Lake, for your first river run. You and he camped along the river, and lying in your sleeping bag under the stars your mind ranged over this new turf—the rocky babble of the river, different from the sleepy meandering of the channels back home; the warmth, that kept your sleeping bag turned down; the cricket serenade, quieter than what you used to hear on the farm, but still nostalgically sweet; and the stars, beautiful even if less bold than your childhood sky.

In the morning Jackson pulled out his ice chest and Coleman stove and you were soon breakfasting on bacon and eggs with toast, and a mug of coffee, too.

"You're pretty handy at this," you commented.

"Been doing it since I was a kid," Jackson replied.

After cleaning up breakfast you put your kayaks in the water, strapped on your helmets, and spread zinc oxide on your noses.

"Remember, if you spill and can't right yourself, climb out and hang onto the kayak and paddle. If you do lose them, your jacket will keep you up. Float on your back with your feet downstream. You want to fend off rocks with your feet, not your head. And if you have to beach yourself, do it at a clear spot. Don't try to grab any streamside branches. I know the current seems slow here, but it's an illusion. The water is way stronger than you, and it will pin you to a branch, and if you get stuck underwater it won't be pretty. All right? No branch grabbing! If you do get stuck behind a rock or something, just relax until the current kicks you out. Don't try to fight the current, you'll lose and just waste your breath. Just wait, go with the current. It'll kick you out. All right?"

"All right."

"Of course it's better to just stay in the kayak to begin with. I want you to follow me, OK? Don't take some other channel of the stream; just stay behind me this first time. If I go to the right of a log, you go to the right, too. OK?"

"OK."

You paddled downstream. You loved the feel of the current, and played around in it, practicing the feel of it. You dutifully followed Jackson, even mimicking his intentional Eskimo roll in a broad, quiet stretch of water. Willows and cottonwoods lined the river and the shoreline rocks were bleached with dried algae. A great blue heron started up in front of you and jettisoned a stream of whitewash into the river as it flapped like a dinosaur downstream, only to be flushed twice more by your advance until it circled up above treeline and flapped back upstream, getting behind your accidental pursuit. A series of kingfishers rattled and chopped their way through the air as you passed, and sparrows and flycatchers fluttered among the willows.

The sun grew hot, and you rolled occasionally just to keep cool. Then Jackson pulled up on a quiet stretch.

"OK, Dennis, are you ready for some splash?"

"I'm ready for anything!"

"No you're not. We've been doing class one. There's a stretch of class two, maybe even a spot of three. Survive that and we'll get to the pullout. So you've got to be heads up. Keep your nose downstream, and follow me. All right?"

You could feel the excitement rise. "You bet!"

"All right. Let's go!"

You followed him down the middle of the river. Up ahead the sound changed. The babbling turned to a rumbling, and you saw water droplets spraying into the air. You watched Jackson slide into an angling green current and pick up speed, and suddenly you followed, eagerly and desperately. The current rushed you forward, and you felt the brief panic of being out of control. But you paddled and ruddered to keep after Jackson, and managed to slide right of a boulder that broke the river in front of you. The water then churned in a low froth, and you paddled with the quick chops you had seen Jackson making. You were heading for a gate between two boulder jumbles, where the current squeezed and accelerated, and the invisible water below roared. Jackson shot through and disappeared. You followed and felt the rush, and then your bow dropped. You leaned back reflexively to keep your bow from a kamikaze plunge into the river, and then you shot into calmer water. Jackson had pulled up in the slackwater, and he grinned at you.

"Say, you did that like an old pro, Dennis!" he called. "You've done this before!"

"Never in my life!" you shouted back, paddling closer to your guide. "Whew! That was fun!"

You paddled languidly another fifty yards in calm water and

beached at the River-run Café. There you bought beer, burgers, and fries, and you assured Jackson that you wanted to do this again.

You drank a second beer while Jackson bought a cheap ride back to his car from the café staff. Then you both toted the kayaks back up for a second run on the same stretch. You were hooked.

"I want to do more!" you said.

And you did. By summer's end Jackson had worked you up the American River to rougher stretches. You became competent in class three and survived one class-four run before the season was done.

"I love this! What a rush!"

When Jackson rode some class-five falls including a twenty-foot drop, you ferried the car and watched in awe.

"You know I want to do that," you told Jackson.

"I know. And I'm sure you will. But not this year."

By August the water levels were dropping fast. New rocks were exposed. Jackson told you that the season was done.

It was shortly after that first kayak season ended that you bought a house on Nob Hill. LC was Elsie now, and pregnant. Business was booming, and you felt like you owned the world!

Five

If you were asked what happened in 1981 you wouldn't know where to begin.

Ronald Reagan was sworn into office, and he appointed Richard Pratt to head the Federal Home Loan Bank Board.

"Do you know what that means?" Paul exulted. "It means we're free!"

"What do you mean?" you asked.

"Pratt understands the S&L industry. He's been our lobbyist for years; Herm knows him personally. He'll be cutting overregulation and allowing us to package loans in ways that let us thrive! It's the best thing that's happened to us in years!"

"So Western Freedom taking loans from its parent will now be really legal?"

"It won't be a problem, you can bet on that!"

"That's what we are betting on, Paul!"

They advertised more ambitiously in the *Chronicle* and on billboards, and business rose sharply.

"I'm processing these loans as fast as I can, Paul, and I can't keep up!"

"Are you verifying income? Some places are approving loans based on *stated income*. Maybe we should do that."

"It would save a lot of time. Also, it would qualify more borrowers."

"Do it."

"You're OK with the risk?"

"We're insured, Dennis! And Pratt is in charge! Make hay while the sun shines! Don't they say that in North Dakota?"

Business boomed, both upstairs and down. You and Paul both worked late every day of the week. After a month of that your wife with a newborn, me, told you she didn't like it.

"This isn't sitting real well at home, Paul. Elsie's got the baby all day, and…"

Paul studied his partner. He began to nod. "Yeah, you've got to take care of your own. Well, what do you think?"

"I think our business justifies another hire."

"Who do you think would be good?"

Dennis shrugged. "I've gotten to know Jackson a bit. I imagine he could be brought along."

"All right. Your storefront doesn't have room for another office. We'll need another space. Maybe a couple blocks over, what do you think?"

"I think… I think another location would increase our business, but might not decrease mine. It's a smart way to grow, but I don't know if I'll get home any earlier."

Paul nodded. "Let's think on it overnight. I'll talk to Jackson tomorrow and see what we can do."

Jackson was brought on board that week. He worked with you for four days, and by then Paul had secured another street-front office two short blocks away. Jackson moved in and soon was as busy as you.

The Warriors improved to almost .500, and the Giants broke .500 with the first black manager in major-league baseball — "And it's high time!" You and Paul agreed.

The next kayaking season took you and Jackson back to the American River and down to the Stanislaus, too. "Before it's gone," Jackson told you.

"What do you mean gone?" you asked.

Jackson looked at him in surprise. "Where do you live, man? You haven't heard about the New Melones Dam?"

"No. Why would I?"

"They're damming the river, flooding up the canyon!"

"Jackson, you're a tree-hugger!"

"No, I'm not trying to save some little fish. But the canyon is, or was, a great kayak run, and they're drowning it!"

"Why?"

"Oh, decent reasons. Flood control, irrigation, electricity generation. All the usual stuff."

"Ah. And who's *they*?"

"Army Corps of Engineers, Bureau of Reclamation. The federal government."

"Government. Well, I guess Reagan has that right, government is the problem. Maybe he'll stop it?"

"No chance. It's been in the works for decades. And the ag districts want it, and that's real money. Little guys like us kayakers, we can't fight them. It's already done, it's filling."

"How long will that take?"

"I hope it takes forever. I don't know. It should be several years."

"But it's still there now. The river."

Jackson nodded.

"Well. Then I guess it's like you said. At least we can get there before it's gone!" You didn't say, *Make hay while the sun shines*. You hadn't seemed to mind Paul saying it, but for you the maxim had a different connotation. It signified community cooperation, not grubbing up the last of something before leaving devastation behind you.

In May you and Jackson drove two cars across the Central Valley farmland, passing miles of tomatoes and cotton and walnuts and almonds, and on up Highway 4 to 49, the gold-mining country. You parked side by side.

"This bridge!" you exclaimed. "It's like something for a ten-lane freeway!"

Jackson shrugged. Highway 49 had grown since the old miners had travelled the foothills in search of gold, but it was still a two-lane road. In the midst of that worn and rugged landscape, the new bridge stretched its anomalously clean white concrete in a mass of construction that arced gracefully over a huge chasm of canyon to reconnect the severed ends of the old road. "It is a lot of concrete," he said flatly, "but I'm looking down, at the water. It's risen since I was last here."

You peered at the lake forming under the concrete span. "What do you think?"

"You can see it as well as I can. There'll be some slackwater paddling at the end. I can't tell how far up it goes. I guess we'll find out."

You hopped into Jackson's car and together made the mountain drive past Parrot's Ferry to Camp 9. You had expected white firs or at least pines at your launch, but instead the road wound through sparse chaparral on rocky red soil, an infertile and hostile landscape that made you think of Mars. You twisted down sere precipices, windows up and AC running, until you finally smoothed into a slope of blue oaks as you re-approached the river. There the trees still wore their spring-green foliage, and a mute scrub jay floated among them. Above, the sun was yellow, and a kettle of turkey vultures turned patiently, like the sixth inning of a low-scoring baseball game.

Through this slow land the river raced, rippling high with snowmelt, fast and smooth like muscle.

"Killer water," said Jackson. "Follow me this first run!"

You double-checked your lifejacket and helmet straps and climbed into your kayak. Following Jackson, you shoved from shore and let the current take you.

The canyon walls soon squeezed toward the river, creating a steep V that rushed the water through, and then they slightly backed off again, and the water relaxed.

"It's an accordion!" you shouted, but Jackson didn't hear as he entered the next squeeze, where a cataract roared. Eager for the rush and wanting to follow Jackson's route you charged after him, yellow paddles flashing. You shot over an eight-foot drop and smacked down into a fast-flowing but smooth pool. Below, Jackson held in an eddy, and you charged to him.

"You didn't tell me you were taking me off Niagara Falls!" you shouted.

Jackson just grinned. "All that matters is your landing!" He flashed a thumb's up.

You passed through gulch after gulch—Grapevine, Marianne, Wolf, and Skunk. Each had its rapids and routes through, but none dropped you like Cataract Gulch had.

"Have you noticed the canyon walls?" Jackson asked in a quiet stretch.

You looked. "What are they, granite?"

"Limestone. You're in the deepest limestone canyon west of the Mississippi."

"Probably in the country then! Can't be any deeper in the east."

"I don't know. You're probably right."

At Deadman's Bar you gazed up at the Parrot's Ferry Bridge high above you.

"That's almost as big as the other one!"

"It's a deep canyon."

You passed under the bridge. The current still flowed swiftly, but white water became rare and then disappeared altogether. The remaining muscle of rippling green water soon went slack, too.

"Damn," Jackson said. "We've got a good mile to paddle still."

So you paddled.

"This is the kind of thing those long-lake kayaks are good for. They hold a truer course, they'll even use a rudder or a sked. Oh well," Jackson shrugged.

You paddled on, and you reflected on the importance of having the right tools: the right kayak for different water, just like the right information for different investment purposes. It was all the same. When an osprey flew over you added the bird to your formulation: the right beak and eyes and talons to live by the hunt. The right tools let you prosper.

You and Jackson made a second trip to the Stanislaus in late

June, but you parked at Parrot's Ferry rather than Highway 49, to reduce the slackwater you had to traverse. The river was slower than it had been in spring, but more rocks were exposed, creating new hazards and challenges.

"Keep to the right on the cataract," Jackson advised you, and as you landed you saw snaggle-toothed stone shards cutting the water to your left.

"Jackson," you said later, "how did guys ever make it down these rivers for the first time?"

"I'm sure there was a lot of shipwreck," Jackson grinned. "That's what culture is, Dennis. The one's who've done it teach the new ones; it saves pain."

You were pleased to make several class-four runs that summer, full of drops and chopping white water. Back on the American River, you were developing your cultural know-how, learning many stretches well, so that you could choose your own path through even the rough parts, sometimes intentionally following the routes that needed the most skill and offered the greatest thrill; and you began to understand the changes in the water, the different opportunities and dangers as water levels rose and then fell through the summer. "It's all risk and reward, isn't it, Jackson," you said.

That was in August. At the end of the year Jacques Cousteau came out with a detailing of the risks and losses in the going uses of water. The book made quite a splash. As if tied to a rock and thrown into New Melones Reservoir. Financiers couldn't be expected to attend to everything.

I had been born in the spring. I've seen the pictures, pre-digital. I was dark-eyed, wispy-haired, and apparently quiet. You said that I studied the world around me, absorbing everything I saw, and you held me close those evenings and rocked and smiled. Maybe something in holding me reminded you of your sister Margaret, and hearing her sing you sang to me. "Lullaby, and goodnight, go to sleep little baby, Dadadumda, dadadumda, daddle-deedle-di-de-oh." It was OK that you didn't know the words.

Mom's parents came to visit. She and her mom monopolized the baby, and you had to sit with Grandpa. Not that Steve was much of a sitter. He stood and looked out our window.

"So that's the Golden Gate! It's not really golden, is it?!"

"No, no it's not."

"In the Golden State even! It's sort of a red, isn't it? That's not good."

"I guess I've gotten used to it."

"That's not good either. Don't want to get used to running in the red!"

You chuckled agreeably. "No, don't want to do that. But don't you think the sun on that bridge looks good?"

Steve nodded. "Yeah, I guess you get used to a thing." He stared at the bridge angling away. The near end gleamed its industrial rouge in the morning sun; the far end plunged into fog. "Sometimes I worry about it all, though. Your business is good?"

"Best ever!"

"Well, that's good, I guess. When was that bridge built, Dennis? Forties?"

"Thirties or forties."

"Heck of a time then. That's when I grew up, you know. I was born in good times, Silent Cal was president, the Roaring Twenties! But it all fell apart when I was still a kid, barely a kid. So I grew up in the Crash."

Hearing what you already knew, you said, "That had to be hard."

He nodded and spoke slowly. "My dad had a laundry business, but who could afford clean clothes then? You've seen the old photos. Sure, folks would try to look presentable, they needed a job! But mostly they needed food and heat. Less and less laundry came in, and I remember hearing my parents talking after we went to bed. 'Ellen,' he said, 'we're not going to make it.' And she said, 'That's not a choice, Ralph. The choice is—How are we going to make it?' She had always tried to push him to be more ambitious. She wanted what any good mother wanted—a bigger house with new drapes and a big front window with flowerboxes on the porch, and new clothes from Macy's for all of us kids. With the Crash she just wanted to survive. But he wasn't that man. 'I already feel like a heel, El. These folks come in without two nickels to rub together, and they give me their one to try to look like something. Thinking maybe they'll get a job as a clerk, or the women as a secretary or a wife to someone with a job. But I know and they know, too, only they can't admit it, that there isn't a job, even to marry to, or that there are thirty people trying to get the one job there is, and then it still won't buy more than soup. How can I take their nickel, El? How can I? They have to eat, too!' Mom had no problem. 'You take it because you're doing their laundry, they came to you to do it! And you take it because you have your own wife and children to provide for! You're not responsible for theirs!' He sighed. 'I'm not? I guess that's what Cain taught Abel. But even so, El, it still won't be enough.' But Mom could have been a Rockefeller, she said, 'Then you need to take your business to people who do have money! They're out there, and they can pay more than a nickel to have their suits cleaned and pressed!'

"And she was right, of course, and it's the philosophy I've always lived by. As a kid I hustled newspapers and even built a little empire. I farmed out the lousy routes where people didn't pay to younger kids, and I took the routes through the neighbor-hoods with fresh paint and Christmas bonuses. When I became a bellboy, I did it at the Grandview Hotel where customers were well dressed and expected to tip good service, not at the Main Street where my dad's shop was. When my brother went into the CCC I latched onto Jeremiah Wilkinson, a customer at the

Grandview. He brought me into his printing business. 'Everybody needs printing,' he said. 'They need their stationery and business cards, but even more than that they need forms, triplicate forms, to keep track of whatever it is they do. The military, hospitals, banks, restaurants—everybody needs printing!' It sounded right to me, and, you know, it became a very lucrative business for us. Me and mine. I feel bad that my parents never got the wealth they wanted, they deserved. But they were big enough to be happy for their children, who all did better than they.

"Yeah, we did better. Roosevelt spent money like a geyser, first on public works and then on the war, but that gave us jobs and productivity that shot us right out of the Depression, so even my brother in the CCC went on to a successful career. He clerked in auto-parts manufacturing, an outfit in Ohio. He says they did just fine; he raised four kids, two of them went to college, and he's set to retire next year. But I did the best. Old Wilkinson was right. And my mom was right, too. You've got to sell where there's money.

"But that's where I get hung up, some, Dennis. That's where I get hung up. Because I don't think my dad was all wrong, either. What about all those people in the black and white photos? They're America too, and they haven't gone away. They're still here, just like they were back in the thirties. And they still need food and heat, and clean clothes, and probably auto parts, too!"

He dropped into silence.

You said, "Well, we have to hope the growth continues, and pulls everybody along."

"Oh," Steve pulled his gaze from the bridge, "I don't know, maybe it can. I just know what's gone before. A new thing started in the fifties, along when you and Elsie were born. Not for me, not in printing; that's always a matter of the right marks on paper. But in Charlie's work—that's my brother, Charlie—he said they started making cheaper material. Wilkinson was bought out

75

and the new owner wanted to make more money. So they used cheaper metals, and sometimes plastic when that took off. They cut corners to get bids from Detroit; they lowered their safety and quality standards, in the products and on the floor. They started automating the manufacture, laying people off. And it all worked, Charlie says. The company lands contracts and gets richer, and he's gotten decent pay. But I just think of every company in the country doing that. All those people getting laid off. And all those products, in cars, in construction, in airplanes and bridges out there, in furniture, in kitchen appliances, in kids' toys, everything! If we're all cutting corners to get the bid, well, we're all buying junk because that's what we're making! Somehow it doesn't seem that can be good."

"They say it moves the economy. You said yourself your brother is well paid."

"Yeah. It's good for business. For each individual business, that is. But I begin to wonder if it's good for all of us together, if we're not just building a thin and brittle plastic reality that won't hold up in the future."

"I suppose it's easier to say that as you get closer to retirement, after your fortune is made."

"Maybe it is, maybe it is. Maybe the voting age should be sixty, what do you think of that?" He turned the question to his wife Marianne, who was entering the room with Mom and little me, but she didn't answer.

You laughed. "You run on that platform, and good luck to you!"

"Dennis," Mom said, "Jenny's up now and it's a good time to take a drive. Let's take Mom and Dad to the Wharf. We can go to lunch."

"All right."

You all loaded into the Eldorado. Mom carefully buckled me into the car seat, pulled on the straps to check them, and the women climbed in on either side.

In the front Steve said to you, "So you're using one of those baby seats."

You nodded. "Yeah, Elsie wants to, and I guess it makes sense."

"What do you think about the chatter to require seat belts?"

You shook your head. "It seems like it should be an individual choice."

Steve nodded. "Detroit's sure fighting it. Says it'll tack hundreds on to the price of a car."

"Well," grinned Dennis, "if it's not good for GM it's not good for America!"

Steve continued nodding.

You kept your eyes on the road, which routed to the Wharf through the Financial District.

* * *

When Jordan was born I, too, was careful to buckle him in. By then of course there were both seat-belt and child-seat laws. I tried to give him the best of everything.

A firm mattress. Sleeping on his back.

Baby food. I bought the organics.

Singing with him. "Rock-a-bye-Baby," "Raffi," and "Row, row, row your boat."

Reading to him. Every night, and daytimes, too. Way before there could have been any understanding of the words. I loved the way he gummed the cardboard *Goodnight Moon*, and I loved knowing, feeling, that he and I were part of the long parade of human existence, of raising and being raised, of loving.

And of course I breastfed him. He was hungry like a baby should be, and sometimes he bit, although his first teeth didn't come in until he was seven months. But we learned how to nurse in almost no time. I got to stay home that first summer, so didn't have to pump until later. That was a nuisance, of course, but that's where we were then.

His eyes were blue as the midmorning sky after a rainstorm, and I could see him listening to me. He started tracking real early, and looking for where a voice was coming from. He'd turn his head, and his wispy-light hair wouldn't lie flat; it rumpled like a last few petals on an autumn daisy. But his eyes would find you and his face would just smile like St. Peter at the Golden Gate; or no, like something more innocent and less ponderous than Peter; just like only a baby.

We bought him a little stroller, blue for the boy, of course, and I took him for walks through the neighborhood. I'd point out the sounds—airplane, crow, car—and he started to react to them. At the park we'd see squirrels and older kids playing on the bars and through the slides and tunnels. We're such little chimpanzees, you know, just playing. And then as we get older—I'd sit with another mom in the winter sun or summer shade and watch the kids play. Not Jordan right away, he was still in the stroller. But he watched, too, and he heard us talking, and I'm sure it was a sound that, just by being familiar in a peaceful time, became a source of comfort. The sound of moms talking as they watch their kids, I don't know if you can beat that for the first year of life.

And all of it was just building his world, showing him that it was safe and beautiful and interesting. I laugh at all the administrative scurrying over education; or maybe sort of cry. Nothing wrong with "academic rigor" that the dervishes always proclaim over, but that's not what matters first. It's just that the child should experience that the world is interesting, and that he or she is capable of learning and loving it, and that he or she is loved. That's what matters.

And the chimps know it better than we. And I guess the bonobos know it better than the chimps. Or knew it. Are there still any bonobos?

I don't want to talk myself bitter now. But ISIL in the news now after the US in Iraq and Afghanistan, and Al Qaeda and its cousins, and all of it just the freshest in the long history of humans hurting humans, back to Vietnam, Korea, World War II, the War to End All Wars (Hah!), the Spanish-America War, the American Indian genocide, the Civil War, the Mexican-American War, the War of 1812, the Revolutionary War. And that's just the US, and that's just recent. It's the whole human history, back to the first ape with a stick, and before that—the chimps give us our glimpse, they kill and eat each other. Education? Pah! All we've done is get better at atrocity, not better at loving.

Get me out of here. The TV, the new dress, the iPhone 6+, the beer-wine-booze-pot-crack. Sugar.

Stop!

Maybe I should take up yoga. What do you think?

Ah, it's not your fault, any more than it's mine. We're all just Forrest Gump's feather.

But we have to be responsible, don't we? Otherwise we're just uglier and uglier.

The sun was so fine, sitting with the other moms, with Jordan in the stroller, watching the children play.

You and Mom must have felt the same with me, back in '81. I know you took me to Golden Gate Park, where we must have had our morning suns, our fresh breezes. We must have rolled through the Japanese Tea Garden. And I remember a bear, I remember it clearly, as big as a house, shaggy brown and standing huge with its teeth bigger than my head; that must have been in the DeYoung Museum. I even remember Stevie, although maybe I'm making the memory up.

Of course I don't remember the spoon-feeding, the diaper-changing, the middle-of-the-night rocking. Nobody does, until maybe they have their own child and then can remember it through the echo. Or maybe they get that through a younger sibling. I do remember you and Mom holding Stevie and, vaguely, lying on the floor with both of us, your eyes and nose big from being close, Stevie drooling. I think I remember him chewing on *Pat the Bunny*, and I was upset, as if I hadn't done the same thing a couple years earlier! And I remember you saying it was OK, so I chewed on *Where the Wild Things Are* and you frowned: "When you're one." And I must be making this memory up, because I was only three then, if he was one.

So much happens before conscious memory. So now I've made it up, creative remembering. But the make-up is not based on nothing, even though the something may be from the future. It is still re-membering, putting the members of my past together, just using later insights to make them, and maybe make them less historical but more true. An inexact science, but more insightful than a chronology of only the documented. A butterfly cannot document its caterpillar days, but still they happened. Or, in our case, dung has no memory of being a peach.

But that's not quite it either. We do become conscious, and if we can avoid preoccupation with the shiny, whirring flies and beetles, we can remember our better selves.

So 1981. I was born, and you loved me and made my world, me, feel comfortable, safe, and full of joy. Reagan was inaugurated, and business boomed. You kayaked, and the hobby became a pleasure that would last for decades. And when I was still crawling, the Forty-niners surprised everybody by piling up wins that led into the playoffs and then, with class and style, to a Super Bowl victory. I'm sure that you and Paul became believers in, say, November, and Paul passed out "Forty-niner Faithful" bumperstickers to both colleagues and clients. Business boomed.

Six

After your great but passing sadness, you started taking me kayaking.

"Just in the lake, Elsie. Near the shore. With a lifejacket. With me. She won't fall, and even if she does the lifejacket pops her up and holds her head above water, and I'll be right there." You were intent on keeping fear from ruining our lives, ruining mine.

Mom sighed her nervous sigh. "I'm going with you," she determined.

"Great!"

"Yeah, Mommy! You can go kayaking, too!" I cried.

"I will not!"

And she did not.

You had had me sit in a plastic kayak in the back yard, practicing my strokes, seeing how the paddle feathered. I had tried on the life vest a million times. It was red with black straps that you latched up snug.

"That's tight, Dad."

"Good! That's what keeps you floating, with your head up."

"But I can swim!" You, you and Mom, that is, had started me swimming when I was two, but I probably wasn't more than a competent and fearless dog-paddler.

"Yes, but this is what we do whenever we're on a boat."

"Hm."

It was a sunny day, so the cool water felt refreshing when I walked in. The beach was cleared smooth, a gravelly dirt. Some other people were getting into a green canoe there, and I could see a man and a boy fishing. I wondered if they caught anything, and I wondered if that would be fun if you and I went fishing. Most of the lake was lined with green grasses and bushes and trees, and people and their dogs walked on a pathway through the green. There were ducks with green heads, too, and gray-

and-white gulls squawking around all over.

I was wearing my blue-and-white bathing suit with the little frilly wrinkles around the middle. Mom said those were so that the suit would look nice as I grew. You had me wear pink-and-black water socks, and I couldn't tell if Mom thought they were pretty or not.

You carried the kayaks to the water, yours and mine, red and yellow. I carried the paddles. Mom carried the lifejackets. I stayed with her while you went back to the car.

The ducks and gulls came in close, and I was afraid of the gulls with their pointy bills and mean yellow eyes. Mom must have seen that, because she said, "They just want us to feed them."

"What do they eat?"

"Breadcrumbs."

"Oh."

Mom sighed. "Maybe we can bring some next time."

"Maybe you can kayak with us next time, too."

"No, I'll watch."

I nodded understanding, mimicking you. "But some day, when you're ready."

"We'll see."

Of course Mom never went. Maybe she would have, though. Yes, I think she would have.

After you tightened my lifejacket we walked to my kayak, the yellow one, and that's when I felt the refreshing cool on my ankles and seeping into my water socks. Mom followed us and stopped at the end of my kayak, resting on the shallow beach.

You had me climb into the boat without your help, although Mom held the stern with both hands. "Hand on the far gunwale," you pointed, "and then both feet in." The boat rocked and scraped on the bottom, as I climbed in and sat, my legs stretched forward inside.

"If she tips over she'll be trapped!" Mom worried.

"No spray skirt, Elsie. She'd dump right out and bob right up."

"Do you know, Jenny, if you tip you climb out of the kayak!" she said anxiously.

I looked at you, but you didn't catch my eye. "I know," I said.

"And if you're tipping, take a breath, Jenny!"

"OK, Mom, I will."

You walked the kayak out to where Mom couldn't reach it, where you were knee deep. From the bow, you tilted it one way and then the other. I automatically tilted away from the spill.

"There," you said, still holding the kayak, "you're a natural balancer! Now try your paddle, go ahead."

I pulled at the water, one side and the other, twisting my wrists to feather just like you'd shown me.

"Perfect! I can really feel that! OK, lay your paddle across your lap and wait for me!"

You pulled me to float near your kayak and quickly climbed in.

Mom pulled out a camera and snapped a few shots. "Be safe!" she called to both of us.

"We will," we both replied.

We paddled side by side along the lake. Some ducks came near us, but not for long. The people in the green canoe paddled past us, and I waved. They waved back.

We kayaked in Merced Lake a couple times more that summer, and Mom stopped coming with us after I didn't die a few times. Then you took us down to San Gregorio in the cold fog to paddle in the lagoon, but that didn't have the current you wanted, so next we tried the Pescadero Marsh. It was ocean cloudy again, but we had some sea swell that rocked our kayaks.

"Woaw!" I let you see my big eyes as my boat heaved.

You laughed. "Pretty cool, huh!"

"Yeah," I said, because what else could I say!

You had me ride the gentle swells for a good while, sideways and bow first and stern first.

Then a seal swam by, surging like the waves up and down, and stopping to watch us, just its head out of the water. I wanted to pet it, but you paddled next to me and made me keep my distance.

"It's a wild animal, Jen. You always give a wild animal its space."

"But it's cute, Daddy! Look at its big brown eyes."

"Yeah, doe eyes. Yeah, it's cute. So you can watch it."

You stayed right by me and we watched it, and the waves swelled in and we bobbed up and down and I didn't even think about them anymore. I thought about that seal and wondered if it would let me pet it, if I was gentle and patient. It dove underwater and disappeared.

"Let's see if we can find some river current," you said.

So we paddled up through the marsh, but the Pescadero Creek inlet became very narrow without any detectable current, so we turned around when we could and tried the Butano Creek inlet. That stayed wider longer, but still didn't offer any current.

I don't know what Mom did in those times we went kayaking. She had her friend Mrs. Anderson, "Annie," that she did stuff with sometimes, but I think they mostly went out in the evenings, and not very often. Mom didn't seem to want to go out with her much, but I heard you tell her, "Elsie, you've got to get over that. What was done can't be undone, and you're not doing any good by being sour. Not any good for either of us."

I think she probably worked on her roses, or maybe just rested.

So I never made it to a river that year, but I continued to take swim lessons. Mom took me twice a week. She said I had to be able to swim if I wanted to go river kayaking. I don't know if that's true, because you said you pretty much float in your lifejacket if you get spilled. But it was true for Mom in any case, and I was glad to learn swimming.

At the pool, and at home, too, Mom spent a lot of time just looking at me. Or that's what I thought, but sometimes I realized she wasn't looking at me or anything, at least not anything visible. I probably understood then, I think I did. But I know I do now. Hell, I spend time looking at nothing myself.

Stevie was one, so I was three. You and Mom read him the stories I liked when I was little, and I liked that because I got to scootch in with you and listen, too. He drooled a lot, but we kept a little white blankey nearby so we could wipe him up. And after the stories I would kiss him and you and Mom, and one of you would take me to bed and one of you would stay with Stevie.

Sometimes I read him stories myself. He was a good listener, and I would explain the books to him. Of course now I know that I was making up what the books were about, but that made no difference. We sat on the cushions Mom had put to the side of the living-room window, and you had hung a lamp down where I could reach the pull on it, and the heat from the old register under the window eased up by us and we read. Dr, Suess and Maurice Sendak and Eric Carle and *Go, Dog, Go*, and *Curious George*, and all the Disney Golden Books and bunches of others; and those were my books, and we read his books, too, the little cardboard ones, including my favorite, *Goodnight Moon*. I loved all that, and snuggling with Stevie, and sometimes now if I'm not careful I can confuse holding Stevie with holding Jordan.

I certainly read to Jordan all the time. When he was just a drooly little blue-eyed, gummy-smiled finger-holder, I held the books that crumbled wet at the corners from teething. I read the story, same story, over and over again. I saw Bill nodding to sleep over those books, trying half-valiantly to read them but, after a day at work, unable to keep the words flowing, his head dropping and checking and dropping to his chest, his eyelids similarly slipping toward his cheeks, his words dripping into nonsense and silence until Jordan jostled for more, which startled him into another brave-but-abortive effort. I imagine Mom watched you make the same forgivable fatherly failure. Or did she? Yes. She stopped working, even if that was primarily to escape her clientele, the abused and confused, the smelly, the barely literate, the incoherent thinkers that disgusted and frightened her. Instead she got me, and then Stevie. We, too, were smelly, illiterate, and incoherent, and probably too ignorant to be confused. But we were not abused.

At least we didn't think so, as far as we thought. Nor by any standards held throughout history. But by your own standards? Your time was unique, your awareness was unique. Your actions should have been, too.

Why should I judge? I shouldn't, I suppose. I can do a better job than yours without condemning yours. But I can't help it. Your life sometimes blazes out at me as a quiet hypocrisy, an evil that—oh, if there were a god, the medieval hell you should endure: your senses enhanced to a divine acuity, and then slow, relentless tortures of ulcer, virus, and vermin; or no, perhaps your increased awareness would self-torture. That would do, I think. But it's hard to imagine such self-reflection and responsibility in you.

I guess I don't wish pain on you really. If there were a god, then, like decent people, I'd want that god to be merciful, not just. That would be soothing, is soothing, even to contemplate. So I should forgive you. Am I that divine? I am still alive. And my forgiveness, whether I give it to you or not, doesn't make what you did, or didn't do, right.

But god seems to be just our own judging and acting. And there is the frightening responsibility, there is the hope. You will not be damned to hell. You will not luxuriate in forgiveness or glory. You will be extinguished. So what you have is your life before you are extinguished. I know I must look to my own, but when I look at yours my stomach turns.

Did I tell you how sweet Jordan felt against my breasts? I'd like to think you saw it. Mom did. And you, even you, a father, must have felt something of it when you held me and Stevie. And maybe you didn't even have to forget that sometimes babies bite! You felt it, directly or watching Mom. And you did all the little things that matter—the reading, the singing, the playing. But it was a time that needed big things, the things outside the walls of home that make home possible. That was your unique time.

I do appreciate the little things. I might have taken Jordan kayaking, too.

Was I eleven, maybe twelve, when you first took me on the river? By then you had taught me to Eskimo roll; instead of leaning away from the spill, twist into it, get momentum to go through it! It was a great feeling! Not that I ever spilled much, at least accidentally. At first you took me on lower stretches of the river. That first time there were only ripples. I know you just wanted me to feel the current, to begin to learn how to use it, to experience how it could cross me up.

Mom came with us, too, although I suspect you'd have rather she not. You were both concerned that I survive, but her concern was a constant crow that saw hazard in every pebble, so that I might as well have stayed at home. Your concern dealt more with the boulders, above water and below. I guess I have to be impressed that the two of you worked at reaching common ground.

"What if she can't turn up when she's flipped, Dennis? She's locked into the kayak now."

"Elsie, first, we're going on a smooth stretch; she probably won't spill. Second, she's done a thousand Eskimo rolls in the lake; she knows how to turn up. Third, she's not locked into the kayak; she can slide out of it anytime she wants, it's even easier under water because you're not fighting gravity. Fourth, I'll be nearby to help. She'll be OK."

"What if she clunks her head on a rock? Then she can't turn up or climb out!"

"That's why she has a helmet, to protect her head."

"But you can't guarantee that she'll be safe!"

You sighed. "No. A bull could fall out of the sky and land on her, squash her flat. But you've got to be reasonable, Elsie!"

"I am being reasonable! You're putting a twelve-year-old [*that's it, I was twelve!*] into moving water. You've always told me how powerful a current is!"

But her tone had retreat in it. She would let you get me into the water.

So we did.

Driving from Sunnyvale—we'd moved there when I was six—to the American River—the geography was all a blur to me. But I remember the marshes, which now I think must have been near Suisun. I remember swirls of ducks and geese, and once you pointed out pelicans. And the blackbirds swarmed in those beautiful flocks, turning black and sunlit gray as they eddied through the air, hundreds or thousands of them turning in serial unison, choreographed by some Russian composer, I suppose; or no, the Russians are that beautiful but not that free. Are there Mexican composers—or, or, who would it be? Just the birds. Americans maybe. It's always some of them, I guess.

We never stopped at the marshes. I never thought to ask. They were something you drove by. And now I'm thinking I must have seen all those birds in the winter when we went to Tahoe, not in the summer when we kayaked. In summer those birds are in the arctic raising their young, up in the six-month sunlight that grows food for them.

I remember going through the fields, too. Yes, I think it was winter, with stubble, not rice or tomatoes, on the ground. But there was a hawk on every telephone pole, and we figured some of them must have been eagles, although we couldn't tell which.

We drove up the American and you pulled in along the river.

The place smelled like rivers do—algae, I think. It's a fresh and clean smell, although not exactly a sweet one.

I couldn't carry a kayak on my own yet, but I fastened my own helmet and lifejacket. You quickly checked them, maybe just to show Mom that you were being careful. She stood nearby looking awkward on the rocks and trying not to be nervous as she had been years before when you first took me out on Lake Merced. Once again she took pictures, now with a digital camera.

We crawled into our kayaks and adjusted our spray skirts.

"OK, Jen, let's go!"

We were in a wide, slow, smooth stretch of river. Out in the middle you said, "OK, flip one now. Just to show off for Mom."

I leaned to my right, positioning my paddle on my left to take the broad stroke that would complement my underwater twist to pop me back up. I couldn't have been underwater for two seconds.

"Way to go," you said.

I waved to Mom. She shook her head, but even at that distance I could see her smile, at once proud and disapproving.

She watched until we rounded the first bend. Then she would drive ahead to meet us at a pullout three miles downriver.

At first the water was slow, although still quicker than a lake. When we saw a fallen tree ahead you said, "There can be branches underwater that you could get hung up on, so keep well to the left." You led and I followed.

We had already discussed, at length, what to do if I got dumped. "Ride the current on your back, feet up to protect against rocks or logs. Gradually make your way to the closer bank, but never fight the current because you'll lose, and avoid getting into brush or trees where there's current, because it can pin you and kill you. Find a clear beach or find a protected bit of stream, out of the main current." I felt ready.

We passed several little beaches, and I thought how nice it

would be to camp there. Most of them already had little campfire rings, and some had stone-and-wood benches around the rings. Often they were a little trashy, with aluminum cans flashing red or blue from the rocky shore, and plastic grocery bags plastered into the willows; but still they lured me with some primitive call for outdoor adventure. I suppose if I were raised to it I could have been a good cavewoman. Our DNA's the same, or nearly. But we aren't raised to it, are we. I wouldn't have a clue.

No, we were in a more advanced time, right? I was twelve, so it was 1993. Your S&L had suffered its losses with all the others, but all the shady dealing was teaching a simple lesson: financial contortions that ruined others were worth it—the taxpayers bailed the contortionists out and made them wealthy. Tough luck to the losers. Milken had been convicted and come out a billionaire.

You and Paul had bilked your clients for all they were worth, too—more than they were worth, and that's where the taxpayers came in—and run your venture into the ground. But you were no fool, were you, Dad. You jumped ship into a job with a ratings agency. There, you said, your experience would allow you to curb the abuses of financial packages that were bound to cause default—the balloon payments, the separation of financial-service salaries from company products, the payment of fund managers for short-term profits, the finance companies taking a generous share of their clients' market gains but sharing none of the losses. You'd made your little killing in the S&L. Now you were positioned to do real social good.

I was oblivious to all that, just as I was oblivious to the swallows skimming over the river and the plastic bags caught in the willows. I don't know whether you saw them. I barely did, and they definitely made no impression on me. But I was only twelve. You knew better, or should have.

We drifted and paddled. Some stretches the water was smooth as blown glass but deceptively strong. There we could cover ground with little effort, just riding the current. Some stretches slowed and we had to paddle to move along toward Mom with the lunches. A few stretches offered occasional rocks to avoid, but I followed you past them. I never felt threatened by the river. I never had to make an Eskimo roll.

We spotted Mom ahead on the left bank, just past a bridge. She'd pulled out a folding chair and was sipping at a Diet Pepsi and reading a magazine. She always picked up magazines at the checkout counter.

I called ahead, and she looked up and waved. When we approached she said, "Well, you survived!"

"Yep! It was fun!" I reported.

"Well, good. Now maybe you can cross river-kayaking off your list."

I wasn't old enough to be sarcastic. I just looked at her uncertainly.

"The mosquitoes here are terrible!" she said, waving at the air.

You and I pulled our kayaks ashore.

We didn't normally picnic. You both preferred to find a local café. But this time Mom had packed ham-and-cheese sandwiches, chips, apples, brownies, and sodas. I think she'd had to occupy herself while you and I were loading for the trip. Now you carried the ice chest down from the car, and I fetched the other two folding chairs. Mom produced a can of bug spray and dosed us both.

"Hide your eyes," she told me, and I did. I'd gotten used to the smell, but it still made my nose twitch as I felt it cool on my arms, legs and around from the back of my neck. "There you are!" she finished.

I started with a Pepsi, like Mom.

"Next time I want some white water, Dad."

"Yeah, a little bit, we'll get you there."

Mom just grimaced. She waved her magazine. "They're still

talking about the World Trade Center!"

"It's kind of a big deal," you said.

"Well I don't like to hear about it. That's your department. But *Jurassic Park* gets OK reviews. We should go see it."

"All right."

"And you know *Scattergories* won't be on TV any more. I'll have to find a show to replace it." Mom didn't object to playing games, but she preferred to watch them.

You nodded.

The wind had shifted, turning upriver. It would be stronger later in the day as the valley heated, but was already warm. A black trash bag stuck in a willow waved at the incoming water. I was close enough to notice.

"Why do people leave their garbage?" I asked.

"They're lazy, or thoughtless," you said. "And the county doesn't help by not having any trash cans out."

"I see trash at school even where we have cans."

You nodded. "Yeah. And it would be expensive for the county to patrol the river."

"White trash," Mom chimed in.

I didn't know the term and thought she must be looking at a different bag than I was.

She left half her sandwich and some chips for the birds, neatly on the wrapping to keep them out of the dirt, and we loaded the kayaks on top of the car. I helped with that, but you fastened the straps.

We drove off and the river was quickly out of sight, even though we followed its drainage.

We stopped for gas at a red, white, and blue station, as we always did. "I prefer them," you'd said. "They cost a little more, but I trust them."

This time it wasn't as polished up as you liked, though. You had explained to me that gas is like a car's food, and oil is like its blood, that keeps it running. Well this station was bleeding all over. Not right then, but over a long period, it seemed. There was oil on the pavement, all over and right up onto the mat heading into the little glassed-in convenience store. I knew that the cars that came there must be leaking oil, and I understood that that meant they were older cars, cars of poorer people.

You frowned. "This place could use a little TSP! Oh, well, we need gas."

I had my window rolled down and could hear the traffic from the freeway. Then I heard two people coming from the next-door fast-food place.

"That's right, bitch! Pay your own rent! And pay for your own goddamn Big Mac, too! And don't ever let me see you again!" He was gesticulating wildly, walking backwards.

She was standing fifteen feet behind him, hands on hips, leaning forward. "Good riddance, you shit-head bastard! You come to my house again and I'll call the cops!"

He was the color of the oily pavement, and she was almost as dark, although her hair looked like it was blonde underneath. They were both wearing unusual clothes that I remember just as bunchy, dirty-colored fabric.

"Your house! Under a bridge, you mean?"

She stared at him and then abruptly turned, at first heading down the sidewalk, then veering toward the fast-food place where a clean-uniformed teenager stood looking, and then back down the sidewalk, walking away, fast.

"And don't ask me for child support, you bitch!" he called. "You said you were on birth control!" He turned and spotted you, who had cleaned the windshield while the gas pumped. He made a pointed glance at our kayaks and strode toward us. You walked down the car and stopped between him and me with my open window that I couldn't close because you had the car key. I could smell him when he got close.

"Hey, man," he said, again glancing at the kayaks. "Could

you loan me ten bucks for gas? It's gotten so expensive now, and I'm traveling."

"Where's your car?" you said.

He chuckled. "Yeah, OK, I don't really have a car. What I want is something to eat."

"Sorry," you shook your head, "all I have is a credit card."

He paused and I saw his torn khaki sleeve lean up on the car. "Can't help a guy out, huh?"

Then the attendant came out of the convenience store. He was a big man in a blue shirt. "Move along, please," he said like he meant it.

There was another pause, and then the sleeve pulled away. "I see," and then repeated more loudly, "I see! You fat cats think you control the goddam world! You own your boats and your gasoline and you charge more and more for it all the time, and guys like me are just left to go hang. I see! I know what you are! You're all working for the government, that's what you are! More bastards!" He turned and was almost struck by a beige sedan pulling into the station. He thumped the hood of that car as it stopped, visibly denting it. Two men popped out, Hispanics, one from each front door. "What the hell are you doing?" the driver shouted. The smelly man turned and ran, just twisting back after twenty strides or so to shout a profanity at all of us.

"I'm sorry," the gas-station attendant said to you and the other two men.

"No harm. Thank you," you said.

You climbed into the car and started to drive. You only fastened your seat belt when Mom reminded you at the corner stoplight there. I turned back. Three men were looking at the beige car's dent in the hood.

You were breathing kind of hard through the nose.

"Those are the sort of people I used to work with," Mom said.

You shook your head. "I've never been confronted like that!"

"You stood between him and Jenny," she said.

"Yeah. I did that." You seemed a little lost. "I don't know what I'd have done if the attendant hadn't come out."

"You'd have given him ten bucks and said goodbye."

"Yeah. Walked him away from the car first."

Mom nodded.

"It's good the attendant showed, though."

We were zipping along on the freeway by then, and you were no longer breathing hard.

So you learned what you would do if some guy begs aggressively at you. You'd try to solve the immediate problem. I remember Andrew in my freshman dorm. He said you're not supposed to drop your food to get away from a bear, because it just teaches the bear to approach people, to beg aggressively. But I know I've never had to make that choice, to fight the bear or give it ten bucks.

Anyway, I learned something different. I learned how we can make problems spiral worse or better. That guy started with a fight with the girl, and he turned it into an ugly scene, first with her, then with us, then with the attendant and the beige-car people. But everyone afterwards was making it better. The attendant shooed the man away. The beige-car guys were looking at how they could fix the dent. Mom helped you settle down. All that made me feel like, yeah there were problems, but the world could work. With consideration, the world could work.

Seven

1984. I was three. So my memories are both close to home and mostly conjectural.

You, of course, were my home. I'd known you all my little life; or not known you, but been learning you. I suppose I first met you, once I was me, *in utero*, back in 1980. They say the child starts to hear as early as sixteen weeks, and I'm sure your voice became familiar, lower and smoother than Mom's, and becoming with hers a sort of auditory home for me; the sounds that shaped my comfort. Did you talk to me then, as you did later? I bet you did. So by the time I was born you were familiar, family. I'm sure I still cried in your arms. Babies do that, I know, and moms are inevitably closer, at that age if not always. Moms are blessed in that way, and cursed.

But in your arms I'd have learned the feel and smell of you, as well as the tone and cadence of your voice; and all of that, of you, would have meant home. I can't remember you consciously from then, of course. You were younger, your arms probably less hairy, a soft thin mat. Your face and torso leaner, your smile perhaps cockier, your hair darker and thicker, but still cut short, I'm sure. And your voice kind and steady as ever, but probably less husky. I can't remember that consciously, but I know they are knit into my being as fully as your DNA. I am your daughter.

And Stevie my brother. You told me that I went to the hospital with you, that we waited outside together. That when I first had the chance to touch him I kissed him and said, "Welcome to the world, Stevie!" And that from the very first I sang to him and read with him and taught him things like pointing and crawling and stacking. I guess that was true. Orwell *was* right about that: *Who controls the present controls the past.* So whether you success-fully primed me to love my brother from the start, or whether you infused that memory into me later, it is the reality that I have;

and I have to say, if you manipulated my toddler past to make my future more beautiful, then thank you for exercising your power in a way that built loving.

Like you loved your sister Margaret, I suppose. We must all construct realities out of fogs of semi-consciousness, fragments made coherent by later words and imaginations. I suppose parents can't help but shape their children, so why not do it toward love.

And of course with loving comes security, and that's what lets children grow. I've seen students fail—a test, a class, a school, an incipient life—and it's not that they're not smart, it's that they're not secure. In their homes, or homelessness; in their families; in themselves, the confidence to try, to risk, to think. They become tentative and then quiet, first in their output and then in their intake. They fail.

You made my world loving and secure. Thank you.

And so I loved Stevie. And you and Mom did, too. I don't remember diapers much, but I remember the plastic sheet under his high chair, splattered with baby food. I remember spooning oatmealy stuff into his mouth with that long little spoon, and wiping his cheeks. I remember the cow mobile over his bed, which perhaps I'm recalling from over mine. I know you let us watch cartoons, which back then was the thing to do. You bought both of us car seats, even though they weren't yet required. All those things that I can only know consciously in retrospect, because for a child they are simply and unconsciously the world. A warm house. Clean clothes. Regular meals. Cuddling and talking, playing games even. Bedtime stories. And later—but not much—opportunities to help, even if the helpfulness was suspect.

Everything. Maybe not the weather, but our take on the weather. *Isn't the rain beautiful! Would you like to make hot cocoa?* Mom did that. And when we'd watch the rain, talking and sipping—she'd have tea, and my cocoa out my lidded cup was just warm, perfect—she'd make sure Stevie was safe, on his blankey or in his carrier where we wouldn't accidently spill on him.

All of that you gave us. Even Mom was good as far as my memories go, or as much as I make them. She only shrank later; but then maybe she had cause to.

She and Stevie and I ran errands together all the time. Shopping, I guess, but going to the park, too.

As far as I know, the bad day was different from no other. You went to work to do what you always did. I'm sure the traffic on off-angled Market Street made its multicolored stop and go, with the electric buses tracking their lines, pushy horns tooting at consideration, tailpipes puffing restlessly, people on the sidewalk striding pointedly or ambling aimlessly checking trash cans, and pigeons puffing at their feet or swirling round their heads. The gray-white fog muted everything, and it was all normal to you and everyone there.

From our house the normal was prettier. We could see the bright red spires of the bridge rising into the sun above it. Those sun-warm spires rose like promises. I couldn't have said it then, but they were hopeful, like a rose in winter or the flash of a hummingbird's gorget as he buzzes the honeysuckle in spring. At the time their striking brilliance against the somber fog was just pretty, and that was enough.

Mom didn't listen to the news in the morning like you did. After you left she always turned the station to music without words. It sounded nice, pouring out from the soft brown of the speakers. She read her news magazine and Stevie and I played on the floor. Maybe I should remember what we played, but I don't. We always played stacking or reading or dolls. He was only one.

Mom put down her magazine and, humming along with the music, opened the refrigerator. She poked around inside and wrote a list on the counter. She looked at the ceiling, smiled, and wrote some more.

"OK," she said, "it's foggy out, better get your sweaters!"

"We're getting groceries?" I asked.

"That's right!"

I chose my pink sweater while she snapped Stevie up in his Forty-niners red and gold. Then she held the sweater so I could slide into it.

She carried Stevie in his carrier, which doubled as a car seat. I carried her purse for her, with her list inside. She locked the house and buckled me into my seat and then buckled Stevie's seat next to mine. The radio, the same music she'd had inside, came on when she started the car.

Soon we were at the grocery store. She unbuckled me first, but I wasn't allowed to get out of the car until she had Stevie, and then I climbed out. I didn't hold her purse in the parking lot. She kept it over her shoulder, and held my hand with one of hers and Stevie's basket with the other. As soon as we reached a cart in the lot she put Stevie into it and we rolled on in. The pavement was jiggly under the cart, and we sang a monotone, "Uh-uh-uh-uh-uh" in tune with the cartwheel's rumble.

Inside we walked row by row. Mom was in no hurry, and rarely looked at her list. She sniffed at melons and held them for me: "What do you think?"

I sniffed but kept my eyes on her to try to guess whether they were good or not.

We half-filled the cart with fruits and vegetables, noodles, Wheaties for you, Trix for us—'cause *Trix are for kids!*—tomato cans, drinks, bread and peanut butter and jelly, boxes of rice mixes, some frozen foods, and three packs of meat that the butcher wrapped up in white paper. When we checked out, the cashier lady smiled at the woman in front of us, and then she smiled at us too, just the same.

Back at the car Mom loaded Stevie first, while I held the cart so it didn't roll away. Then she put all the groceries in the trunk, and then she buckled me in. "Don't forget your purse," I reminded, but she never forgot that.

The music came back on and we were driving home.

Somewhere something happened. I don't know what. At first I was told someone ran a red light, but later it had something to do with a lane change, too. I don't remember this at all, I was too young and it was too foreign and too fast. I have a memory: we were still in the car, and the music was playing, Mommy bleeding on her forehead, turning to us: "Are you OK, Jenny?" and I nodded, but when I looked at Stevie he wasn't there, his whole basket was gone, and then Mommy was scrambling in the seat beside her, and she lifted, tilted his cream-colored basket up and she screamed, "Stevie!" and she started feeling inside the basket where I couldn't see, but then I could see her hands come away red and his blankey red.

There were people at the door and they took me out, a man, and I screamed to stay with Mommy and Stevie, but he held me, and people all around, and Mommy and Stevie were out then, too, Mommy still holding his basket, and pretty soon sirens and a policeman, and then an ambulance with its red light twirling like an accident, and I was with Mommy in the flashing red light but the ambulance-man had Stevie, and Mommy just cried looking at Stevie so I cried too. "It'll be OK, Mommy, it'll be OK."

The hospital was empty-looking. Even with lots of people it seemed empty, with bare walls and floors, and the places to sit looked like they didn't know what a person was; they were stiff, like pictures of chairs. But we sat in them, cold and hard, after the doctors felt us with their cold hands and asked us questions. Mom got a bandage on her forehead. "But it's just surface," he had said. I didn't need anything, and he patted my head and said, "There's a good girl. You wait with your Momma now."

They kept Stevie, and you came and sat with us. You hugged Mom first, nice and long, and she cried and said some things, and you listened gently and shook your head and walked her back to her seat, and then you leaned toward her and took me on your lap, and that was much better than the cold chairs. Maybe I fell asleep. When the doctor came you stood up and went to him. I stayed with Mommy, on the chair that was still hard but was warm from you sitting there. Then you came back and knelt by me and said, "Jenny, I want you to wait here. Mom and I are going to talk with the doctor." I nodded and Mommy got up with you. She cried then, talking with you and the doctor just down the hall a little. Then she nodded and turned to me, but then turned back, and you came to me and knelt by me. "Jenny," you said. "Stevie was hurt very badly in the accident. His head was hurt and he's not going to live." And you were almost crying, trying not to, and I started. "We have time to go say goodbye to him." And we all followed the doctor down the empty hallway.

Stevie didn't look like Stevie. I mean, he sort of did, but he had a bandage over his forehead and greenish tubes out of his nose and arms and from his shirt. When you held me up I couldn't cuddle with him like I wanted to say goodbye, so I cried more. Mommy and you both kissed him just on his cheek over the tube, so I did that too. Goodnight, Stevie. Goodnight, Moon. We all cried.

You didn't go back to work that day, or the next. We stayed home and it was sad. Mr. and Mrs. Anderson came over the next night, and she brought some boxes of big saucy meat, and rice with all kinds of vegetables in it, and there was a salad; she leaned down at me smelling of perfume saying, "with cheese and tomatoes and olives and egg slices and a bunch of other colors. And after that," she said with a flourish, "this is the most luscious cheesecake you have ever tasted. It's from Worth Their Weight in Gold Cheesecakes, and they are."

Mom shook her head and was getting teary-eyed, and Mrs. Anderson patted her shoulder and said, "There, there, honey, you've got to get your mind off it."

Mom still shook her head but didn't say anything, and pretty soon Mr. and Mrs. Anderson left.

Then Mom said, still shaking her head, "I don't want to take my mind off it. Off him."

We ate a little of the box food that night and a little more the next day, but I think you threw most of it away.

I learned what a funeral was. There was a long time in the church where the priest looked sort of sad, and Stevie was there in a metal-looking box called a casket, a little one. We were there and Mr. and Mrs. Anderson, and two other men from your work, and two women from Mom's old work—Mellie had seen it in the paper and she told Helen—and one man in charge of the casket. And that man and the priest and you and Mom and me, and Stevie, of course, we all went out to the cemetery where the priest said some more prayers and asked if Mom or you wanted to say anything, but you didn't. There was a hole there in the grass, but we didn't stay to watch him buried.

It was gloomy and quiet around the house. You went back to work, but Mom couldn't smile about anything. She didn't play music on the radio. We sat in the living room and tried to be company. "The doctor said we could have kept him on the respirator," she said to me stonily, "but he wasn't ever going to be Stevie again. Your father thought we should, maybe there'd be a miracle. But our baby was gone." I didn't know what to say. She continued, "Did you hear what happened, Jenny-dear? The car seat broke. There were different latches in back to slide the seat belt through. The one I put it through broke. That's what killed your brother."

That evening she said to you, "We should sue the seat manufacturer. So that it never happens again."

"Elsie, the belt was in the wrong latch. It could happen to anyone."

"That's the point!" she was suddenly enraged. "It could happen to anyone! But it shouldn't happen to anyone! It's poorly designed! Carelessly, murderously designed!"

You probably had to chew through your North Dakota sense of personal responsibility and sufferance to swallow her argument, but I guess you did. "I see your point. Well, if you want to talk to a lawyer…"

She did. She found Chase Raymond, Attorney at Law. "And I don't want it just to be a lawsuit to get some money!" she said. "I want it to change the way they make the car seats so they will be safe!"

Mr. Raymond nodded. I'm sure that to him that meant huge punitive damages. He sent a letter to the company.

Mr. Hendrickson from Customer Relations replied with condolences, but denied responsibility, since it appeared the car seat had not been properly attached.

Mr. Raymond re-emphasized that the product was defective due to a design that promoted misattachment.

Mr. Hendrickson said that Mrs. Self's was the first complaint they had had, so it did not appear that misattachment was a widespread problem.

Mr. Raymond requested records of all complaints regarding the car seat.

Mr. Hendrickson declined.

Mr. Raymond served notice.

All of this took many months.

Mom and Mrs. Anderson began to go out again. A lunch. A dinner. Another dinner.

"Elsie, dear. You can't let your roses go."

"Oh, I haven't. They're just resting."

Annie raised her brows.

"OK, I've let them go a little. I'm working with an attorney to get the seat belts better designed."

"Yes, Paul mentioned something about that. How's it going?"

"Barely at all, it seems. But I know these things take time."

"They can take longer than you've got, Elsie."

"What do you mean?"

"I mean, I'm not sure a lawyer is the right way to go. Lawyers sue for money, not change."

"But money is the root of change, isn't it?"

"Yes. But working on it day in and day out will make you old and bitter. But the company doesn't get old, or if it does it just hires a new set of lawyers. It'll outlast you."

"You think I can't win then."

"Oh, you could. But I'd put my money on the big horse every time."

Mom stared ahead. "Well I'm not ready to give up."

"You shouldn't be, dear! But let's talk about something more pleasant! This croissant, for instance. Isn't it to die for!"

Mom winced a smile and nodded.

The next day she pruned her roses. But she also called Mr. Raymond to schedule an appointment. He was available in two weeks.

For two weeks she quietly steamed. When she walked into his office she got right to her point, "Mr. Raymond, how is the case doing?"

"It has been difficult. I think they are going to move to settle."

"Settle? I don't want a settlement! I want them to make a safe product. I thought I had made that perfectly clear."

"Yes, but I don't think we could win a suit. The product is too new, a new design. There is no record of complaints, and without that record we can't demonstrate a design flaw."

"One child's death is not enough to demonstrate a flaw?" she asked brittlely.

"I'm afraid not, Mrs. Self."

"How many children's deaths is enough, Mr. Raymond?"

"More than we have on record, I'm afraid."

"And who has such records?" she asked.

"It would be the company, of course. That's where the complaints go."

"So we complain to the fox about the missing hens!"

"That is how it is, Mrs. Self."

"Is that a new arrangement since you first took the case?"

"Ma'am?"

"Was there ever someone beside the fox to complain to?"

"Not really."

"Then why did you take the case!"

"I do think we can get a reasonable settlement, Mrs. Self."

"Wonderful! I can get paid to go away, but these killers will keep peddling their poison! Doesn't the government do anything about things like this?"

"Not really. They haven't defrauded you. The Better Business Bureau would field a complaint like that. But product safety? The rule is *caveat emptor,* buyer beware!"

"Do you think that's right, Mr. Raymond?"

"It doesn't matter what I think."

"Yes it does! Aren't you a citizen?!"

"I am. And I'm a lawyer, and I recognize what I can win and what I can't. We can win a decent settlement, Mrs. Self. We can't reshape the business-customer framework."

"I see." She was still hot, and resented having water thrown on her flames. She steamed. "So they can sell anything, feed us rat poison, and we have no recourse."

"There has to be a record…"

"So, they lose the records. They make an inconsequential change so it's not the same product. They are invincible."

"You know what they say, 'What's good for GM…'"

"Yes, yes. And small business is the backbone of America. And what are children, Mr. Raymond? Pebbles to be stepped on? Mud for business to make its footprint in?"

"Mrs. Self, I can see you're agitated. I will press this issue and bring it to a close as quickly as I can."

"Sure, Mr. Raymond, sure. You do that. And then take your fee out of the settlement. That's how it works, isn't it? Don't cheat yourself?"

"Of course, ma'am."

And she vexed her way home and pruned the roses down lower, almost to the ground. She scrubbed the floors, hard. It's a good thing she didn't scrub the windows because she might have broken them. She served TV dinners.

"What's up?" you asked her.

"My good lawyer, after all this time, says we can't win in court. He's going to settle."

"Can part of the settlement be to improve the seat design?"

"*Caveat emptor!* That means No!"

You nodded. "Yeah, Paul said something about that."

"Paul? What's he got to do with it?"

"We were just talking." You hesitated. "Sometimes business is a small world."

Mom looked at you suspiciously. "And what small world is this?"

"The folks you're suing do business with us. They're heavily invested in our products."

"Oh! O-ho-ho! Oh! And Annie knew that, too!"

"I suppose."

"And you knew it. And Paul knew it. Everyone but me! Let me work my hysteria out, is that it? I suppose you'd talked to Raymond, too. Didn't you!"

"Honey—"

"Didn't you! You bastard! You god-damned bastard! Get out! Get out of this house! Get out, now!!"

You didn't move. You looked at the floor. "What should I have done?" you asked.

"I said get out!" she screamed.

But you didn't move. To your credit, you didn't move.

And she still screamed, but not *Get out!* "You should have talked with me! You should have told me your conflicts! We'd have worked it out!"

"You were pretty set on it. And at first I didn't know. What company owns which, who's who. It gets complicated. And I thought your plan was good. Then later I learned…"

"But still didn't tell me. You're something, Self, you're sure something!"

You waited before saying, "I'm sorry."

"You're dishonest. Stay away from me, you filthy…" She turned and ran to the bedroom, where she closed the door.

You looked at me, not looking good. "Finish your dinner."

We ate in silence.

It seemed she didn't talk with you for weeks. And when Annie called one time—I know, because I answered the phone, just the way she'd showed me, after it rang and rang—she listened for a while and then said No, she wouldn't be available.

Finally on a Saturday morning when there was no Golden Gate above the fog she said, "This is a cold city. I want to move."

Now I think back on it, you were probably glad to get that much from her. It wasn't sweet, but it wasn't *I'm leaving you.*

You looked out the window where she was looking. "All right."

She continued, "We don't have any friends here. At the funeral, there were no friends, except maybe Mellie and Helen, and I don't even do anything with them. When your sister died back in North Dakota, didn't you have friends at the funeral? Didn't your family have friends?"

"Yeah, we did. We'd lived there a long time, of course. Everybody had."

"This city's friendless and cold."

I'll bet you were thinking North Dakota's colder, but you said, "We can move, Elsie. We can do that. Honestly, I'll move wherever you want."

She didn't melt into your arms with relief or forgiveness or anything. She just nodded. "It'll mean a longer commute."

"I can work anywhere. And I don't mind driving."

So you and she started talking again, and slowly worked your way back to friendliness. That was a thing to see, a thing I respect and honor you for. I don't know if it made you stronger together, but I think it probably did; not because you'd be better, but because you'd have greater faith in the sticking. I respect that. I wonder if it was something you got from your childhoods, something that disappeared as your generation aged and developed mine, the throwaway society?

Eight

1984 was the bad year, the year that stole Mom's spirit. Not the way that George Orwell had described 1984. Orwell was right about a lot of things, but not that. It wasn't the government subduing the citizens with an authoritarian pseudosocialism. It was the citizens opting for the cut-rate inhumanity crowned by the kings of commerce. It was my brother dying because the Kingdom of Capitalism was upon us, and its only value was profit, so it couldn't afford a design or material that actually protected children, and it subdued the petty government to its rule.

Most of us lived like Orwell's proles, close to home, to diapers and dishes, birthdays and bike tires, only vaguely aware of the forces molding government. But you were a lord in the Kingdom—not a king, but a duke or some lesser noble—and you joined your fellows in this whole new level of profiteering through finance, fashioning it as a zero-sum, even negative-sum operation. You and Michael Milken, and other rising stars in junk-bond rip-offs. T. Boone Pickens, another take-and-break corporate raider who just now tried to foist his greenhouse gas on us by buying a voters' initiative. Carl Icahn, making his first billions by taking over companies like TWA and stripping their assets, driving them to bankruptcy, turning employees' jobs into their loss and his private treasure hoard. Ivan Boesky, who did us the service of evoking enforcement of laws against insider trading by so brazenly breaking them, and so earned himself a one-hundred-million-dollar fine, which left only that much or so again in his pocket.

But you were still just honing your skills in 1984, even as the pillaging was rotting both the S&Ls and society.

You sat that 1984 evening, once again staring out the window into the darkness, once again intermittently rapping your fingers on the soft arm of your chair. You weren't a knuckle-rapper; your style was more muted, self-effacing. You were one who, if you were going to blow up a bridge, would prefer to time the explosion so that it would occur when you were far away, eating sushi downtown. But the upholstered chair protected your almost silence. So you rapped.

I watched and asked naively, "Daddy, are you missing Stevie?"

"Mm? Oh. Yes, I suppose I am."

"I miss him, too." I climbed into your lap and you held me.

Mom brought you a cup of tea, and you smiled a penitential, bucking-up smile at her, taking the tea, warming the both of you, and me, too.

But your seeming distraction over Stevie was fake. So why should the tea and Mom bringing it have warmed you? I think dishonesty must enhance psychological compartmentalization. That would be a necessary adaptation. You can be dishonest but still enjoy the kindnesses of decency.

So it works that way, whether it should or not, as long as you're rotten enough. I didn't know it then, of course, that you were a liar. You knew Mom would love you for your apparent distress over both Stevie and your subterfuge with Mr. Raymond, so you used it, you got your tea and comfort. Weirdly enough, your dissembling gave three-year-old me warmth, too, so now I don't know whether to excoriate you or thank you. But I know it was dishonest. You weren't thinking about Stevie or Mom or me or your own behavior.

Your mind was elsewhere: it wasn't spectacular yet, it wasn't in the muddling media, but the S&Ls were starting to fail. FSLIC was bailing them out. They were merging to try to stay afloat, but most of the mergers were still voluntary. It was in just the next week that your venture with Paul, Western Freedom, was reabsorbed by your parent company US First. Freedom had grown ever more clever and reckless in its loan generation, and now too many clients were defaulting. You couldn't keep your Ponzi structure going.

But it wasn't the string of broken customers you left behind that had you staring out the dark window or rapping quietly on your armchair. It wasn't even the closing of your private S&L. You weren't really bothered, so much as calculating: How should you map out your next move? How could you keep making a killing?

Because that's what you did. I was too young then, and Mom was too trusting or needy, but now it is as clear as driving alone with a broken car seat.

Nothing for a month. You and Paul and Jackson wouldn't even talk about it. You'd know. Nothing for a month, maybe six weeks. You'd just take down your shingles and move back into your US First desks, which had never been emptied. Process the FSLIC paperwork to receive payment covering your bad loans. Refer your desperate former clients to their lawyers, and perhaps suggest to them that bankruptcy really isn't all that bad. After all, many debts are discharged, most of your personal possessions are exempted from liquidation. Chapter seven, is it? The state doesn't want to ruin families. Bankruptcies are just a way of doing business. No big deal. Don't get tied up in scruples.

And after a month of that you'd bring the next scheme up in a team meeting. Paul would introduce it; did, I'm sure.

"Have you heard what Salomon Brothers and First Boston are doing?" he asked.

"Oh, I read something about that," said Ken. "I didn't really understand it. CMOs, it said."

"Right. Collateralized Mortgage Obligations. It's complex." Paul nodded. "Basically we make a loan and sell it to a commercial bank. They sell it to an investment bank, where it can be securitized. That means they repackage it as bonds, using the mortgages as collateral. And those bonds can be sliced up with all different levels of risk and reward. There's something, a desired risk level, for every investor, and they're bonds so they feel safe. So they sell."

"And the bonds are secured by the original loans," said Phil, thinking out loud.

"Yes," Paul affirmed.

Phil continued, "So if those loans go bad—"

"We're already out of the picture. We've sold the loans," said Paul.

Phil nodded. "And so has the commercial bank. So only the investment bank, First Boston, you say, has a risk."

"But they've sold their risk to the investor," Paul said.

"So the investor has the risk." Phil nodded, then shrugged. "And we're all OK then!"

"That's right," confirmed Paul.

"So," continued Phil, "we can make loans like you were doing at Western Freedom, but we sell the risk away."

"You're a genius, Phil. That's exactly it," said Paul.

"I told you you should have hired me," said Phil.

"Well, now we can all get a slice of this action."

"It's high time!" Phil affirmed.

"It's exactly that," Paul nodded. "Make hay while the sun shines!"

And did Paul once again using that expression bother you yet, as a transgression against your upbringing, against people joining together to bring in the crop before rain ruined it, one farm family helping another for the common good? When people actually lived as neighbors, as community, and so built community? Did it move you to reconsider your actions? Apparently not. You shrank your community. As long as you could foist the risk off on *someone else*, let *them* rot. Even devise their rotting, as long as it enriched your smaller selves.

So US First beckoned the bankrupts once again. You didn't

have to convince them of anything. You didn't have to lie. There's a sucker born every minute! But PT Barnum only swindled away an afternoon's wages; you took four years of their earnings, you ruined them.

Too bad, eh? There's always wine, or meth. *Caveat emptor.*

You make me so proud of you, Daddy.

Oh, but you were smart about it, weren't you. As Paul had laid out, you sold the risk. Some other sucker would fall for the finances you contrived. Why, I bet the city-council candidates asked for your endorsement! Such an upstanding fellow! You and your company brought in such a good stream of cash, good tax money, all to the betterment of the city! You were what everyone should be! Why, I bet you made charitable donations, too! Something for the indigent, with whom your dear wife had worked. A hero of the age!

But somehow more people tumbled into hardship, lost their jobs, their retirement, their homes.

You knew what was happening, so you stared out the window and plotted. You knew the failure was coming, so you looked at options, you cultivated contacts, and when the FSLIC lost too many billions covering bad loans like the ones you were selling, becoming bankrupt itself, you had a place to go. US First hadn't folded yet, but half the country's S&L assets were in default, and yours would follow; but you wouldn't be there. "Timing's everything," you and Paul had agreed, and you left US First within two months of each other. He went into the Securities and Exchange Commission. You went into Strump Securities Ratings Agency, the Moody's and Standard & Poor's sort of thing. But of course you kept in touch. Keeping in touch was good business practice.

But I was a child and oblivious. What I saw in those years was that we moved to a new home. I liked the name: Sunnyvale. Now the sun shone in my window in the morning, through the pink curtains, turning my whole room into Tinkerbell Town. That's what you called it when the rosy glow and the morning furnace and the rows of dolls Mommy plunked on my shelves made the room so cozy. I liked Tinkerbell Town.

I started school, too. Mrs. Sweetwater read us stories and we colored and had recess. I remember one morning the whole playground was strewn with beans, little white beans. Mrs. Sweetwater said beans were good for us, so I collected three of them and planted them in the yard at the edge of the grass. They sprouted, too. I watched them and watered them with the hose. But you didn't know, and you mowed them. I was sad, but Mom said even you can't know everything. I thought she was wrong.

I don't remember much else from preschool. Not consciously, anyway. Or kindergarten. I know that those years, and even more the years before them, are the definitive time of a person's life. It seems so strange that they should be lost in the fog of precon-sciousness. It's like we are formed in the dark and then bring that cloaked form into the light of consciousness for just a little while, really. How are we supposed to make a better world from such an unreasoned menu? What even *is* better?

I didn't ask those questions then, but you had a sort of answer. You got me into T-ball and soccer. I watch those little kids now and wonder if I had a clue what was going on. I imagine I did, because I stuck with it. I don't remember learning to read, although I do remember reading, and I don't remember learning to add or subtract. I do remember playing soccer. The grass thick and, on early games, soaking wet so if you fell you were drenched and sometimes mudded up. Perry's Realty. Purple uniforms. Kicking the ball, or sometimes only trying to because there were so many other kids in the way. Plump red grapes after the games, served up from brittle plastic trays. Welty's Insurance, green uniforms. Playing midfield and forward, scoring maybe.

The grapes were good. But at home I was not a fruit-and-vegetables girl. I liked mac and cheese, hotdogs with lots of ketchup and mustard, and ice cream. "Enjoy it now while you're young," Mom said, sounding like Marley's ghost gone cynic. Mom was not at core a spiritless person. But her light shined only in shards after Stevie.

I didn't complain about the grapes. They were what our team moms served, and everybody ate them. One time we had a spit-fight with them, but that got kinda gross, even for me as a kid.

We went to Hawaii a bunch of years, to Honolulu. You must have felt lordly. Profit through the Eighties and then came the Roaring Nineties: the internet took off, free trade was expanding, what wasn't to feel good about? I was old enough to play, and you had taken me kayaking, river kayaking on the American River that June, and then it was sea-kayaking in Oahu in August. It was the sheer pleasure of new challenges, new experiences, limitless possibilities. We had surfing lessons at Waikiki, where even Mom got in the water, up over her knees. She mostly liked the meals and mai-tai's, though, dining out every night and never having to cook. I don't blame her. I still remember that restaurant with the view of Diamondhead one way and the airport the other, all along the water. You proposed to Mom at a beach, and I'd guess that strip brought back memories, even if they were clouded.

After that trip we went lots of places, a different place every summer for the next bunch of years: Disneyworld and a kayak trip through the Everglades with a gallon of mosquito repellant; I was playing U-14 that year, and you flew me back for a game. Next Washington, D.C. and all the monuments and memorials. Then New York and Boston, separate trips. Seattle and Vancouver, one trip. The Inside Passage with whales and porpoises, and up to Denali where we saw brown bears, moose, and mountain goats. We talked about Paris, but you didn't want to be on the plane that long. You funded my study abroad there instead.

I graduated from Fremont High and then went off to Irvine. I had played soccer for the Firebirds, but did not for the Anteaters.

Irvine's a minute from the beach, and I jumped pretty heavily into sea-kayaking, especially when the gray whales were migrating. They swim every year from feeding grounds in the arctic to calving grounds in the Gulf of California. They're beautiful and curious. By law we kept away from them, but sometimes they approached us. I had one spy-hopping at me just thirty feet away. She was a curious little one, and looked me right in the eye. I wanted to talk with her, and often have imagined such conversations. Whales have a whole different wisdom from ours, I'm certain.

Some of their wisdom fits, or should fit, with ours. Females usually mate with more than one male; a lot of the Irvine women appreciated that model. And when they breed they can do it several times, belly to belly for up to an hour, another point of appreciation; but they do have a practical difficulty—they have no arms and they're in the water, so they can float apart: whale wisdom—to solve the problem a nonbreeding male bumps up against the female's backside to keep her where she wants to be. So accommodating, the whales!

A point of dubious appreciation.

But they do only have a period once every two years. That is a good idea! And all the girls get pregnant at the same time! I don't know if that's a good idea; the kids could play together. I guess it works for them, because it lets them feed in the rich winter waters of the north and then travel together to give birth in the south when the water's warm.

I wonder how they synchronize? I wonder what climate change is doing to them?

I should have been a marine biologist.

Was I raised to be useful, Dad? You were, but then the farm wasn't available to you. You went into larceny instead. I at least kept my options open. I was an English major.

I know, people make fun of English majors. Thank you Garrison Keillor; now *there* was a bright spot in your generation!

Back in those years, at school, I maintained that non-English majors ridicule our pursuit because they think it is easier and therefor of less value; when the truth is that easiness, which is individually variable, doesn't matter; and that the value is immense, a breadth and depth of thought and expression that the narrower studies miss. I don't particularly maintain this anymore, but I still think it's true. People might, like you, study business and learn how to rob from the poor, or even the rich, but they seem not to know how to adequately feel their plight or passion, which is different from ours in being muted by inarticulation and made bleak by its vacancy of humane ethics. Or they might understand string theory, but have little sense of how to make human life richer. In contrast, the competent student of literature learns, feels, the commonality of humankind, and perhaps beyond, of whales and all the world. There is a humane and poetic insight that good literature offers. It is not foolproof, and should have the benefit of science to check its tangents; but it is an insight that gives an esthetic and moral vision that science often cannot provide until too late for positive action, and that business doesn't even look for except as a pathway to profit. It is an insight that is readily available to the masses of people— hence, *easy*. But we have killed the poetry, the stories, and replaced them with cold and greedy formulas that may win the elementary principal's adulation, may reap the bigger profit, may inflame the righteous soldier in us, but overlooks or denies or disregards the raping of beauty.

Whales don't rape. We should learn that wisdom, that practice.

I remember studying fables. They were efforts to pass on cultural wisdom. Aesop: *Don't kill the goose that lays the golden egg.* Uncle Remus: *When you git a invite ter a bobbycue, you better fin' out when an' whar it's at, an' who runnin' it.* Cultural wisdom. What wisdom runs through our heads now? Advertisement catch-lines. Stuff to preen and loot by. We have put business in charge of the country.

I tried to live both wise and small at Irvine, and living brought me to Bill—Bill Alhouse. Like me, he was a product of your generation. Like me, he wanted our generation to do better than yours. Like you, he sold out. But that was later.

I didn't even meet him on campus. We met at Newport Beach, and you couldn't get a much prettier place to meet when you're young, or any age, I suppose. It had the fun shops, the crystal ocean, a cool onshore breeze under a friendly sun—it was friendly at that time—and all that impeccable Southern California cleanliness, as alluring as youth and as real as Hollywood. We fell in love.

I taught him kayaking. He was a ready learner. He hadn't kayaked before, but he'd been in Boy Scouts and knew the basics of handling a paddle. At first he rented a kayak, but later bought his own. His car, used, had come with a roof rack, and it could hold both our kayaks, so we became quite mobile along the south coast.

One time we were out not far at all, not a hundred yards, and a herd of sea lions came over us. They were migrating north, and porpoising through the water fast, determinedly. There were hundreds of them, each two or three times our size, their chocolate bodies looping in and out of the water. At first we feared they might land on us, but after ten minutes we under-stood that they paid us just enough mind to avoid plopping on us. We shipped paddles and sat amidst that downpour of porpoises. After twenty minutes in their porpoise-storm we were still surrounded by them, still adrift in their looping world.

"They're making a sine wave!" Bill exclaimed. "Over the water and under, over and under!"

"They're making thousands of sine waves! I wonder how many there are and how long they do this, how far they go."

We gazed at them. Northward the herd already stretched almost out of sight. To the south there was no seeing its tail end.

"I don't know," Bill said. "They must be traveling, what," he looked at his watch and the northern extent of the leaping mammals, "maybe eight, ten miles an hour? They look like they could keep going all day."

"I'd think jumping out of the water like that would get tiring."

"You'd think. But maybe the air resistance is so much less than water's that it's worth it to jump."

Every now and then one would fly by real close—the females sleek and streamlined, the males brawny and scarred. They rocked our little boats.

After forty-five minutes we gently paddled from their midst and in to shore. The sea lions were still passing by, living out their wisdom in the blue sea. We drove inland to live out ours in the off-blue sky.

He taught me downhill skiing. For that we drove to Mammoth. I started snow-ploughing on the bunny hill, but graduated to the mild slopes. After getting me going, Bill couldn't resist a couple of his own runs down the higher, steeper chutes, and in subsequent trips, if it had snowed the night before, he went directly there, "to catch the powder at its freshest." I understood that. It was no different from what you did going kayaking when the river was up.

Snowboarding was becoming popular then, but Bill had no interest in it. "I'm a purist," he said. "Skis."

I liked the skiing, and usually the drive up there, too. The sun would be rising over Nevada and the morning Sierras swept up steep and white to our west; there was a sense of cold, but it was warm in the car. It all made for a feeling of life and beauty. But on the way home the scene usually changed. Afternoon winds picked up, and the whole basin was doused in dust. Apparently before even you were born Owens Lake had been drained to send water to L.A. The lakebed dust rose in unconscious recompense.

Bill and I were both seniors when we met. I don't know if

there was some undertow in our psyches whispering that it was late, that soon we would lose the college venue for meeting potential spouses. And we didn't fall madly in love at first sight. But we played together, we talked, we built our coffee habits, and we decided that staying another year at Irvine would be a good plan.

Bill worked toward his masters in biological technology. "I actually would love to go into genetic engineering," he said.

"Why would you do that?" I asked him.

He looked at me blandly. "To have a job. To make money."

"Is that all? There are lots of jobs. Why that?"

"It's interesting. I think I'd be good at it."

"If it's not worth doing, it's not worth doing well!" I fenced with the stolen adage.

"OK, Ms. Clever. Um, I could help feed hungry people."

"But genetic engineering! You're feeding them poison!"

"It's not poison! It's making a more nutritious food. Or making it last longer. Or grow better," he defended.

"But that's not what they're doing! They're engineering crops that withstand their own poisons! *That's* what they're doing."

"Well the whole thing has to be financially viable."

"But financial viability doesn't make it worthwhile."

"No," he conceded. "But it will increase food availability."

"And how do you know it's not poison?"

He sighed. "All right, finally I don't. It hasn't been around long enough. But I have no reason to think it is. And listen, we know for sure that people are hungry. I'll be working on feeding them! That's a good thing, isn't it? Would you rather let them starve?"

"No. Let them eat cake, you're right."

"And what's your final solution?" he attacked.

I didn't answer then. The answer tasted bitter. I just muttered, "People need self-discipline."

It turned out, however, that Irvine specialized more in biomedical than genetic engineering. "Making prostheses, or designing diagnostic tools," Bill told me, shrugging. "That's good, too."

So his goals were malleable. At the time I considered him flexible, a good thing. He studied what was available, and soon slipped into computer imaging. He spent long hours pecking at the keyboard and rolling the mouse, and staring intently at the monitor.

I didn't object to tech, but I felt my interests were more human. My pursuit was a teaching credential. I wanted to help kids grow up to be happy, well-adjusted, and competent adults. Bill had nothing bad to say about that.

A year later we moved to San Jose. In late August I found a job teaching fourth grade. School had already started, but we'd been warned that schools often wait to hire because they don't know just how many students will show up. It's a lousy system, because the first week or so the kids are shuffling around with substitutes or classes being split and reformed, and also the new teacher doesn't get any time to prepare for that class, that age group. But that's how it is, another unsolvable problem. I jumped into it pretending I knew what I was doing, but I didn't. I had vague visions of talking with them sweetly, and they, enthralled by being treated with respect and understanding, would respond with similar sweetness and patience, and we would prance in merriment toward universal enlightenment. Two weeks into school the charm wore off. Another week of growing chaos and a rising panic at my monumental incapacity, and Mrs. Gard, fifth-grade teacher, stopped in my room after school.

"Is it everything you dreamed it would be?" she asked.

"Oh! It's OK. I'm learning."

"No you're not!" She laughed. "You're still reeling, and will be all year! Don't take it to heart, honey. You don't raise babies without soiled diapers. It's all a dirty business, and we all go through it. It does get better."

I stared at her. I knew she was speaking the truth, but I didn't know whether she was an ally or a hostile sniper.

"Honey, I just want you to know, we all know it's hard. At least if we're honest. But listen, don't beat yourself up, the kids'll do enough of that for you. Just laugh a little, that's all you can do, and don't try to fix everything by tomorrow. Do what you can, of course, and fill the rest of the time with the publisher garbage."

"You don't like the books?" I asked, trying to hide any note of fear, for the published texts and support material were my lifeline, the things that I could assign and have a prayer that the students would put their heads down over them and *be quiet*.

"The books and all the pre-fab activities? They're mostly garbage. Not all bad ideas, but since they're pre-fab the kids don't have to think their way through it. So they just try to fill in the blanks with whatever you or Johnny next to them tells them to. They don't learn, not mostly. Learning takes time, figuring things out, for them and for all of us. So, teacher: first you survive. Second, when you can you take a pre-fab here and there and rewrite it so it's yours, it makes sense to you. That's when you can *teach* it. That's when you can *listen* to the kids and hear what they're not getting. That's when you become a person to them. That's when they can learn.

"But you can't do all that at once, honey. Don't try. Heck, bad teachers, including way too many administrators, never get past the garbage. You'll be a good teacher, you will. For now, make sensible what you can, and listen to the kids."

"The kids are not always cooperative," I risked.

She laughed a rolling cascade. "Not always? Well, you must be special! Honey, laugh with them when you can, bust 'em when you have to—for their good, you know—this is their childhood, their time to learn how to live in society, not later when stupid behavior loses them a job or lands them in jail—laugh with 'em, bust 'em, and try to make your curriculum make sense to them. You do that and even this year you'll do them good. And next year you may even enjoy it every now and then. All right, hon?"

"I don't know whether to laugh or cry!"

"You can do them both, honey."

And she hugged me, and I did.

Oh, those first years were hard. Mrs. Gard, her advice was spot on, but it's easier said than done. You just can't hear it when—. It's like you're drowning and someone's calling to you from shore with instructions on how to do the crawl. You can't get it just then!

And I know the kids can feel the same way. That's where Mrs. Gard was really right. They have to have time to work with information or an idea. Otherwise it's just another wave busting down on them.

And that's where all the Standardize Movements go wrong. People are different, and alive, and I think most of us want them to be. So you have to let the teachers build learning in the unique, organic ways it develops each year. As Mrs. Gard, Janice, said to me a few years later, "If it ain't organic, honey, it's poison."

Not that I object to standards. They were so helpful to me at the start, and still are! They tell me what to teach! But the high-stakes testing makes tests the goal of study. That vision happens to kids, to administrators, to teachers, and to parents. And it's all wrong. The point is to foster adults with a habit and facility for learning; it's not to pass the test when you're twelve years old. No matter what the test publishers lobby.

But if you haven't been in the water you don't know how to swim. And some people don't get past the dog-paddle regardless.

Hard years. I don't even know what Bill was doing. He worked at a medical technology company designing eyeballs or something. I know his work didn't drown him like mine did. And I know he never knew what I was doing, either. He couldn't. It's not that he didn't care, but that he was on terra firma, not in the water.

But I stuck with teaching and he stuck with software, and we stuck with each other and eventually decided to get married.

I'd been told weddings are crazy, and Mom was out to prove it true. You and Bill had become friends, or friendly anyway, and you both told me just to let Mom do whatever she wanted. "The marriage is for us," Bill said. "The wedding is for them. Let your mom have it."

I tried, even though I didn't agree. *It's my wedding, after all!* Wedding plans seemed to give Mom a purpose, and she shifted up from neutral into a high gear. She wanted the ten-foot-tall wedding cake; she got it. She wanted a thousand guests; she got a couple hundred anyway, including people like Paul and Annie, with whom she had long reconciled, in the way that foundation on a face reconciles wrinkles. She wanted the most expensive champagne and the fanciest hall for the reception. She got them all.

I reserved for myself the dress. I allowed her to speak, but I made the choice. So I didn't get the strapless with the lace-draped hoop-skirt. My dress was simpler—a smooth flow of fabric from shoulder straps to V-neck bodice, not overdone, a dished waist, and a slightly flared skirt. I liked it then and I like it still, although I don't have it anymore and don't regret that.

You walked me up the aisle. In retrospect, I think I was a Disney princess. The wedding went off without a hitch, or with only the hitch intended. Bill wasn't a dancer, but we already knew that and got through the reception just fine. Your friends and Mom's mostly drank too much, but Bill and I left them to you. We lit out on our honeymoon, first to Niagara Falls and then on to New York. It was Times Square, the Rockefeller Center, the Empire State Building. It was a blast, and I was giddy!

Nine

The venue was a wedding, and my giddiness was that of youth, so excusable and probably even healthy. The world, however, is older, and should have had a more sober hand on its tiller. Instead it was like me, or like your friends, that cloud of smiling two-dimensional faces with a matching depth of thought. They partied-hearty and then vomited on the country. They drank too much, and then charged the country to nurse their hangover.

Only in college, away from you, was I learning what was happening all those years of my growing up, what you were doing.

Sure, I'd known you commuted to the City. You liked the drive, you said. You came home evenings and kissed Mom and me, in that order. You usually attended my Saturday soccer games, and summers we kept kayaking, at least once soccer was over. You treated me like an intelligent person, talking adult things like finance and politics with me. In many ways you were a model dad.

And I knew, almost subconsciously, that you prospered financially. We had everything. But at college I began to understand your context. Ivan Boesky had been caught conducting insider trading. He testified against Michael Milken, and they both went to jail. Of course a couple years later they were both released, Boesky with a couple hundred million, over four thousand years' wages for the average American. Milken even more. They had bilked the American people and ruined uncounted lives. They accepted their punishment and their pay. Of course, you didn't tell me any of that. I learned it later, from Bill. Or no, it was from Joey.

You were a smaller fish, and easily dodged the coarse-mesh S&L crime net. No, you were not Boesky or Milken, a flamboyant highwayman who robbed and throbbed. You didn't go to jail or come out a billionaire. You bilked your clients quietly, using the complexity of the system and the mood of deregulation to commit your theft legally, or at least legally enough. You stripped the economy bare as a burned hillside, but when the resulting mudslide rolled through the neighborhood, you were gone, clever devil. Homes were ruined, but you were unscathed. You had moved into ratings, a new and cozy arrangement.

At Strump's Ratings Agency you were a client of the securities banks, and not responsible for, or at least vulnerable on account of, S&L failings. Now you had another role in the game of investment wizardry: to be hired by the securities wizards, you had to provide a service they wanted—high ratings on their securities. So in honest capitalistic competition with Moody's and Standard & Poor's and whoever else was out there doing ratings, you raced to give the highest appraisal possible, justified or not. So the stock market rose, justified or not.

Just like the glasses rose at my wedding.

So the hangover was inevitable.

But you oozed past it, through it, around it, without negative consequence, it seemed. Like the others, you made out by impoverishing the broader public; and like the others, you congratulated yourself on your wealth, and wore it with the affected indifference of a small-time baron. You always leased the latest model of vehicular grandiloquence; leasing was the thing at the time. Your lawn was as carpet-like as Monsanto could make it; I often couldn't play on it because of a fresh round of spraying. Mom sometimes wore a dress more than once, but often did not; she assuaged any remnant sense of Yankee thrift by complimenting herself on her copious donations of dresses, slacks, hats, and boots to the Salvation Army. For my part, I could go to school without filing for financial aid—although I'm sure you would have filed, if you'd thought you could get anything out of it. Your effort was to be adequately legal, and legality became for you and your associates—I can't say your friends; friendship implies caring and responsibility—what served for morality.

You stayed in ratings until the myth of the New Economy was firmly established. The dotcoms were rising like bread dough on a warm day; no, faster, like mushroom clouds over the future, and the word among the cognoscenti was that there was no gravity, that price was divorced from value and could rise forever. High securities ratings, the stock market rising, business activity rising, and you and yours, the hot bulls of the economy, convinced Government to repeal laws that had protected consumers ever since the Great Depression. That's when you left Strump's to enter the securities market. Sunstar Securities, your sibilant service to humanity!

I was in my mid-teens. You were in your prime. You had everything. You could sell snake oil, even poison, and write the laws to make it legal. So you embarked on a career of creating complicated investment products that promised high returns. At least that's what you said—or not *said*, but *intimated*. Intimation is more alluring, and besides, you could point to it and to your written disclaimers to thwart any legal action taken against you. You were good, I'm sure of it. And your eager public, even other bankers, once again trusted you—you were the expert, after all— and bought your products. Did you sell to Orange County—the old home of the navel oranges you loved—their lost billion and a half of taxpayer dollars? That was lost pensions, lost county services—road maintenance, health services, law enforcement, court services, an airport, mosquito control, flood control, libraries, parks, air and water quality—nothing of real value, right? Or did you settle for ripping off just ninety-five million from Wisconsin workers? Or no, did you specialize in stealing from private enterprise—greeting cards, pharmaceuticals, banks—institutions holding people's jobs, and homes, and retirement hopes. Oh, even the banks and mutual-fund managers lined up to invest crazily and create other people's losses. Because that's what it was. You and the teams of investment managers, the securities banks, you weren't losing a dime. You were raking it in, losing the money of your investors, not yours. You had separated your profitability from your customers'. You knew that board oversight was a thing of the past. Boards of trustees, the supposed protectors of investors, were lost through dilution in mutual funds and even more by computer-based trading, millisecond fast, so that shareholders came and went multiple times just over lunch, without even a dream of exercising corporate oversight. So fund managers shepherded in whatever board members they wanted, and you could do whatever you wanted.

And that's where you went ugly.

Not that there weren't real problems to work on. NASA informed Congress of the imminent rise of global warming. In all our talks, I never heard of it, much less saw any attempt to deal with it. The Soviet Union broke up into many nations. How did you, your generation, help those new nations? And that's *help*, not *exploit*. I didn't hear about it. Genocide in Bosnia and Rwanda— what did you and your cronies do to alleviate that travesty? No, you were busy drilling for more oil, and creating nutrition-free food, and marketing drugs for rich-men's diseases; you were busy making money and defining that as wealth.

That's what you talked about with me. How to make money, not how to do good with it. You rattled against government, even if it was a democracy. Your energy didn't go into making the world a better place; it went into reinforcing the anti-government malaise that Reagan had crystallized: passing a Constitutional amendment to keep Congress from giving themselves a raise, as if their pay upset the general well-being as much as your corporate activity did; and raising as big a ruckus as possible over any government failing, or even personal failing like Bill Clinton's that you could pin on government, all while you and yours fleeced the public as payment for playing on Nero's fiddle.

But the attempt was made to bomb the World Trade Center.

Did you ask why? I didn't see it. And then the Oklahoma City bombing. And then the Unabomber. And then it went to Columbine and all the string of school shootings that that started. Didn't something seem wrong to you? But no, your concern was narrower. You were making money, and therefor you were good.

Oh, but you didn't get mired in office-talk with your family. You switched to other topics: the Forty-niners were in their glory days, and the Bulls, oh too bad you had to give up on the Warriors. And the other stuff on TV: Viagra, for crying out loud, which you couldn't avoid talking about with your teenage daughter because there it was, piped incessantly into our living room. And even Britney and Justin. All those momentous things. And when something that mattered did trip into the news, it came and went, because newscasts were of the ephemera, not the important.

And that was my world, because you were my world. And I can't say I didn't enjoy it; we do that sort of thing, enjoy what we find. Nobody wants to be morose. But don't you see how shallow you were making my world, and I suppose your own, too? Don't you see what you did? Not by what you did, perhaps, but by what you didn't do.

You made money. But shallow people, no matter how much money they have, can't sustain a culture, much less a democracy.

Or apparently an economy that serves its people, either. Back in the Depression, civic leaders wanted to end the conditions that created poverty. They did a pretty good job, too, passing laws and living with a decent concern for the common good. They separated investment banking from regular banking, and they didn't create derivatives to tempt and confuse and bilk people; and borrowers actually had to qualify for a loan, which kept them from getting in over their heads; they avoided usury, which was almost guaranteed to run folks into the poorhouse; and they paid living wages and offered pensions! But starting around the time I was born you were in the business of dismantling their protections as *government interference*. The failure of the S&Ls was your baby as much as I was. But after they crashed, when I was learning my times tables, you didn't correct your mistakes like your parents and grandparents did. No, you cried gleefully that we had a New Economy, and you continued to rewrite the laws and shortcut prosperity. Oh, you weren't particularly trying to create poverty, I suppose. You were trying to create your own wealth, and everyone else be damned.

But it was all peachy for us—you and Mom and me—wasn't it. At the time I was unconsciously proud of you. The trips to Hawaii—but I didn't learn any Hawaiian history, for better or worse. The vacation to Disneyworld—where I suppose I learned that the thing to do with money is buy whirly rides and cotton candy. We zipped down to the Everglades, too, where I was accidentally impressed by the heron that let us walk right by, close enough to its dagger-beak that I was a little scared. And we kayaked through the mangroves, where I imagined there were baboons in the trees. You didn't teach me that baboons lived in African savannahs, not Floridian swamps. And you certainly didn't teach me that the development of Florida was drying out the waterflow that made the Everglades possible. No, the Everglades were another park, just like Disneyworld. I was thirteen, old enough to have begun to learn. But your choices had removed your power to teach me so much of what mattered.

The next year was D.C., and understanding began to leak in to me. I suppose it was normal to focus on the monuments and times past there. What did I learn? I learned that I liked Lincoln. He was so sad and good. Mom bought me a booklet about him. I still have it. What caught my teenage melodramatic sense was, *To ease another's heartache is to forget one's own.* Maybe some people would say those words like a butterfly, La-di-dah, but not Lincoln. He was a mule in the traces, not a butterfly, and he just kept pulling. Easing heartache was an idea that didn't leave him.

He rendered it differently in a more famous speech. *With malice toward none; with charity for all; with firmness in the right, as God gives us to see the right, let us strive on…to bind up…to care for…* Yes. That, and just above it, *It may seem strange that any men should dare to ask a just God's assistance in wringing their bread from the sweat of other men's faces.* Of course, he was talking about slavery. Now our leaders call it freedom. Freedom to abuse another person's work. Freedom to rip people off.

But I had to learn all that later, not then and not from you.

Still, thank you for taking me to Washington, D.C. I can say that. Your manner was always blandly generous.

And the next year was New York City. I guess I'd gotten to like history by then. In both D.C. and at Battery Park I was seeing all those war memorials, and that seemed OK, but like most people I really liked the Statue of Liberty and Ellis Island. How cool are they? Lady Liberty, with her torch held high and the broken chain at her feet, the beautiful symbol of freedom! And certainly the best monument one nation ever gave another— Thank you, France! And later worded: *Not like the brazen giant of Greek fame, With conquering limbs,* but the Lady Liberty, the welcoming *Mother of Exiles…Give me your tired, your poor, Your huddled masses yearning to breathe free…Send these, the homeless, tempest-tost to me.*

Not exactly *your* sort of poetry, *your* sort of sentiment. But you were smart enough not to take issue with it directly. No, what you did was co-opt liberty. You dressed it up in *storied pomp*, the flag and the soldiers; and every election your candidates touted support for our boys fighting for our freedoms, support for our veterans! But after the elections you eagerly went about stealing the wealth of other nations, "Westernizing them," so that you created the conditions where the boys would be called out to war again. Iran. Iraq I. Iraq II. Afghanistan. Syria, Iraq III. Oil wars, wars to charge our protégé nations for our victory and for the infrastructure and cultural upheaval we foisted on them. That was your wisdom. Maybe I can excuse Afghanistan, but the others were pretty exclusively for American wealth; yeah, the one percent's wealth, scarcely even yours. Not America's broadly, and certainly not the Middle East's. And you were the cadre who made it happen.

But I didn't know this then, and you didn't show it. Rah-rah Liberty! You bought me a flag, and your representatives in D.C. voted to cut veterans' funding, cut funding for everything, and support American business establishing itself in foreign countries. Always the smooth argument that the trade will benefit both sides. And always true: there's a one percent in every country. Or where there's not we can destabilize the government, whether it's democratic, socialist, or fascist, and create one. You don't usually have to destabilize the fascists, though. Those dictators know where their bread is buttered. They already comprise a one percent who will do business with you.

Yes, Father, I have learned the character of your love.

But again, I didn't know it then, didn't experience it at the time. What I knew was that you took Mom and me to New York. We saw sights that thrilled and inspired me, gave me a love for words and their hope and beauty. I loved you for that, and I don't object to that love now. You weren't malicious, just unconscionable.

I was fifteen and just starting to be conscious. Maybe you did do something right, to waken my awareness. Even if it was accidental.

The next year we went to Boston, and there we traced our pre-revolution roots. "It's a funny thing," I said. "I always liked Sam Adams. He seemed like the action guy, and his cousin John was the boring one. And in a way that's true. But now it seems like John was more patriotic."

"How do you mean?" you asked.

"Didn't you read the plaque?" I exclaimed.

"No."

"The Boston Massacre was phony! The British were just protecting themselves from a mob that attacked them. But then Sam had his buddy Paul Revere make an engraving of it that looks like the Brits are mowing down innocent citizens. So then the Brits were tried for murder, and it was John who was their defense lawyer! And he always held that as one of his top achievements!"

You laughed. "That doesn't say much for his accomplishments as president!"

I scolded him. "It does say something about his respect for law!" Even then I knew I sounded like Mr. Parenti, my history teacher, but I knew you couldn't know that.

"English law! If it were up to him we might never have broken from England then," you said.

"Maybe not. For queen and country," I bantered.

"We'd have to brush up on our bloody English accents!" you said.

"Blimey."

You reprised the conversation when we visited the Boston Tea Party site.

"Well!" you said. "I didn't realize that they were dumping privately owned tea! I thought it belonged to the British government, that they were protesting the government!"

"Well, they were," I said. "It was against the taxes on the tea." I'd just studied this stuff in school, and it was a good story.

"Yes, I see. Hmp! That tea was private property though. Somebody's enterprise."

I don't know if you were quite bothered exactly, but at least piqued about the destruction of private property. "Hardly seems patriotic..." you mumbled to yourself.

The conversation must have kept turning around in you, because that evening at dinner you said, "You know, that bit about the Boston Massacre, I knew that. Someone told me, maybe your Uncle Jake, years ago. I'd forgotten."

But that tidbit didn't sound to me like Uncle Jake.

The next year was our outdoor adventure. We cruised up the Inside Passage. First we flew to Seattle, and then at dawn we boarded the *Guillemot*, a small cruise ship operated by its owners, Randy and Christie Granberry. They were nice. They'd been doing tours for eighteen years, and they seemed to love it. He mostly piloted the boat, and she mostly oversaw the guest amenities. *How conventional!* They had a crew that helped with things like keeping the sitting deck clean. The *Guillemot* just had one deck for passengers, not like those gigantic cruise ships that have many decks with swimming pools and tennis courts. Mom had wanted a cruise like that, if she was going to go anywhere, but you convinced her that for the Inside Passage the smaller ship would be better: "Save the liner for a trip in more open water; we can do that in the Caribbean." I don't know why you wanted the smaller boat.

I don't think we were ever out of sight of land on that trip, except when it was foggy in the mornings. Almost we were never out of sight of an island. Right out of Seattle we were staring at Bainbridge, and then Whidbey, dead ahead north, and then the San Juans. You were a map geek, and always showing me our route on a map that Randy had mounted behind glass on a wall, there in the viewing room with the big windows all around. We did this trip in August, so it wasn't bitter, and we mostly stayed outside. The sun shone on our first afternoon, but still there was a breeze that felt pretty cool for us Sunnyvale girls, so Mom and I kept our jackets on—not zipped, but on. You were in a sweat-shirt, and kept scanning the shoreline with your binoculars, looking for moose or something. You'd been looking for orcas from the first, down in Puget Sound, but Christie told you that there was too much boat traffic to expect them down there.

We churned up the east side of Vancouver Island through Georgia Strait. Harbor seals we'd seen all along, but saw more now. Still no orca. But there was a retired couple on the boat, Mr. and Mrs. Blankenheim, and they were birdwatchers, crazy birdwatchers. They'd see some speck out over the water and get all excited, or else they'd just bring their binoculars down and shrug, "Second-year glaucous-wing."

A glaucous-wing, they taught me, is a kind of gull. And they're *gulls*, not *seagulls* like we've known all along. The glaucous-winged gulls take four years to mature into ivory-white adult birds, and while they're still young they have different muddy markings, "Just like children in the yard," Mrs. Blankenheim said. You latched onto the Blankenheims, but I kinda thought they were weird. Maybe just old.

There wasn't anybody my age on the boat. There were two couples with little kids, and a handful of retired people, one of those couples with their grown kids and spouses with them, and us, so I felt a little out of place. Randy and Christie were nice, though, and showed me how things worked on the boat—I even steered it a little, out on the Pacific Ocean—and so I met the crew, two people who weren't too much older than me. They were friends with each other, though, and three's a crowd. So I pretty much hung out on my own.

That first night was almost a full moon, so it was bright traveling up the Johnstone Strait, which is a narrow sleeve between Vancouver Island and a bunch of smaller islands east of it. "Imagine if all this area were snowy," you said. "It'd be bright like daylight, under the moon."

"Is that how it was in North Dakota?" I asked.

You started, as if I'd unveiled subconscious thoughts. "Yes," you said, "it was."

"Do you miss it? North Dakota?" I asked.

"Well, snow in the moon was pretty. But no, not really. That was yesterday's world. This is pretty sweet right here."

Mom joined in. "What is the latest with your brother?"

We were now several years into the Internet Age, and even

Uncle Jake had discovered email. He and you were in touch much more than you had been before, even if the state of the art was dial-up.

"Not real good. He rambles around. Sometimes there's not enough rain, or not at the right time, and maybe he should plant red wheat or barley, even—drought-tolerant crops. Other times you just can't compete as a small farmer, you need ten thousand acres minimum, and should have a hundred thousand. Mostly it's money. He says it's not the bank in Pullup any more, it's the bank in New York, or New Jersey, says he can't keep track anymore because they buy and sell each other, and I guess he got sucked in by a decoy ad that he thought was from whoever owns his mortgage, and he got doubled up in debt, and anyway he's in bad shape. It's a tough time. I really don't imagine he'll hold the farm much longer."

Mom nodded. Apparently this conversation wasn't new. "What will he do?"

You just shook your head. "I'm not going to ask. He doesn't know."

"Couldn't you help him, Dad?" I asked.

"I can't make it rain like it used to," you said. "I can't buy him a ten-thousand-acre farm. I can't change the way finance works."

I stared at you, and then at the path of the moon on the water. Your answer was unsatisfactory, but a better one was beyond my grasp.

The dark water slipped along under the boat. The shoreline that wasn't snowy slipped by, too. The moon that had seemed so beautiful suddenly seemed over-bright, harsh and glaring.

We reached the Pacific Ocean proper the next morning. The *Guillemot*, after travelling the protected interior waters, began to rock gently as the waves rolled by us. "It's like a cradle," Mom said. "I thought it would be colder."

We travelled through the North Pacific sun on the tranquil sea. The Blankenheims reported a whale spout between us and land,

and I thought I saw one then, but couldn't be sure. Mrs. Blankenheim showed me the white patches on the pelagic cormorants, and I did see those.

It was a quiet day, and I felt bored. I lay on the deck. Some gulls hung about the ship now and then, coasting and flapping. I could tell that some were adults and some were young, but I couldn't tell if they were glaucous-wings. I wondered if they were bored, too, or if they weren't smart enough to be bored. Some people seemed that dumb. Couch potatoes. Morons. The Blankenheims didn't seem very bright, chasing after little spots of feathers. But they didn't seem bored, either.

That was the afternoon that Randy invited me into the pilot's cabin and let me steer the ship.

"Have you gotten your driver's license yet?" he asked me.

I nodded. "Two months ago."

He chuckled. "Who taught you, your dad?"

I nodded again. "And Mom, too."

"That's good. That's good. Well, you'll know how to steer this then, it's the same thing. Here you go."

He stepped aside gesturing me to the wheel.

It was like any steering wheel, but blue and white vinyl. It didn't waver when he released it, and when I put my hands on it, it felt firm and steady.

Randy watched me and said, "It wants to keep doing what it's doing. That's called inertia."

I nodded, having heard the term.

"Now look up ahead," he said. "See that? That's Bonilla Island. Which way do you want to go around it?"

I felt my jaw tighten. "Which way should I?"

"Either is good."

"Let's go right, closer to Banks."

He raised his eyebrows. "How'd you know that was Banks?"

You had told me. "I saw it on your map," I said.

"Oh, in the Observation Room. Well good. And good choice.

OK. Just turn it a little bit then, just about that far." He held his finger and thumb about two inches apart. "Slowly."

I slowly turned the wheel.

He nodded appreciatively. "If you turn it slowly enough the passengers don't even feel it."

I bobbed my head.

"OK. Now straighten it back out."

I eased the wheel back to straight. "It doesn't do that on its own, like a car?"

He turned his palm over and back. "It will. But it's easy to oversteer a boat on its turn. You know, a car turns the wheels up front. On a boat it's the rudder at the back. It's a different motion."

I pursed my lips as if I understood.

When it came to dinner time you poured me a taste of wine. "The captain told me you steered the boat!" you said.

"About two minutes."

"And you didn't sink us!"

The Dining Room adjoined the Observation Room, with its same extensive windows. The sun set low, golden, and tranquil. The adults were being served more wine. The little kids were plunked in front of cartoons in the Observation Room. I sat there too, not feeling right in either group. I watched that sunset and wondered about adulthood. So what do you do? You grow up, raise your kids, and then drink wine? You win or you lose, which is measured by money—Uncle Jake losing the farm or Dad going on a cruise? Is that what adulthood is?

The sun turned a rose red, and two long-winged birds flapped across it, low on the water. I zipped my jacket and stepped outside to leave the cartoon noise. The air was colder, but there was still no wind. I sat in one of the lounge chairs on the deck. The sun sank slowly. No more birds broke its trail of light.

Once we made it into the islands up the panhandle I didn't steer the boat any more. The islands were all around us. On Randy's map they looked like oyster crackers crinkled over the soup. He steered the boat close along those islands. We stood near the Blankenheims, you with binoculars in hand. We saw our first orcas with them, a pod of maybe a dozen, we couldn't tell for sure. They flashed black and white in the sun when they humped up out of the water.

"Aren't they beautiful!" Mrs. Blankenheim said without taking her binoculars down.

"I wouldn't want to be in the water with them, though," Mom said.

"I guess not." Mrs. Blankenheim grinned. She extended her binoculars to me. "Here, Jenny, you take a look."

In the black circle of the binoculars the orcas glistened. "What would they do if I was in the water with them?" I asked.

No one answered for a moment, and the whales rose and fell in the waves, travelling parallel to us. I returned the binoculars, not wanting to appear too interested.

"They might not do anything," said Mr. Blankenheim. "The resident pods mostly eat fish. But, they all eat meat, so I don't suggest you find out."

You said, "I wish we could get closer."

Mr. Blankenheim nodded. "So do I. But I'm glad we don't. Got to give them their space, too."

You nodded, not in agreement, but in recognition of what sort of person Mr. Blankenheim was.

And it was funny, because I remembered when I wanted to go close to a seal and you were like Mr. Blankenheim: got to give them their space. Had you changed, or was it just that you felt safer in the big boat? Safer for me, perhaps?

Mr. and Mrs. Blankenheim stayed out for hours, scanning every rock outcrop we passed. They showed me pigeon guillemots, which the boat was named for, and which stood like red-booted schoolchildren on the black cliffs. Also murres, bobbing in the water, and scoters and brants. They got excited about three little marbled murrelets—"They nest in the tops of the tallest trees!" she said—and some rhinoceros auklets in breeding plumage. I liked the puffins with their crazy bills and stylish do's.

You liked the eagles. We saw several, grown and young. They're like the gulls, with the young ones being splotchy-muddy until they finally get their white heads and tails when they're four years old. Randy piloted us into the mouth of the Stikine River, and we saw lots of them there, perched all over the trees, and we saw some of them hit the water with their talons and maybe bring a thrashing salmon out, but mostly missing; or sometimes the salmon, especially if it was a big one, rip its way out of the eagle's grip. Once we saw an eagle hold a big one, but it couldn't lift it, and it just started flapping its wings like oars and paddling to shore. Watching it, you nodded with respect, the same way you later nodded when we saw an adult eagle steal a fish from an osprey. The osprey hung onto its fish a long time, but the eagle, twice its size, kept chasing it, and finally the osprey dropped the fish. The eagle dove and caught it in mid-air.

"The osprey are better fishermen," Mr. Blankenheim said, "but the eagles are bigger."

Eagles became pretty old hat. We still liked them, but after a while you stop going *Ooh!* when you see them.

In Glacier Bay we rented kayaks and spent the day paddling through the Beardslee Islands with a ranger. Mom stayed on the boat.

The ranger's name was Tom. He was dark complexioned and dark haired, outdoorsy-looking, and very comfortable in his kayak. He first checked us all out in our kayaks to make sure everyone knew how to handle a paddle. He didn't make us do Eskimo rolls, though.

"OK," he said. We'd all heard it already, but now we were on the quiet water. "We'll be staying close to shorelines, but we want to stay at least a hundred yards from any wildlife. That's for both your protection and theirs. Your binoculars will bring you closer without disturbing the wildlife. Try not to be loud, but if you see something, just say what and where, like on our right at two o'clock there's a bear eating a salmon. Something like that. OK, and it's OK to spread out, because the animals have young now, and they're hungry, and I haven't lost my quota of visitors yet, OK? Everyone understand?"

There were chuckles. Seven of us: Tom, you and me, another couple from the *Guillemot*, and two other guys—turned out they were college buddies from fifteen years earlier.

It was a rich day, and I told you it was too bad the Blankenheims couldn't be there. You nodded equivocally. Tom pointed out harlequin ducks, which are crazy-quilted little birds, and there were cliff-loads of cormorants and gulls and puffins, and we got closer to the marbled murrelets—the hundred-yard rule didn't seem to apply to birds, although we didn't charge through them, either. Maybe forty or fifty yards. Those birds just looked like little corks on the water, a little tweaked at each end where the cork had ripped into two pointy ends.

"Those little birds are crazy," Tom said. "They nest inland, maybe many miles, up in some old-growth tree. Mom finds a mossy spot and hunkers in and lays a single egg, just one. Then she and Dad take turns sitting on it for a month. They each sit a day at a time, and the other gets to fly out to sea and catch fish and eat. Then after a month the chick hatches. Then Mom and Dad are flying back and forth all the time, usually a trip to the nest with each little fish they bring."

"That can't be too efficient!" you interrupted disparagingly.

I felt embarrassed by you. I know that's a normal feeling for kids at that age, but you actually didn't embarrass me very often. But I did feel it with Ranger Tom.

He handled you well. He shook his head. "Birds don't get to choose how they live. Only humans have real choice.

"But the marbled murrelet story isn't over," he continued. "After a month, the parents just stop returning to the nest. Imagine you're that little bird. Thirty days old, all by yourself, up in a tree in a sea of trees. And you can't hop around like a robin and catch bugs, you don't have the legs for it. So these little monthlings jump into the air and they fly, beat their little wings like crazy on their maiden voyage, all the way to the ocean! Then once they're there that ocean better be alive, 'cause they've got to feed themselves!" He looked across the water where a small group of them floated, each spending as much time under water as on it. "That's those little fluff-balls."

I tried to picture them trying to feed themselves and discovered a question. I was kind of self-conscious asking, but I said, "Do they fly underwater with their wings, or just paddle with their feet?"

Tom said right off, "Good question! You know how I know it's a good question? 'Cause I don't know the answer. I know penguins swim with their wings, like flying underwater. And I think dippers do, in rivers. But I don't know about these guys."

I felt bad for asking him a question he didn't know the answer to, but he didn't seem bothered.

We passed a weathered totem pole that faced us from an island on our left, to the west.

"What tribe is that from?" one of the paddlers, a man in a blue coat, asked.

"That is from *Homo europeaninnius*. Somebody tried to set up a hunting and fishing lodge there, before the park was formed. It failed. His dock is gone, but his dock marker is still there."

"Weren't there Indians, Native Americans here?" the same man asked.

"Most of this north of us was ice. Maybe from here south you had some Native Americans, the Tlingit people they say, until ice moved in at the tail end of the Little Ice Age, maybe as recently as three hundred years ago. Maybe some of my people came from here. I'm European, but I'm also Native American, Chugach, from west and north of here."

Blue-coat nodded, taking a last look at the European totem pole.

Later, as we approached a creek, Tom said, "On our right, two o'clock, there's a bear eating a salmon." He grinned and shrugged at his guests. "I've been here before." Then he continued, "Really, some things are fairly predictable. As long as the rivers run and the salmon run, then there's a good chance the bears will be at a good spot where the salmon pool, maybe below a cascade in the river or something. The bears know where to find them."

"So what kind of bear is that?" the man from the *Guillemot* asked.

"That's a brown bear." Tom nodded. "Not a very big one, though. Young male or sow."

"Can they swim?" asked the woman. "I'm not really nervous, I know we're far away."

Tom nodded again. "There was a brown bear that was getting into people's trash, so it was relocated to an island seven miles across the open sea. It turned up back home, and I don't think anyone gave it a lift."

Even you, Dad, seemed to appreciate that feat.

We floated and watched the grizzly. She hunted by swatting at the water when she saw a fish. We saw her miss, or half miss, several times before she sent a big salmon toward the bank. She lunged after it and pinioned it with both paws. Then a cub appeared, ready to eat its lunch.

"They learn how to hunt from their mommas," Tom said. "Some swat like this girl. Some pounce, jaws first. I like that style, they come up dripping with maybe a big old salmon in their jaws.

"Anyway, let's move on a bit and we'll find our own lunch site. I don't think we want to crowd the brown bear."

We paddled on. We'd already spotted several seals and sea otters, and where we beached for lunch we saw river otters, too, well out into saltwater.

All the kayakers scattered along the shore. You and I sat with Tom.

"This whole area," Tom said. "Well, every place has its own story. Here the animals are still finding their places. And their places are changing. Just two hundred years ago glaciers came all the way down to the ocean all around here. They had never retreated after the Little Ice Age five hundred years ago. Now they're retreating fast. Almost all of Glacier Bay was ice, a sheet four-thousand-feet thick when Captain Vancouver came here. Now it has melted away, sixty-five/seventy miles up the inlets. So, that melting exposes soil, and after the ice melts plants move in, the mosses and lichens right below the glaciers, and then grasses and forbs, and then maybe the alders and willows, and finally, if it's not disturbed by fire or storm, the spruces and hemlocks you see all along here. But it's all new, and the animals can't really move in until the plants have. So the marbled murrelets haven't been here long, nor the brown bear or river otters. They were around, but not right here. So they're all just finding their places."

You scratched your chin. "So what you're saying," you said, "is that climate change is happening, and it's opening up new habitat."

"For now, around here, mostly yes. Although someone's gain is almost always someone else's loss. The marbled murrelet has a cousin, the Kittlitz's murrelet. They nest near the base of glaciers, and almost all of them nest in Alaska. They are in serious decline." He turned his hands up. "Also, the Far North is already packed with geese and ducks and shorebirds, and polar bears and arctic foxes. If their land is 'opened up' as you say, and other plants and animals move into that space, where will they go? There is no Farther North."

You had the good sense not to say something stupid like, "Survival of the fittest." But I know you thought it. Even then I knew you thought it, although perhaps at age seventeen I couldn't have articulated my knowing. Would you think the same of his people, the Chugach? Not fit enough to live? And if so, of whom else?

You got up and walked away, probably to give yourself some space, or to pee behind a tree, or to find another animal.

Suddenly alone with him, I glanced at Tom self-consciously.

He shrugged. "Where you from?"

"California. Near San Francisco."

"You go to school?"

"I'll be a senior." I didn't like saying that. I wanted to be older, in college at least.

He nodded.

"Where are you from?" I asked.

"I grew up in Valdez. You've heard of it?"

"Yeah, something…" Why *didn't* I know more?

"You heard of the Exxon Valdez. The oil spill. That's the place. Nine years ago, you were just little."

"Yeah! I saw pictures. It looked horrible!"

"It was. When the spill happened…" He shook his head.

"Tell me about it."

"OK. My father and brothers, they worked for the pipeline, still do. They make good money, too, way better than I do. My dad took my mom to Seattle last year, they went up the Space Needle and everything.

"But my uncle didn't. He fished. He went belly up after the spill. Lost his boat and everything. My cousins worked on beach clean-up for a long time, swabbing up the oil that coated the shoreline. You know, we get big tides around here. The ocean squeezes into the inlets and rushes up twenty feet or more, vertical rise. Depending on the shoreline, that makes a lot of mudflats, almost as far as you can see, or a lot of tidepools, miles and miles and miles of them. And all those miles that have to breathe got coated in oil. They died, the places died. There were the big things that make the magazine pictures—the otters and seals and cormorants. But all the little things that feed those things, the shellfish, the sandcrabs, the urchins, finally the plankton. That's what everything lives on. And they died." He snorted and gazed over the tree-lined water. "But the world is resilient. They have come back some already. Not all the fishing, but a lot of things are coming back. Not soon enough for my uncle, though." He paused and looked at me.

"Go ahead," I said.

He nodded. "My uncle couldn't fish and he went downhill. One night he got drunk and fell asleep at the wheel. Froze to death off the side of the road. My dad said it could have happened anyway, but even he didn't pretend it really would have. And now my cousins are up in Barrow, trying to do up there what Exxon did down here. Can't get away from it, making Alaska dollar-rich and life-poor.

"I couldn't work on the beaches, I was too young, and the oil was too toxic. But I still saw it and got into it some. We used to fish in the lagoon near my house. The lagoon became a cemetery, a mass grave. Our own little Auschwitz. We—my friends and me—we'd pull dead birds out of it all the time. New ones, for a long time, that landed in the lagoon and got coated. At first I thought the colors, the oil rainbows on the water were pretty. That idea went away real fast though.

"And Exxon still hasn't paid a dime of its fine. So you get what the message of that is.

"And now rich people can still come up here and see what's pretty, and then go back down and ruin it with their dollars and their votes. Call government the problem and let the oil companies do whatever they want.

"So that's how I got here. Partly it's, I don't know, selfish, I guess. I get to be out where I can pretend things are OK. And partly I just want to work at something worth doing. Yep, government work. I mean, I don't blame my dad, he does what he can; he doesn't have a lot of choices now. But I'm trying to help people love this land so maybe they'll go back and vote for someone who will protect it. If we don't do that...

"You know, there will be more Exxon Valdez's. Here, Barrow, off Mexico, the Mediterranean, the Barrier Reef. It'll happen, and the more it happens the less things will come back." He snorted again. "I don't get it."

Back then I didn't get him. But I liked him. He cared about the wild land and ocean all around us, and they were beautiful.

"We should probably start heading back," he said, standing. "Nice talking with you, Jenny."

On the way back in our kayaks we saw a moose swimming in the water, crossing from one island to another.

You shook your head at it, in awe, I thought. "That can't be an easy way to make a living!"

Ten

It was later, through Charlene, that I better understood Tom the Chugach, the Glacier Bay Ranger. Tom was living a form of desperation. Charlene was studying it.

"You go in with all the glitz of modern convenience," she said. "Televisions, trucks, central heating, internet, travel. You don't have to work to make them want it. And then you offer them a job that they think will give them that glitz. And then in a single generation they lose their old ways, and you've got 'em. The fishing and maybe the fishery, too, is gone. Or how to flay the whale. Or make the dug-out canoe. Or how to keep the meat without a refrigerator. Or how to cook without an electric stove. Or how to socialize without a TV to steer your thoughts and park them for you. You just destroy them, make them dependent, all in one generation of gentle abuse. We used to conquer people militarily, like turning Africans into slaves or Native Americans into reservation drunks or Aussie aborigines into — what, we stole their children! But now we're more clever. We just sell them things. It's the age of white-collar conquest through capitalism."

So Tom, I figured, was lamenting the loss of his Chugach heritage and trying to live in the strange new world.

But that was all later, my sophomore year at Irvine, when I roomed with Charlene, and could see Tom and Joey and maybe all of us struggling with the loss. Charlene always spoke about things in terms of *us*. *We* invaded America. *We* wiped out the buffalo. *We* are melting the glaciers. She knew that neither she nor I had personally gone out and chiseled the natives or cooked the air and oceans. But it was our culture that did, the entrepreneurial capitalism of Western Society, from which we benefitted; so she was right to hold us responsible, perhaps not for the sinning but for righting the wrong. That was good about Charlene. *We* is a good habit. But I don't think I first got it from her.

I was starting, just starting, to understand things back in high school. Senior year I had economics with Mr. Newell. I don't remember much from that class: supply and demand, which I kind of got, and something about M-1 and M-2, about which I have no clue and honestly don't care enough to learn.

But Mr. Newell talked about externalities, too. I remember that. It's what you don't count even though it's there.

"So let's say I sell fresh eggs," Mr. Newell said, his thin brown tie against his yellow dress shirt. "A lot of people want fresh eggs, so there's a market. I keep the chickens right on my truck and drive door to door and deliver the eggs fresh and warm, right out of the hen. People pay premium, top dollar for those hen-fresh eggs, and the mommies come out and have their four-year-olds hold the egg still warm out of the hen and it's all sweet and organic-feeling, so they're paying me and I'm paying for my gas and chicken feed and doing all right. But, bad news: I end up with a bunch of chicken crap, too, right? Now what am I going to do with all that? I've got a couple of choices. I can keep a tray under my hen cages and catch all the crap, and maybe I can sell it, maybe as fertilizer, and if I can do that then great, it's more income, right! But if I can't sell it I still have two choices. I can pay the garbage dump to accept it; but I don't want to do that, that's an extra cost! Or maybe I can just rake it out of the truck as I go so it doesn't accumulate and leave me with a big mess at home. I don't get anything for it, but it doesn't cost me, either. It just goes away. *That* is an externality. It doesn't count for me or against me."

Todd Alcatraz was the smart guy in my year. Most of us were just taking classes, doing what we had to do, not hating Fremont High, but just vaguely under the impression that we were marking time until life started, which was definitely after high school. Mrs. Russell, my friend's mom, always clucked that high school was the best time of our lives, and Janis and I always died at that. It was a sentence to eternal monotony, and Janis swore that if it was true she'd just "I don't know, run away to some cult, anything to break the boredom." I'm sure she found better options. And in retrospect, I'm sure Mrs. Russell didn't go to college.

But anyway, Todd Alcatraz was a genius. I don't know if that means he was born with Einstein genes or that he just thought about stuff, but either way, he was always a couple steps ahead of the rest of us, who maybe were just trying to memorize what the teacher said, at least enough to pass the class. Todd said, "But Mr. Newell, wouldn't that kind of upset people, if they get chicken poop piles left in front of their houses?"

Like most teachers, at least the good ones, Mr. Newell liked it when students actually seemed to think about their topic. He replied, "Well it could. But usually if it's only a little, or you learn to dump the poop, as you call it, where the people don't complain much, you can get away with it. You're right, though. You don't want to dump more than a shovelful on South Bernardo, somebody'll complain. But other places—" He shrugged.

"Yeah, like Casa de Amigos!" Jaime quipped, referring to the mobile-home park between the freeways.

A handful of our classmates chuckled like orcs, but Mr. Newell spoke over them. "But it's true! Honestly, we don't have a really run-down neighborhood here in Sunnyvale. But most places do. And those are the places where successful operators dump their chicken poop, because those people don't have the resources to make trouble for them. It's a big issue with noise pollution—where do you site the factory?—and huge with water and air pollution. Right now businesses have a place to dump their waste, and they don't want to lose that. That's why they lobby Congress and elect candidates who oppose environmental regulations. They're trying to reduce their costs. They haven't found a way to sell air pollution, so they're trying to at least keep it an externality."

"Is that white-collar for *they want to poison us*?" jibed Jaime.

I guess Jaime was pretty smart, too, in his way.

Mr. Newell told him that no, he didn't think anyone really wanted to poison anybody. "But life is competitive, and any successful business has to cut its costs."

Todd took up the banner. "But externalities are bad, then. They mean we can trash a place."

"Yes, but they also mean your business can survive. And that means the business provides a product, and jobs, and tax income for government that provides roads and fire protection and police."

"And we'll need those police, because we're all going to live in Casa de Amigos!" Jaime cut in for a few laughs.

"So—there's got to be a balance!" said Todd. "Can't we run our businesses so they're clean?"

"That's what the mainstream environmental movement's about. But going to wind and solar is expensive," Mr. Newell cautioned.

He always cautioned. I guess he was a middle-of-the-road kind of guy. But he threw out wild ideas, and that was fun. I guess he was a pretty good teacher. He maybe got some of us to think.

For then, though, it was mostly Todd, and Jaime. And a little bit the people that laughed at Jaime.

Todd had a way of biting his lip and looking at the ceiling. He did it then and said, "But if all businesses had to do it, take care of their externalities, wouldn't that level the costs, so every business would still be able to compete, just everybody'd be at a cleaner level?"

Mr. Newell nodded. "Yes, it's called leveling the playing field. It's what happened with seat belts. They weren't an externality, but they were an extra cost that government mandated. The auto industry fought hard against that mandate, resisting the cost, but it passed. They all had to do it, all the manufacturers, so none of them were at a disadvantage for doing a good thing, and people kept buying cars. It didn't hurt the companies.

"But, we do have a more global economy now. So American companies are competing with foreign companies that aren't under our laws. So those sorts of mandates—seat belts or clean production, or for that matter minimum wages for employees— would have to be included in trade agreements. So then—" He looked pointedly at Jaime—"Then we could begin to clean up the Casa de Amigos not only here but in Mexico and Indonesia, too."

So that conversation stuck with me, one of the standout things I learned in high school. Basically, it was that we could solve problems if we took care of our crap. They didn't have a question on that in the standardized tests, but it's what mattered. We can take care of our crap.

I told you about that classroom conversation, and you were your typical equable self. Your salient comment was, "Yeah, but it's a tall order to clean up Mexico and Indonesia. You know, it means the governments have to be up to monitoring their industry so they follow the mandates. A lot of these governments can barely hold on to their presidential palaces!"

Of course, later that year you voted for George W. and his promises to defund our own government so we wouldn't be able to monitor our mandates either. Way to go, Dad!

And there must have been something about meaningful classroom discussions like that that bothered you and your buddies, too. That was about the time you rolled out your war on public education. Make testing the point of school! Fault the school for serving low-income kids! Point out the rare cases where schools with heroic efforts were able to overcome poverty and raise their test scores, and pretend those test scores equaled successful education. Clamor for higher academic standards, while the glaring failure of our society is less a matter of academic failure than social fracturing. Our children face a relentless alienating barrage of advertisements that define them as needy or inadequate, unless of course they buy Gummyhead's Plastic Life-enhancers, and political leaders protect that corporate degradation and try to confuse and abuse the flagging middle class, offering privatized "choice" as a way to further disinvest from neighborhoods rather than put resources into uplifting them! Yeah, it's all hard in Mexico and Indonesia! But what's harder still is my parents' willful choice to weaken our society. *Look what we can manipulate! Look what we can accumulate!* Look at what you're doing, for God's sake! Have you no sense of what it is to be a struggling child? Have you no sense of community?

That summer, right before Y2K—good old Y2K, always gotta have something to fret about—I graduated from Fremont High. I was good, set to head to Irvine. You were still tolerable, as long as you weren't around too much. But back in North Dakota they'd had a rough year, as you'd expected. Uncle Jake lost the farm that year. He started roughnecking. The oil boom was on in North Dakota, the start of fracking there, I guess. Another good idea. It had only been eleven years since NASA told Congress that climate change was real, that it was happening, and that it promised to upset ocean levels, ecosystems, and economies; and of course that means human beings! But your generation's reaction wasn't to deal with it! It was to ignore, deny, get what you could while the getting was good. Make hay while the sun shone, because soon it will shine too hot to grow hay. *Oh, but we didn't know!* You didn't know because you didn't want to know. You could look the other way and pretend everything was just fine! And you could make sure others didn't know, either. You could hire liars to muddle the knowledge in the public's mind. You could continue to swamp them with idiot TV that served the dual role of replacing both intelligence and socialization. Great! Maladjusted idiots! Congratulations, Dad!

Or really, was it worse than that? Was it not that *you didn't know* but that *you didn't care*? You just shrank your sphere of concern. You didn't care about the world. You didn't care about plants and animals. You didn't even care about human beings. You didn't care about America. You didn't even care about your own children or grandchildren, except as they decorated your life. You just cared about yourself, maybe a little for those within the reach of your short arms and failing eyesight. Anything beyond that puny reach was somebody else's problem. Just leave your crap on them.

You made yourself a worm, with a myopic world view, and worse than a worm, with toxic castings.

Yeah, your brother lost the farm. Sold it to a bigger company and became a day laborer. There's the American dream! How did you create that economy? Or more to the point, why didn't you prevent it? Oh, I know, because money had already become all that mattered as a pursuit, you proved that with your S&Ls and Securities Exchange ratings; and now it was on its way to becoming all that mattered as a civil right. Money could buy out livelihoods, it could litigate farmers into bankruptcy, it could legalize poisons and assault rifles on the street, it could buy senators, because money was becoming what you've made it now, speech, sanctified by the First Amendment, and if you've got enough you can out-megaphone any other voice. Uncle Jake's voice for instance.

So he lost the farm and started fracking, bringing home his boom-bust paycheck, making more money for oil companies who had used up the gushers and were now after the hard-to-get oil under the ocean or in the arctic or locked in rocks. Never mind that this oil was feeding the climate change that would kill animals and economies, and create desperation and terrorism. Never mind all that. Never mind.

Your nephew, my cousin, came to stay with us. Jake's boy Jim, a refugee from loss, an immigrant to the golden state of opportunity. He hadn't wanted to inherit the farm anyway, had no interest in manual labor. He wanted to study computers, so he came to California, to Silicon Valley. You and Uncle Jake had talked, and the idea was that he could live with us and establish residency. After a year in California he would qualify for in-state rates at the UCs and CSUs.

You and I picked him up at the airport. He was awkward, but friendly. He had short blond hair and wore a dark plaid shirt, blue jeans, and spotless new tennis shoes with unfamiliar red and blue logo stripes on them. He was one of those lean boys, not quite scrawny, but gangly without being tall, more stretched than tall, like he hadn't grown into himself yet, and you couldn't tell if he might just cave into his own chest. He was twenty-one, and talked with that funny Midwest accent that flattened sounds out, just like the flat plains they live on.

"You heve lots of cars here," he observed on the freeway. "Ded sed you would." And when we turned into our driveway, "You don't have a fleg at your house! I raised the fleg every day at ours."

You said, "Well, we could fly it, I suppose. I guess our focus here has been on the economy, helping people prosper. We think that's kind of patriotic, too. But maybe you're right, I've got a flag rolled up somewhere."

"I'm sure ours is flying at home."

"I'm sure it is," you agreed.

Mom got him situated in our spare room, and then we all sat and talked while a casserole baked in the oven. "Casserole, that's a Midwest dish. I want him to feel at home!" she had said. Having her nephew seemed to have stirred some vitality in her.

You asked, "Well, Jim, while you're establishing residency, I suppose you'll want to work?"

"You bet. Something in computers would be great." He was too long and skinny for the padded chair he sat in, and his head kind of dangled forward from his neck. But he didn't look like a vulture. He wore a big, broad, naive smile.

"What's your experience?" you asked.

"In computers? Oh, I'm on ours at home all the time. Ded and Mom make me go to bed, or I'd be on it all night."

"What do you do on the computer?"

"Games. I can do anything. I'm a level-five ninja. And I love the graphics."

You nodded. "Have you taken any programming classes?"

"No." He grinned self-consciously. "I just like the games."

"You know, we have community colleges that are very inexpensive. You might want to start taking some classes right now to build up your background."

"Oh! Could I really do thet?" He looked stunned, like Alice in Wonderland or Charlie in the Chocolate Factory.

"Sure. We've got DeAnza and Foothill Colleges, right close by. You could take some beginning programming, or, you know, might want to become a master at Microsoft Office."

He looked a little confused. "A Master?"

"I'm sure there's some sort of certificate," you explained.

Jim screwed up his face in puzzlement.

"Microsoft Office is the whole—you've probably used the Word program to write papers."

"Oh, yeh," he nodded. "Yeh, I've done that."

"Office includes Word and also Excel and Power Point. They're other programs that businesses really use a lot. Being strong in Office would make you very marketable."

"Marketable," he repeated.

You sighed quietly.

Mom said, "If you'd like to do that, Jim, I'm sure the summer session starts soon. I could take you over tomorrow and we could see what's available."

Jim's head bobbed. "OK, yeh. Thanks, thet'd be great."

Jim was older than me, but he didn't seem to have gotten out much.

Mom and I took him to DeAnza the next morning. Yes there were some classes starting the next week. Jim signed up for a computer-literacy class and beginning programming. Mom paid for him, out of state and all.

"Well, thank you," he said, his head bobbing. "I'm real excited about all this!"

Then we went and bought him a bike so he could get to classes, "at least through the summer," Mom said. She wanted to get him a real good bike, but even I knew better than that. We got him a medium-quality road bike and a good lock.

The next day he biked to DeAnza and back, just to make sure he knew the way. Mom had given him careful directions, and when he came back and said, "You sure have freeways around here!" she was aghast.

"You didn't ride on the freeway, did you?" She held her hand to her mouth.

"Oh, no." He grinned shyly. "But I never got far from one, neither! There's freeways all over here!"

"Well, I guess there are," Mom said.

"I expect a guy could get lost," he said.

That night you brought a laptop home from work. "Jim, we were phasing this out at the office. You're welcome to it," you said.

It was a normal PC, a couple years old, but Jim looked like he'd gone to heaven. "Really? Thanks, Uncle Dennis! You guys... Just thank you! You keep helping me!"

"You're welcome to it," you said again.

You showed him how to log into it.

"And how do I dial in?" he asked.

"Dial in?"

"Yeah! To get on the internet!"

"Oh!" you said. "You don't have to dial in. It's always on."

"Really?"

"Really. Just click that little blue e."

So pretty soon Jim was in his ninja game. He pulled away from it for dinner, but didn't watch TV with us, and then stayed up late. I know because I saw the light under his door. No one told him to go to bed.

I don't know if we should have. He slept in until lunch the next day, which was a Saturday. And then he did it again on Sunday.

"I guess I missed church," he said. He looked rumpled.

"That's OK," you told him. "We don't usually go."

"Really? My mom and ded go every Sunday."

"They're conscientious people," you said, and I'm sure Jim didn't hear your ambivalent cynicism.

He nodded.

Mom suggested to me that I might try taking him somewhere.

"Where?" I asked.

"Well…there must be a park…"

"We're not seven, Mom."

"I know. Maybe bowling, or miniature golf."

"I think I've done those once each in my whole life!"

"Well there you go! Here's an opportunity to do them again."

So Jim and I played miniature golf that afternoon. We had to wait about an hour for our turn, and then neither of us was very good. It seemed like what it was, just trying to kill time, but it was OK.

Getting back into the car he said, "Hey, do you smoke?"

"What? No, no I don't."

"Well. Do you mind if I take a minute here in the lot? I mean, I don't want to smoke up your car."

"Oh, sure. You go ahead." What was I going to say?

He lit up and sucked. We both stood by the car. I, at least, felt awkward, like hanging out behind the backstop at school.

"It's been a little too long," he said. "I try not to smoke at your house. Just a little out the window."

I nodded.

"I'm kinda surprised your ded doesn't smoke. Mine does. My mom, too."

"Yeah, my parents don't."

"I like it."

"Yeah? It's not good for you, you know."

"I know. I don't believe that, though."

"What do you mean you don't believe it?" I'd had a science teacher who used to get passionate on that topic. *Believe is what you do with things you can't know. This is a matter of evidence: what does the evidence show? It shows that the Earth is round. It shows that tobacco causes people to get sick and die. It shows that burning fossil fuels causes global warming. These things aren't beliefs! They're what the evidence shows!* "It's what the evidence shows."

Jim shrugged. "I still don't believe it. There's a lot of do-gooders out there that want to run our lives."

I shook my head. "There's a lot of bad-doers who don't care about our lives."

"Follow the money," he said, taking another long drag. "All those people in Washington D.C. making money off telling us how to live."

"But it's the tobacco companies making money, not the government," I said.

"They got you snowed," he rejoined. "It's all the Man. They got my ded's farm, too. And then they tax these cigarettes so you almost can't afford them. Who says they're not making money?"

"But—senators and congressmen get a salary. They don't get paid more by raising taxes. The taxes are used to run the country. The military, roads, that sort of thing."

"Welfare!" he said, as if he'd won the argument.

There was no point in talking with him. "You about done there?"

"Yeah. Thanks for waiting."

"No problem." I looked askance at him. "You should try to think clearly, though."

"My ded says I think all right."

I nodded at him. *Your dad who lost the farm.* But I didn't say anything. Heck, lots of people were losing their farms. And lots of people smoked. Jim wasn't a bad guy. It was all part of a bigger problem that I hadn't figured out.

I thought about it driving home. The traffic was bad, and it was slow going. At stoplight after stoplight I looked at the rows of tailpipes spitting poison, just like Jim had with his tobacco smoke. Rows of cars spitting gas, rows of people. People talked about population. Was our problem the numbers of people? Is that how nature limits us, we get suicidal like lemmings supposedly do, and smoke tobacco and cars? That couldn't help.

"How was miniature golf?" Mom asked when we got home.

"Yeah. It was fun," I said.

"Yeah, thank you," said Jim.

I went and looked up population growth.

Sunday-night football hadn't started yet then, so at dinner we talked a little. I said, "You know, the traffic was bad today, and I just looked up world population. Did you know that when Jesus was alive there were only two hundred million people in the world? That's like one thirtieth of what it is now!"

"Didn't God say, 'Go forth and multiply'?"

"And then when the US started there were about seven hundred-fifty million, still not a billion. And now we're at six billion!" That's what it was then.

"We must be doing something right!" you quipped, thinking you were funny.

"But there are traffic jams!" I protested. At least I could count on you to get my metaphoric language.

You shrugged. "I think it's a great testament to our age that we're able to feed so many mouths and keep them healthy."

"No! People are starving and dying of preventable diseases!"

"Well, we've still got to get better at what we're doing. But with the Green Revolution—you know about that, right, Jim?

You're dad didn't shy from increasing his yield by using pesticides and fertilizers. Those tools moved resources from grasshoppers and weeds to people! With the Green Revolution and with medicine—well, without them this many people couldn't live!"

"I'll say! There weren't even three billion people alive when *you* were born. Over half the population growth has happened since you were born because of your Green Revolution. Doesn't that scare you?"

"Should it? Maybe it should make me proud."

"I don't think anybody likes traffic jams!"

"What would you prefer, mass murder to get rid of the extra people? Forced sterilization so they would never be born?"

"No." I think I whined a little. "But we have to do something."

"Tell me when you've got it figured out."

"OK. I will!"

I kept thinking about it, but didn't have anything I could say out loud.

After dinner, Jim went back to his ninja game and his open window with the closed door. He had it figured out: run away.

Eleven

I fell in love with college immediately and with Joey Rogelio almost as fast. *Rogelio*, I liked saying the name, with the Spanish G. Rogelio. It seemed exotic, and he did, too. Apparently it's supposed to be a first name, like *Roger*, but somehow it became his last name. I guess we have *Rogers*. Anyway, he was dark-skinned and soft-spoken and thoughtful, and he lived just upstairs.

Oh, I didn't really love him right off like a lover. But I remember him right from the start, when the RAs had everyone introduce emself. *Emself.* That was the term they used. Eric the English Major explained, "Our language doesn't have a gender neutral singular personal pronoun. So we have invented one. When the person could be either male or female, use *e* for he or she, use *em* for her or him, and use *ez* for his or her."

"We call him Eric the English Major," Tanya, another RA, explained. "English is such a useful subject." Tanya was in business.

E, em, ez was maybe a little ahead of its time, but *Eric the English Major* stuck. I think it was the assonance.

So we were supposed to say our name, where we were from, and one interesting thing about ourselves. I said that I was a Class IV kayaker. No one knew what that meant, so I had to explain. Sort of a chance to brag, I guess.

On his turn, Joey smiled, almost shy, his white teeth bright against his brown skin. He said, "I'm from La Puente now, but before that I'm from the road. I was a migrant worker until I was fifteen."

"Really!" exclaimed Eric the English Major. "Where did you go?"

"All over," Joey said. "In the winter down in Imperial Valley. Then in spring up the coast, berries and vegetables. Then over to

Bakersfield or Fresno, fruits, nuts, vegetables, and up the Valley. Back down for oranges in the fall." He shrugged.

Eric looked almost envious. "That must have given you a lot of rich experiences."

"In its way," Joey said noncommittally.

"I'm sure it did!" smiled Tanya curtly, and she nodded to the next freshman, a sharp-angled blonde.

"I'm Tabby," said the blonde, "and I've been on every continent except Antarctica."

"And where are you from, Tabby?" asked Tanya.

"Torrance."

But my eyes were still on Joey, who seemed to be listening attentively, but I felt that his head was somewhere else.

At lunch I saw him come off the cafeteria line and look around. Most freshmen came through with a roommate or friend, but he looked alone. I waved him to my table, where I was sitting with my roommate Cathryn. Cathryn was a socially oriented person, always ready to giggle at a double entendre, and a creature of our time, primed to chatter about celebrity insights.

Joey saw me wave and gave his habitual slight shrug. He approached our table and, setting down his tray, said, "I'm Joey, and sorry, I forget your names."

We introduced ourselves as he sat down, and I added, "So, Joey, how did you get from migrant farming to UC Irvine? That's not easy!"

He shrugged and smiled. "It wasn't so hard. I had three years of high school all in the same place, in La Puente. So what about you? How did you choose Irvine?"

How did you choose Irvine? He turned the conversation to us. That was good. And his question was intriguing, too. Was it just first-day banter or was it bitterness, raising the likelihood that Cathryn and I had choice? Was it resentment?

Cathryn jumped in. "UC by the beach, what more could I

want? I'm going to major in tanning!"

He smiled amiably, his teeth again bright against his skin.

They were clean teeth, perfectly aligned. He couldn't have had braces, though, could he?

I guess I hadn't developed a sense of humor, probably still haven't. I said, "I wanted to get a little distance from my parents, you know, and I guess, well, this seemed like something different for me." *You know, and I guess, well*—Why did I say that? But at least it wasn't *like!* But gawd, *get a little distance,* I don't know what his relationship with his parents is! I added quickly, "Not that I don't like my parents! I do! They're great! And Northern California, too! This just seemed—well, I want to see different things."

"I can understand that," Joey said.

"Everything's different!" Cathryn exclaimed. "Look, we're all wearing different clothes. We're from different places, we have different majors, different interests. Some are tall, some are short, some thin, some—not. Some like Leonardo, some like Will Smith."

Joey nodded. "Some like diamonds, some like pearls."

Cathryn clapped. "You've got it!"

"Some like real estate, some like the stock market," he continued.

"Yes! *Viva la difference!*"

"Some like parathion, some like carbamates."

Cathryn's lip curled. "What are they?"

"Different pesticides."

"Ugh! Why would you want to bring up something like that?"

"Just talking about things that are different! They even kill in different ways, and have different risks!"

Oh! He is bitter!

Cathryn looked askance at him. "That's not an appropriate topic of conversation at the table. Table conversation should be light."

"Really? Like—who's better, Britney or Drew?"

"Yes!"

"Like the history of the *Titanic,* but not free trade without health and wage regulations, or all that other complicated stuff?"

Cathryn's face clouded over. "I'm sorry life's been hard on you," she said with sarcastic complaisance, and then turned to me. "That's all for me, I think. I'm not hungry any more, and I don't really want to delve into the sordid stories of poisons. They should be left out in the fields where they can do some good, don't you think?" Back to Joey. "Some people live in the world of sordid things. I prefer finer things. You mentioned diamonds and pearls. Those I know something about, thank you."

"I want to, too," he said. "So far I know that diamonds are mined by slave labor in Africa. I don't know about oysters, but they're probably in farms that pollute some estuary in a poor community."

Cathryn pushed away from the table, looking at me. "I have to go now. You have a wonderful lunch, if you can stomach the menu!"

As she walked away, back erect, Joey raised an eyebrow at me. He could raise just one, like Spock. He didn't shrug.

I did. "Everybody's different." I thought that was clever.

Apparently he did, too. I don't know why we hit it off then, as if there was some instant understanding between us. Or why, for that matter, he had an instant antipathy for Cathryn. Her dress? Her air, I guess? I don't know. But he didn't bait me as he had her. After she huffed away we didn't talk about life as a migrant farmer or for that matter as a daughter of a Bay Area investment banker. We talked about the Orientation Week schedule and getting classes and choosing majors. He already knew what he wanted to study.

"Economics. I want to know how people get poor and how to stop it."

And now I can't help thinking what you would say. *Quit*

buying things you can't afford and investing in risky products! Risky products: things that you sold. And almost everything else advertised on TV. Things they couldn't afford: clean water. Clean air. Staying in one place for education and community. Retirement savings. Children.

Children for God's sake!

But at the time I just got as far as "That's cool!"

Still, Joey and I had struck a friendship. We never did have a class together, but that year we ate with each other often and went to campus films and just hung out.

We explored the place. Irvine is a beautiful campus. *Everything* is well kept, the grounds, the buildings, inside and out. The lawns are like fairways, or maybe huge putting greens. There are no untended shrubs, and the trees are all pruned up so the view is open and there is shade to sprawl in. The place is clean and refreshing. We walked through Mason Park, right by the campus, and around the lake.

"Is this Heaven?" Joey asked me. "I mean, everything is green, there's not a cloud in the sky. It's like a park here!"

"I think it is Heaven," I said. "And it is a park."

"Oh, yeah. Mason Park."

The lake was crystal clear, without any of the algae scum that sometimes develops on small lakes. The trail hugged the shoreline, and no bushes obscured the view of that crystal water. The sun shone, but the mild ocean kept it from being hot.

"This is what I'd wish for everyone!" I said.

He smiled brightly—but was there a cloud hidden there, always?

Gradually I learned his story. He had come to the United States as a six-year-old, slipping over the border behind boxes of auto parts.

"I don't think I remember that, or maybe just a little bit," he said. "I think I remember the dark and closeness. There must have been thirty people, and it must have stunk. Maybe my parents would have come sooner but they couldn't do it with a crying baby. As it was, Teni, my littlest sister, she was two. There were seven of us: my dad and mom, and then Edgar, he must have been nine, and Sandra, then me, Niki, and Teni. It wasn't hot when we came, though. It was raining, hard. It just would have been dank and sweaty. Edgar remembered it better, and he told me all the time. He said there was a big pot for everyone to use, and you had to put the lid right on it when you were done. We were lucky because with the kids we were farthest from the pot. They didn't want anyone to tip it over. But what could farthest have been? Fifteen feet?

"But we made it, and my dad and then all of us got work, not Niki and Teni right away, but they didn't know it. And I guess really they did work, too. You're paid by the harvest, so if they threw in a tomato it counted. My dad's cousin had a green card and he helped us. We started following the harvest. Made friends that we'd sometimes see in different places, too. That was fun.

"It was a fine life, for a kid. My parents always worried about the poisons on the fields, and there were times when we weren't allowed out until the next day, and they knew the owners wouldn't let their own kids out there, but the fruit was ready and had to be picked, and we could do it or let someone else, and it's not like we had a savings or some steady income and could decide to sit this one out. So we'd pick. Dad said we might as well, 'cause we're just sitting right next to the field breathing it anyway.

"But we didn't care, me and Edgar, Edgar and I. We had great times. Just exploring. Sometimes there'd be a ditch nearby where we could catch bullfrogs or crawdads, or sometimes even fish, little sunnies usually. He showed me how to catch them. In those ditches we could herd them up. Sometimes we could make a cardboard wall to help. And he had quick hands, Edgar. He could grab them and hold them. And we'd eat 'em. We'd boil the crawdads. They're as good as lobster, and *they* can sell for three dollars a pound! Mom always complained they might have poisons, 'cause those ditches are right along the fields. But Dad said, no, the poisons would wear off and dilute. I don't think he believed it, though. He just didn't have a lot of choice. And we all seem OK.

"One place, up out of Merced, there was a kid with an extra fishing pole, and there was an irrigation pond we could get to. We kind of had to sneak in and out early there. But there were small-mouth bass in that pond. We'd dig up earthworms and those bass, they were fun to catch, and they were good eating, too!

"Dad and Mom worried about the sun in the fields, too, in the summer. Some farms were good about shade tarps and fresh water, but a lot of them weren't. We saw people keel over. A hundred and ten, and you're just trying to fill your sack, and water's a quarter mile away. Old folks, especially. They'd get carted off and watered up, and sometimes they'd come back out later that same day. They were tough as tortoises, some of those old guys. But even tortoises die."

He turned quiet, remembering something. Then he smiled a close-lipped smile. "My brother told me a story. I don't know where he heard it, or made it up maybe. It was about a boy named Raphael. Raphael worked at a big ranch where there were cattle and vaqueros, and he learned to ride horses and throw a lasso, and in the evenings there was a room in the house with a whole wall of books, and his parents would read to him and then he would read to himself. At night he watched the stars with his brother, and sometimes a vaquero would sit with them and tell them the stories of the different stars. Raphael was very happy. But then they drove the cattle to market and when they came back they had only a thousand pesos, which sounds like a lot, but is not for all your cattle sold. They said the slaughterhouse would not pay more because they had cattle from the jungle who cost less, and so they could not pay us more. And so the vaqueros left the ranch, and the wind blew the sign, *Raphael's Ranch*, down into the dust, and there was no more food. So Raphael couldn't live as a man, so he turned into a coyote, and he hunted rabbits, and it was OK. He still went into the house evenings and read the books, and he still watched the stars at night, although no one told the stars' stories any more. He hunted the rabbits and it was OK. But then more people came and they turned the road into a highway and knocked down the old house and the books, and they put up a store and a whole strip mall. And then there were parking lots, and so the rabbits disappeared. So Raphael the Coyote couldn't hunt rabbits anymore, so he turned into a tortoise, and he walked out behind the strip mall and hid under a bush, and that's where he lived.

"That's the story my brother told me."

"The tortoise lives," I said.

"Under a bush." He shrugged. "So when we were picking we all got a little school, here and there. I think it was toughest on Edgar and Sandra. They were the oldest. When my dad got the job in the warehouse we stopped moving. We've lived in La Puente ever since, nearly four years now. But that was too late for my brother. He wasn't even close to a GED. So he couldn't get a job, and the army wouldn't take him, and he wouldn't have wanted that anyway. He wasn't... He wasn't a hard ass. He didn't want to kill people."

We were sitting under oak trees, on campus. He looked out over the clipped green lawns to the sparkling patios and shining halls. People were walking every which way, following the paved walks—to lunch, to class, to the gym, home.

"These people can walk in any direction," Joey resumed. "They have choices, they'll graduate with jobs that are legal, where they'll be able to feel good about themselves. Edgar didn't have that. Oh, I guess he could have gone back to the fields. But that's not real. You get a TV, we got one, and you see all the glamor and the things you should buy, and going back to the fields is like losing, like giving up, like saying you're a loser. None of these people here have to make a choice like that, even conceive of a choice like that. They have to decide what color sweater to buy, or where to go at spring break. I'm not saying it doesn't feel alive and difficult to them, but it's a whole different world.

"And besides, there's not as much picking work as there used to be. It's getting to be all machines now. Everybody talks about making jobs, but they rip out the old orchards and throw away the ladders, and they plant little trees, close together, and buy shakers so they don't have to hire pickers. And there are machines for the field harvesting, too. Sometimes the machines bruise the vegetables, but they sell them processed and nobody can tell.

"So the jobs aren't there. He could have picked, but... I don't know if he'd have done any better." He stopped talking and stared across the campus, then smiled self-consciously.

"Your brother?" I asked.

Joey didn't shrug. "Where we live it isn't like this. There's a gas station across the street, and it's an intersection where there's oil a quarter-inch thick, and there's always traffic, you never don't have traffic noise. You look out your window, and the thing you can like is the lights in the rain. If it rains hard enough the stoplights look like Christmas. But it doesn't rain that much; mostly it's just dirty city, full of people wishing it was better but not knowing how to do that, just barely scraping by, and that takes all of them. Dad and Mom, they work, they take care of their kids. Heck, I'm in college! But they don't have any savings, they don't have any retirement. What are they going to do?" He looked down at his hands. "That'll be my job."

"They'll have Social Security and Medicare," I said.

He stared at me, thinking. "I don't think so. They're paid in cash. Both of them."

"Oh."

"So what they have is us. They took care of us." He again looked at his hands.

"Our apartment was OK. It was crowded, but Mom kept it clean. She showed my sisters how to clean and cook, and I learned, too, because I saw Edgar not learning and I didn't want to be that. I liked doing the laundry, because it was warm in the laundromat and usually quiet, except for the hum of the machines, and that was OK, kind of nice, you know. I could read there.

"But it wasn't all right. Niki and Teni were still in elementary school, and they'd have Award Ceremonies every quarter, and Edgar'd go see them because Mom and Dad had to work. I know it ate him that they couldn't. He'd tell me that all the bankers—that's what he called them, basically anyone like the people on this campus, buttoned-up, you know, even if they're just kids that pretend and hope they're not—but in La Puente they're still not even like this, because they're still Mexicans, and they're not this buttoned up, just trying to be. So all the bankers would be there to smile and take pictures of their kids, but Mom and Dad couldn't be there, and how was that fair? So he wanted to get a camera.

"Edgar was kind of lost. He would have been fine in Mexico, where everybody knew who they were, what they were supposed to do. The man was supposed to work, the woman was supposed to cook and take care of the children, and they were all supposed to go to Mass on Sunday. But that was gone here. Mom and Dad both worked. The music was different. The jobs were different. The work style was different—no families, no relaxing, just *productivity*. Entertainment was different, off TV, and all produced, not making your own stories and music. I don't know how that can happen, he was only nine when we came to the US. Maybe he saw it in our parents. They came for jobs, a better life. They probably think they found them, I don't know.

"There are lots of guys like Edgar. They don't have a place.

They can't hardly read, so they can't go to school, which they can't afford anyway, and they can't do…because… You know, if you put Edgar out on that lawn, you know how he'd look? How he'd feel? And then if you put him in a classroom with these people? That's impossible! He'd know where he stood. Even if everyone was polite, he'd know.

"So he became a tortoise. I guess a coyote, first. He tried working with a friend as a mover, but they couldn't get jobs, and his friend's truck was always breaking down, so that didn't work. The McDonald's didn't want him. He started being out late and getting bad-mouthed at by our parents. Mom told him he had to be respectful, but he wasn't, and she said he had to come home at a decent hour, but he didn't. She and Dad talked, 'What do we do? If we throw him out he'll be on the street, but if we let this go he'll be worse.' Finally Mom said he had to go. 'We have other children, and they deserve a home without him coming in all loud and mean.' Dad agreed, and told Edgar he had to go, but he could come back when he would be respectful. He never got respectful."

Joey grimaced and continued. "He got into stealing, and then there were drugs. I don't think he used much, but he pushed. No, that's not true, he used. And then it got more violent. He and his buddies. There was a turf war. They got guns, spent more time over in Chino, in places where you have to be in a gang to survive. I don't think Edgar ever killed anybody, but I know he robbed store owners. And if he had to, gang on gang, I'm sure he would have killed. Those people were his… They weren't his brothers. They can never be that, he didn't catch crawdads with them. But they're his homies. That was how he could live.

"So those were his coyote days. And now he's a tortoise. He lives under a bush." Joey paused before continuing, "He's in prison. Two years, maybe one. But even when he gets out, what will be different? You can't take a guy without this kind of experience" —he waved at the campus— "and expect him to live this kind of life. It's not real. But this is the only kind of life allowed now. All the jobs are going away.

"So I don't know how it works, but that's what I want to learn. That's why I'm studying economics."

I was quiet, considering Edgar and Joey. And inside I sort of laughed—laughed or cried?— thinking that most people would study economics to get a lucrative job. And that was what Joey needed, a good job, wasn't it? Understanding was all good, but a job is what you live by day to day, your bread and butter. Maybe understanding is a luxury, available only for those who can afford it.

I actually thought that. I know because after teachers for years had been telling us to keep a journal, I'd finally followed their direction in college. I have it written down. And although it is dismaying to know I thought that—as if our understandings aren't what we are feeling and living by every minute, as if they're not what makes life beautiful, as if understanding might not have given Edgar a different place to go, as if a job without understanding of one another is worthwhile—the fact that I thought the job alone was the first pursuit, that fact gives me hope. It shows that people can change. Even people like me. Even people like parents, Dad.

We were at the beach. I remember it as sunset, with the sun resting like a boat on the ocean, and the waves just little lines of ripples across the sundown gold. Too many of my memories of Joey are as sunsets. Beautiful, but sunsets. "Tell me about your sisters."

He laughed. His self-conscious smile had changed, frequently now breaking into a little chuckle that I think was both merriment and despondency. "My sisters! Well. Sandra is married. She got pregnant early, and they decided to marry. My mother was very upset, and she told Sandra she didn't have to marry. I think she wanted her to go to college, too. She said she and Niki and Teni could take care of the baby. But how would that have worked, with school and her job? And an abortion, I don't think Sandra ever considered it, and I'm sure Mom didn't. That would have been a hard one for her to take.

"At first I was worried about the guy, Raul. He seemed nice enough, but, well, he looked like he could be a friend of Edgar's. I mean, I hope all my sisters marry nice guys, and Edgar, he's my brother, and really, he's a nice guy, too. But nice isn't enough. Raul was one step ahead of Edgar, though. He had a diploma. So at first he didn't have a job, but my dad, people like him, and he talked with his boss and now Raul works in the same warehouse as Dad. But Raul gets paid by check, so he's already ahead of Dad. So Sandra's doing fine."

"You know," I said, "I don't want to have my well-being defined by my husband's job."

He looked at me and nodded. "Of course. You have options."

The golden boat had sunk into Atlantis, and the western sky was pink, the calm sea a reflection of pink going into night.

"Does Sandra ever get to watch the sun set?" I asked.

He looked westward and then dropped his eyes. "There are not so many views where we live. The sky is up, but not out so much. The buildings are not like downtown L.A.; that would be even worse. But there is no view like this. The buildings block the views."

"Would she enjoy it if she could see it?"

"Yes, I think so. You know, you learn to love what you have. Or at least live with it. She's like most people. She watches TV." He shrugged.

I was trying to picture her, her life. "Is her baby born?"

Joey nodded. "A little boy. Edgar. Named for our dad."

I nodded. "And maybe his namesake uncle will be in better shape by the time little Edgar gets to meet him."

"Maybe."

"But he'll have another uncle no matter what."

Joey nodded cautiously.

I think you, Dad, would prefer a guy who nodded absolutely, strongly. Not because you don't recognize that there is a tentativeness in life, but because a guy who sees things black and white, or at least affirms that things are black and white whether he sees them that way or not, is *safer*. He won't rock the boat. Or she, or e won't! E'll just do what e's supposed to do, and that keeps the sun shining, even after it should have gone down.

We rose from the darkened sea and turned inland toward the city lights. The sand squeaked under our bare feet. We were hand in hand.

Waiting for the bus I said, "Maybe sometimes you could bring your nephew to the beach so he can see the sky."

"Yeah." He nodded like he could envision it. "Yeah, I'd like to do that."

Then we were on the bus, and I rested my hand above his knee. "You never told me about Niki and Teni."

He put his hand on mine. "Niki is kind of a quiet girl. She is very studious, very responsible." We lurched along in the bus. "She will go to college," he added.

"Good for her!" I said.

Joey nodded.

"Do you know what she will study?"

He shook his head. "She doesn't know yet, either. Probably something so she can get a job. Maybe she'll be an accountant."

"There's nothing wrong with that."

"I'm not sure of that," he said.

Was this in our sophomore year? That's where I find the thoughts in my journal that would echo this conversation. But no, it was spring of freshman year.

"What do you mean? She could still enjoy the sky," I said.

"I think accountants build a world where the sky gets small. You know, not just accountants. All the finance and marketing, the way money is accrued. No one makes money on an open sky, so they make it small, they replace it with things that create an income stream."

"Is that what you're learning in your econ classes?"

"No! I have to figure that out on my own. But it's what what I'm learning means."

"It's the way things work, Joey. That's what you wanted to learn."

"Yeah. So I could make it better."

"You're a hard one," I sighed. "So you don't like Niki?"

"What? Niki's my sister! I'd do anything for her!"

"Even if she's an accountant."

"Especially if she's an accountant. She'll need it more." He grinned against the bitterness.

"So you'll bring her out to watch the sunset with her little children."

"No." He turned somber. "She'll be able to afford the sunset herself. I'll just have to work harder to get her and my nieces and nephews to appreciate it. More of the sky will have been replaced."

"I hope you're wrong, Joey."

He nodded. "So do I."

"What about Teni?"

He brightened and laughed in sudden sheer enjoyment. "Teni is a jalapeno, a habanero! Teni *is* the sky! Teni owns the world!"

"Then I suppose she doesn't need to go to college!" I said.

Joey slumped back on the bus seat. "Two things," he said. "You are suggesting that the reason to go to college is to get money to own the world, own in a very fiscal sense. That is accountant-think. A better reason to go to college is to be able to enjoy life more fully, to understand and appreciate what life is about. And secondly, if she does own the world she had *better* go to college, or else the world is being run by fools!"

"Well, I'm put in my place!" I said, and I thought I sounded like my mother, which was very annoying.

"I like the place you're in," he said, and squeezed my hand.

"And not fools, that's wrong. But people who aren't educated, in a world run by people with diplomas."

I didn't ask more about Teni, at least not then. I thought how amazing Joey was, to have thoughts like that in spite of his background. We got off at the bus loop and walked to the dorm, still hand in hand.

Joey came by my room as infrequently and briefly as possible. He didn't like Cathryn. "She's money. You are too, but that's not all you are. She's money without people."

One time when she wasn't there he looked at some class notes she'd left on her desk.

"*Global trade,*" he read out loud. "*Expected to grow. NAFTA, WTO. Purpose: profit, NOT cultural exchange/learning fuzzy-wuzzy. Advantage: low wages, low regulation. EU good—standardizes. Trade Negotiations: have alternate plan so can play hardball. Clear, high demands. Point is not reciprocity but profit. OK to include favorable points in fine print only. But be ethical, no lying. Be aware of cultural values in gift giving.*" He looked up. "Do you know what this means, Jenny?"

"I wasn't listening."

He looked at me almost angrily. "*Include favorable points in the fine print only. But be ethical!* That's '*Be sure you're legal when you screw them!*' This is what she's learning in class! No wonder she's subhuman!"

"She's not subhuman!"

"She's inhumane. She's inconsiderate. That sounds subhuman to me."

I scowled.

"*Be aware of cultural values!* That's *Be careful in your bribes!*"

I shook my head.

"And that's what she grew up on and that's what she's getting in class now."

"Joey, it's just business."

He lifted the pen from Cathryn's desk and added a note to her notes. When he stepped away I read it. *First Global Trade deal in America: Manhattan Island for $27 in blue beads.*

I remember we were at Mason Park on an evening, following its paved trail around the lake. The white rocks that wrapped the shoreline seemed to glow under the cool dusky sky. I heard a robin chirp, and it took me back to the American River. It must have taken Joey somewhere, too.

"There should be frogs," he said, suddenly standing still.

I stopped, too. Cars hummed on the nearby streets and highways, but the park was still. "Wait, I hear one."

We stood silently.

He shook his head. "I can't hear it. I've heard them louder than a train, all around like you're in the middle of an ocean of them. Have you ever heard them loud like that, especially after a rain, louder than thunder, and they just keep going? There were so many of them some places, millions. Sometimes on a levee Edgar and I could turn and face a field and it was only loud in the creek behind us, and then we could turn and face the creek, and it was blasting, not quite painful, but really loud. And it would go like that for a mile, all the way 'til the creek went into a tunnel."

I nodded. "I heard frogs sometimes camping with my dad, when we went kayaking. But not like you're describing. You were in the valley, slower water."

"Frog water. But this should be frog water."

"It's a park," I said. I looked around, and the manicured lawns, the brushless borders and expanses, the trimmed-up trees, all that had seemed so park-pretty and still lovely in the softer tones of evening, all took on a groomed and sterile air, as if some surreptitious poison was slipping through the veins of the grass and up through the roots of the oaks. "I don't like to think about it," I said.

"No one does," said Joey.

Twelve

I don't know why I liked Joey. I mean, he was good-looking and considerate, but so were lots of boys. Maybe he just seemed exotic at first, and then he became substantial. I don't know. I liked him. But I didn't tell you or Mom about him that first summer.

Mom had started a collection of little statuettes, and she spent her time dusting them. You were putting in long hours. The Dotcom Bubble was bursting, and you had to revise your mantra of a New Economy, the mantra that claimed that virtual reality had replaced physical reality, and value was separate from goodness.

Jim had taken several classes at DeAnza by then, and he had been accepted at San Jose State for the fall. He still lived with you and Mom, but was excited about moving into an apartment in August.

"I've already found two roommates," he said. "They have an apartment close to campus all lined up, and I'm going to split it with them."

"That's great!" I encouraged him. "How did you find them?"

"Online. I know a lot more now, about how computers work and all."

"That's good, Jim."

"It'll be good to get my own place, too," he said.

"Right. And meet some people, too." Mom had said that Jim never went out, just holed up in his room with his computer.

"Yeah." He nodded, bobbing. "I got a job, you know."

"Mom said. With the Humane Society?"

"Yep."

"Tell me about it."

He bobbed his head some more. "They liked me because I had experience on a farm. So I feed the puppies and kitties and take them for walks. There's a closed-in yard where I can take them. I just have to be careful where I step."

"Don't they clean up?"

"I do. But sometimes, I mean, you can't keep up with every puppy poop, you know?"

"I guess. It must be sweet to take care of the little fuzzballs."

"Yeah, I guess. Anyway, it gives me some spending money, you know?"

"Will you keep working when school starts?"

"No, no. The job's here in Sunnyvale. I can't afford a car yet."

Or school, I thought. I already knew from Mom that Uncle Jake was sending him money for school. Uncle Jake seemed to be making decent money. Or at least plenty of it.

We didn't eat dinner together. Sometimes Mom cooked, but between you working late, and sports, or else news, on TV, and Jim being a recluse, and me having been gone, and Mom just feeling done with it, we ate whenever, wherever.

So it was Jim who, over a peanut butter and jelly sandwich, told me he was slated to work through July and move into his apartment on August first. But it was Mom who told me ten days early that Jim was done with work.

"I asked why, and he said they had a new person coming in and wanted to train him and they couldn't afford to keep both of them." Mom shrugged, but her shrug wasn't like Joey's. Joey's was an armor, an *I-don't-care* to protect him from the vulnerability of actually caring. Hers was a sort of helpless *what-are-you-going-to-do.*

Jim's was like hers, an *I-don't-understand-the-world.* I tried to talk with him every day that summer—catch him in the hall, call him out for a bite to eat, whatever opportunities arose.

"Hey, come here!" He called me into his room on a rare morning he had the door open.

It smelled only faintly of cigarette smoke, and wasn't unduly messy.

"Did I show you my gun?" he asked. "It's an old-style pistol, a six-shooter." He held it up for me to admire, but I lacked the skill.

"It was my dad's. It was Grandpa's."

I nodded, as if in appreciation. "What do you do with it?" I asked.

"Same as you do with any gun, shoot it! I've shot birds with it," he said. "Not here. Just back home. It's a target gun, not like in the game." He nodded to his computer. "At home I had a rifle. Dad and me went hunting every fall, except now I'm in California. Do you know where there's a range around here?"

I shook my head. "I suppose there is one."

"Yeah. Maybe I'll have to find that."

But as far as I know he never did, and I never saw the gun again. He didn't keep it out and about.

Another time I asked how his parents were.

"Yeah, they're doing great. They sent a note with the check to start up my apartment. Dad says his work is no fun, just a whole town of men who don't want to be there, but good money. Mom's shopping for a new countertop in the kitchen. So I guess they're good."

"Good! How about your sisters?"

He shook his head. "Mom didn't say anything. So I guess they're OK, too. Gretchen's probably fixing to get married."

"Oh, I didn't know she had a boyfriend!"

"Well, I don't know either. But that's what they do, isn't it? She'll probably go and get pregnant, and then the guy'll marry her."

"They still do that in North Dakota?"

"What else? I mean, anything else…"

"Anything else might keep her options open."

"What for?"

"For anything she wants to do!"

Jim shook his head disparagingly. "What else is there to do?"

"Travel! Study anything she wants!"

"She doesn't want to study anything." He snorted. "Especially computers."

"And don't boys learn not to get girls pregnant?"

He leered and shook his head.

I shook my own. "Don't you get into trouble, Jim! And hey, what happened at work?"

"Work?"

"The Humane Society."

"Oh. I had an accident."

"What happened, Jim?"

"I had a puppy out in the yard, and I wasn't looking. And I kinda stepped on it."

"Jim!"

"Well, I'd kinda wondered what it looked like inside, and there it was, just a little one, smaller than my boot."

"Jim...!"

"I didn't really do it on purpose. I stepped on it, right across its back. It smashed almost flat. I think I broke its back, but it didn't die right away, so I stepped on it again. I thought if I crushed its head it wouldn't suffer."

"Oh, God."

"It was messy then. I didn't know what to do. It was all smooshy and broken. Little brown puppy fur mixed in with the bloody lumps of brain, and the broken bones were white. I looked at it all, but the heart wasn't beating any more. I couldn't even tell for sure what was what. The paws were still there. I was going to take one, a clean little brown and white one, for luck, like a rabbit's foot. But I didn't have a knife, and I knew I couldn't twist it off without getting bloody, so I didn't. I just got one of the baggies for poop and I threw him into the poop can. I don't know what I could have done better."

I just stared at him. "Are you OK, Jim?"

"Yeah! I'm fine!"

I looked at him questioningly.

"I am!" he protested. "I've seen animals die on the farm. I had to kill chickens. And people die all the time in Ninja. I'm used to it."

"That's not healthy, Jim."

"What? Knowing that things die?"

"That kind of dying."

"Pfeuh! What other kind of dying is there?"

I chewed on my lip. "It's the focus, Jim. You've got to focus on living. On making life good."

"The puppy was an accident." Briefly he hung his head like something innocent, like a schoolboy caught slipping a fish into a girl's lunchbox, maybe a hundred years ago. But then he looked up assertively. "And the chickens were my job! And there's nothing wrong with playing games!"

I shook my head and backed away. What else could I have said? I was—disgusted?—appalled? Repulsed. Maybe frightened. I left him. He could go back to his computer games—who knows what he was doing there?—and he did.

I didn't tell you or Mom. Maybe I should have.

But that's why you drove Jim to his apartment the next week. I didn't want to be with him, especially alone with him.

So I didn't meet his roommates or see his neighborhood. You told Mom it looked a little rough, but a boy had to find his way. You had a little shrug in you then, too.

I'd have gone stir-crazy that summer except I'd picked up a job scooping ice cream. They say those used to be high-school jobs, and they still are, some. Where I worked we had older folks come in applying all summer long. The manager accepted their applications but never called them back. He never said it, but I know why. Who wants old people scooping up their ice cream? That was his thought. Gotta do what the market wants.

Anyway, nobody there killed puppies, or at least they didn't talk about it. And nobody there was you or Mom. So that was all good.

But I was ready to go back to school by late June, and certainly by September. You had offered to put me up in the apartments— my own room, really nice—but I had decided to go in an off-campus house. I was rooming with a friend, Charlene, and there were lots of other people around, including Joey. After looking at Jim and how he lived so weirdly isolated, I felt all the better about being in a place that forced more contact. I'm sure there's a balance between time alone and time with others, but at that point I felt like I'd rather risk time with others.

We didn't have to declare majors yet, but everyone was sorting it out. I didn't know what I wanted to do, so I was leaning toward an English major. I figured it offered a window into who people are, and kept job options open. Joey still wanted econ so he could fix poverty. He wasn't really that naïve, but that's what he wanted. Charlene was studying biology, but she wasn't pre-med. She wanted to teach, but maybe in outdoor education, not a classroom. I didn't keep in touch with Cathryn, but I knew she was business.

Funny, now that I think about it. Cathryn was probably the richest, money-wise, of any of us, and more than anyone else she just wanted to make more money. I can understand that attitude from have-nots; if Joey felt that way it would make sense. But from Cathryn? I guess she had accepted your generation's ethic, Dad: possess more.

Anyway, I took plenty of breadth courses, and that quarter, probably influenced by Joey, I took a course on Contemporary Economics. That was the course that gave me my best under-standing of some of what your generation did, the focus on dollars. It was nothing new, really; you just did it so well, and on such a scale. Destroy habitats and livelihoods, because if you don't somebody else will, and they instead of you will profit from that ruin. Call it free trade: forced labor, the slums, the lock-in factories, the child slavery. Make it illegal to legislate tariffs against abuse or pollution, since those tariffs would violate free trade, the biggest god on the block, manufactured in Hell. Make things cheap so people will have to buy replacements, or engineer incompatible parts or built-in deficiencies or forced upgrades so people have to buy new before the old is worn out. So their incomes go away in junk purchases, so they remain poor and poorer. So more manufacturing is required, concentrating wealth and spreading out poverty and pollution. So we destroy the climate as our legacy. So we levy slap-hand penalties against occasional companies—that's to shareholders, to retirement savings, to people like Joey and Charlene instead of against the CEO's who commit the sins! And buy governments so your actions are defined as sins only, beyond our courts, not as crimes. Neat system you wrapped up there, Dad!

But of course people know, if not in their brains then somewhere down in their hearts, their bones, or their bowels, that everything in the universe is connected, that whatsoever we do to the least of our brethren we do unto God, we do unto all. We know that if we paint with poison the house will be toxic; if we make poisons we'll eat and drink them, and we'll get our cancers; if we live by the sword we'll die by it; if we live by chicanery we'll die swindled, or worse, only as swindlers.

So I was studying contemporary economics in class and with commentary from Joey, and learning contemporary ecosystems from Charlene, and still hoping with both of them because we were young and strong. But not everyone is strong, no matter their, his or her, ez age.

You know the story, at least part of it. You told it to me, to some extent. No awareness or suspicion until he seemed odd, furtive, even more reclusive, at Thanksgiving; growing quietly unnoticed, like cancer. My cousin Jim. Your nephew.

Apparently his roommates were a little seedy indeed, weren't they. And of course he had no resources. He was a stranger, an isolate. Maybe he would have had friends back home, in North Dakota, but I doubt it. I can picture it. He moved in. He grinned like a fool and played ninja. He started classes and still played ninja. What did he eat, peanut butter sandwiches? Who were his friends?

"Hey Jim-bo, come have a little fun with us! What are you doing with that computer all the time?"

"Yeah, like it's a woman!"

"Shit, you can't spend that much time even with a bitch. They wear out, you know. Get out here, Jim-bo!"

And he'd finally come out, head hanging, sheepish grin.

"Jim-bo, this is good shit. Come have some fun with us."

"Yeah, be a roomie!"

"Oh, I don't know that stuff. I smoke cigarettes is all." His nose wrinkling, his shoulders bobbing.

"Well you can smoke this, too. Here, see!" Taking a sample draw on the pipe.

Jim scratching his nose. "I don't know."

"It's time to learn, Jim-boy."

But the big one, the boss: "Ah, let him be. You don't have to do this, Jimmy. You do whatever you want."

And Jim nodded and almost turned back to his room, but you can't live virtually, it's a diversion but not a life, and here he was with real people inviting him into their company. So he shrugged and walked up and held out his hand for the pipe. Was he scared? Right down to his toes, but no. He was young and adrift. He didn't have friends, he didn't have health, he didn't have prospects, he didn't have religion, he didn't have a nation. He wouldn't have said that, but all those things in his life were too thin and brittle to help him navigate the real world. They don't have to be thin and brittle, but they were. His country was raising the flag, but not making sure that it stood for something good. "Freedom" had long since become doublespeak for "right to abuse." His faith was church on Sunday, and even that remnant had been chucked aside in our house. His prospects—what did he know that could enrich his life? Only the imaginary world of his computer game. Did that release serotonins in his brain? Maybe. Did it socialize him? Apparently not. His health—oh, he was young, still growing, but already committed to sucking cigarettes, which made sense because it fit with who he had to be: he'd sucked poisons all his life on a farm growing the American Dream as reconfigured by and for Monsanto, and you don't just chuck who you are, you hold it close; when the going gets rough you latch onto it all the harder, like a life-vest, because the instinct is it's *all you've got*, so he had started the long slow suicide of tobacco just like the long slow suicide of the farm, of toxic fields and finance where the ducks and foxes disappear, and the farmers follow, bequeathing all first to the bigger company and then to the impoverished, regimented future. And friends? Did Jim have friends back in Dakota? He never mentioned them. No, I think he was friendless there, too. His evenings there were a precursor to his time here, alone with his screen. Joey might say he had lost his culture. Not like Mexicans coming to the US might, or Asians, or Africans ripped out of the Old World at America's dawn, not like they who lost their stories, their food, their faiths, hurricaned away in the tumultuous New World. No, the hurricane came to him, right there in the Breadbasket. Farming changed from a living to a business, and business had become not sustaining but hungry, ravenous, the cancer of the communities that fed it, poisoning its denizens, bankrupting its farmers, yielding the land to some grander lord while the locals sank into serfdom. And that hand in hand with television, which supplanted thoughtfulness with jingoism, Aesop's fables with advertisements, cultural wisdom with commercial exploitation. That was the gift of his parents' generation to Jim. And then the internet came, too, for Jim a grand feast of games, of distraction, of imagination, of time becoming isolated.

Anyone, especially any young and ungrounded person, might have reached for the pipe: growing up is a perilous process. More often than not, the endangered grow past it. But sometimes, through weak friends, weak family, weak culture, or bad luck they don't.

So Jim smoked, and smoked again, whatever was in the pipe. He grinned and probably giggled, and his new chums laughed to see a new dope. And the weeks went, and at first he made it to all of his classes, then began to miss a few, just here and there, and what's called partying became a bigger piece of his life. His party scene wasn't social, with the drugs and alcohol no less toxic, but mixed with a potential for some lifeline friendship. Not so for Jim. He no doubt was a reclusive user, sharing the hollow of his pipe with himself alone, a performer not a friend to his chums, his pushers, who laughed on the sidelines, and then he would retire to his computer where his warrior began to fail, to die, how many times did it die?

He failed a midterm, and then another. He was lost in his exams, probably would have been without the drugs. What did he have? No one was there for him, no church, no country, no family, no friend. All he had was commerce. The pushers. The incoherent economy that had taken the farm and now required him to learn words and rules he had no aptitude or interest in. The relentless ads and TV shows that showed him what was of value, and it wasn't him, even if the ads claimed he deserved the latest rip-off. But he had a gun. You can't count on a civil society in modern America, but you can count on a gun.

It's fashionable for the lost these days to go down in a blaze of unsocialized incoherence, to inflict on others their own dysfunction, to kill. Newtown. The Washington Navy Yard. Virginia Tech. Aurora. Fort Hood. Columbine. Kinston. Seal Beach. Manchester. Appomattox. Carthage. Omaha. Red Lake. Oklahoma City. And on and on. "Never again" is cried out, over and over and over. But the forces of profit rule, the cries of the people for self-governance are drowned out in the megaphone of money and the legislative silence it buys, and the guns and the asocializing commerce propagate, and so "Never again" is cried again, and again, with ever-increasing hopelessness and cynicism. And the larger society may merit its shooters as the natural fruit of its desocializing commercialism, but the bloodied individuals and their bereft spouses and children and parents don't; and no one, not the NRA or the lost shooters or the CEOs, the killers with guns or the killers with commerce, deserves to act that way.

And Jim was a quiet boy. Such a bold action as confronting people with a gun would have been contrary to his personality, his imagination, and certainly to his training as a hunter.

Had he thought about the gun? He knew it was there, tucked down in his drawer, accessible but inconspicuous. Loaded? Probably not; he'd have known. Safety on? Absolutely. All of that he'd have known, been quite conscious of. But had he thought about using it? Probably not.

The classes made little sense to him. Another test, a final exam, was a matter of random bubbling. At the edge of his consciousness stalked the likelihood, the certainty, of failure in school. Disappointing his parents, no home to go back to. No job prospect to go forward to. What was he going to do? What could he do, without modern skills, without a farm, in an economy and society that offered no shining eyes for people like him?

And then another reincarnation of his warrior avatar died. He, the warrior, had already lost a level. The world was closing in. How could he fight it? What was the problem? The problem was him. The warrior was capable, it was Jim who was weak. He was the one who couldn't fight, who couldn't succeed, who didn't fit. But there was a way to win, or at least not lose.

Was he high? What matters is he was low. He pulled the gun out of his bottom drawer, the pistol he had shown me, its black barrel clean, cold, and smooth; his father's gun, his grandfather's. He checked the chambers. Why did he fill them all? Did he, who certainly knew better, not comprehend the finality of his action? Was it a last recognition of his own incompetence? He closed the cylinder. He held the gun in his hand, marveling at its power, the power he lacked; its balance, its decisive functionality. Unlike him, it would work at what it was supposed to do. His warrior would do better without him. His parents would not have to support him. He would stop smoking even, since that was a problem. It was all good. He would win.

So he put the muzzle in his mouth. All unconsciously he must have envisioned this ahead, rehearsed it. He didn't hold the gun to his temple first, to test the feel of it. He went right to the mouth, pointing up. Perhaps he'd read or seen movies. He didn't think to go to the bathroom, where the spatter could have been collected in the tub. Jim didn't think that far ahead.

The splatter sprayed over a stack of textbooks and notes, his computer, and his unmade bed, with sheets and blankets Mom had bought him that would now go to trash. Everything to trash.

You called me the next day, Friday of Dead Week. Maybe I should have studied that night for my upcoming finals. But I didn't. Maybe loss and destruction, like anything else, love company. The company of more loss and destruction. I remember a feeling of a great plexiglass wall closing in on me, not bringing panic or complete blindness but a dumbness and unclarity of thought, not exactly emptiness but viscous slowness. *Any man's death diminishes me because I am involved in mankind.* Jim was my cousin. My world contracted and grayed.

Friday night, even of Dead Week, a terrible moniker, you can find a party on campus. I wasn't really after a party. I was after memorylessness. I called Joey and told him of my cousin's suicide. I asked him to come with me. He did. I guess I wasn't as bent on death as Jim, but I was related to it. I knew the parties could be particularly dangerous for the overindulged. That was where I was going. That was where I went.

I don't know whose bed I may have awakened in, or whether I might not have awakened at all. As it was, I came to in my own bed, under the covers, still in my clothes. Lying there, from my small, gray, nauseous world, *Thank you, Joey.*

You and Mom flew the body back to North Dakota. There was no reason for me to miss any finals, you told me. But still, even though I'd never felt particularly close to Jim, I thought of him and sometimes spoke with him, as though he were not just another hole in the fabric of humankind but could communicate even about his own death. Jim, I'm sorry I wasn't there for you.— *Oh, it's all right, you were OK.* Scratching at his nose.

You had been considerate of him, just as you were and are of me. You and Mom supported him financially, well beyond any bare minimum. You were alert to his schooling needs and gently guided him forward in them. You considered his recreation, his transportation, and his need for independence. You gave your time and resources as he could use them, and your guidance where you could.

But it was all imbedded in the larger world where he didn't fit, where he didn't have a place to go that he reasonably, or emotionally, could go. He wasn't cool, and coolness, always a prime motivator, had become more overwhelmingly consuming with the push of commercial requirement abetted by invasive technology. He had found the happiness of a higher-pixel screen, but pixel-deep happiness doesn't support life. He had the culture of free enterprise, the culture that exploits everything and everyone, the sort of free enterprise that slave traders practice.

He had your congenial pat on the back, but a culture based on exploitation, and it took him from his home, it had already taken the home he grew up in, and it took him from being part of a healthy society, and it took him into drugs, and it killed him. Neither the bottle nor the pixels nor the drugs could deliver happiness, inclusion, love. A culture of warmth and decency and care is what delivers life, and Jim didn't have that. He had the culture of Use and Be Used.

Oh, but Jim was weak. Yes, he was. You and I are stronger, aren't we. So it's survival of the fittest, eh, Dad? Aspire to be wolves not dogs, and certainly not humans, eh? Shake off this thin veneer of civility and be who we really are. All the Hitlers and Hannibals and haters, that's who we are, right, Dad? No, even you know that that's only a possibility, not a necessity. But you fed it anyway, to the point where you couldn't protect your own nephew from its horrors.

Or your daughter either.

Thirteen

But I had good times before the bad. Joey and I grew closer that spring, making an unstated pact of companionship against the vicissitudes of the world. I think I was falling in love. Still falling when in June he came to visit us in Sunnyvale. He swung through from I-5 on his way to Oregon, where he had relatives working. He was hitchhiking.

"Isn't that scary?" Mom asked over dinner. She was going thin since Jim died, but not yet fragile. She'd had you pour wine for all four of us.

"Not usually," he replied. He had lost some of the grinning teenage awkwardness he had when I first met him. He seemed more confident. "Most people are pretty good."

"But it only takes one bad one," she countered.

"Oh, someone might rob me or something? Yeah, that's possible. But not likely. I'll take the risk. You know, nothing risked, nothing gained."

You laughed. "In my business we're always trying to avoid risk."

"Yes, for yourself, your company. But not always for others, that's not how business works. I want to build myself to be a benefit for others. I think sometimes we have to take risks with people, or they don't have the chance to choose to be decent."

"Well don't shoot yourself in the foot hoping someone else will be decent!" You scowled genially.

"No, I don't think being lame would help anyone. That's a risk, not a goal."

"Still, I would think you'd want your own car," Mom rejoined foggily.

"At some point I probably will," Joey replied. "But for now I can get along without it, and they're only a cost, personally and environmentally."

"A cost, a convenience, and, if you want to have an impact, a necessity," you counseled.

Joey shook his head. "Necessity for what? I can walk or bike to classes. I can hitch to Oregon. That all saves on resources, if we're just decent to one another. That's the world I want to help build."

"You'll miss out on opportunities," you cautioned.

Joey didn't see that he was getting into deep water, or didn't care. He shrugged. "But I'll be supporting other opportunities."

"Like what? Careers and vacations both require taking charge, creating opportunities; not just riding along on whatever happens!"

"Sure, but Jesse James could say as much. He created opportunities for himself, but…"

"But we shouldn't create opportunities by ripping people off? You think that's what I'm saying?" Rare anger flashed in you.

"No! Not at all! Or, well, yes!" Joey was taken aback, not understanding the sudden ire. He struggled for words, placating ideas. "People are different. Some people are Robin Hoods! Others are just Jesse Jameses."

"And you're going to save the world by begging from the drivers and giving to the hitchhiker!"

Joey shook his head. "No, I won't save the world. I can only make my contribution."

You stared at him. "It seems to me that the people who pick you up and *give you a ride* when you're standing on the side of the road, they're the ones doing the giving!"

Joey nodded. "They are giving, but they're not the only ones. They're giving kindness. My job is to contribute a worthiness of their trust and helpfulness."

You broke out laughing; I saw the crowns on your teeth. But then you studied Joey briefly and seemed to make a decision. You smiled. "And maybe you can contribute a few bucks for gas, eh? Here, more wine?"

Joey hesitated, then flashed his awkward youth-grin again. "Thank you. And yes, I'd like to contribute for gas. That'll save the driver, too. Economy of scale."

You poured, and he felt that he'd been reprieved, but he didn't know from what, or why.

Mom served apple pie a la mode for dessert. "A good American standby," she said.

Later we—Joey and I—took an after-dinner walk. The long summer evening blessed Sunnyvale, the world, with a warm and dusky beauty. The cars in my neighborhood were occasional rumbles of muted color, and the hum of boulevard traffic might have been a river.

"What was your dad mad about in there?" Joey asked.

I grasped his hand, twining my fingers with his. "You know, they have their old ways. They think that progress is owning more things, and when you said you didn't really want a car, well that upsets their sense of how the world should be."

"So they don't like me."

"Oh, don't worry about them. I like you!" And I kissed him right there on the sidewalk. He held me and kissed back, not hungrily but sweetly.

And I knew that public kissing would be distasteful in your eyes and Mom's, but I didn't care so much, even though I could feel the same inhibition. But then, it was a dusky hour, too, not broad daylight.

I took Joey to the same miniature golf course where Jim and I had gone. It was much more fun with Joey, but I couldn't help feeling echoes of my cousin. Those shadows would pass, I assumed.

Joey stayed for two nights, sleeping in what had been Jim's room. You went to work and Mom found ways to absent herself—she shopped, I think. The morning I drove him to the freeway onramp Mom said goodbye from the kitchen. You had said goodbye the night before. No one had said "Nice to meet you."

At the onramp we gave a quick kiss, but both of us turned away self-consciously. It was daylight, but that wasn't the source of our awkwardness.

"I'm sorry it wasn't more fun here," I said.

He shrugged.

I wanted to wait for him to get a ride, but he said no, that would be weird and maybe even dangerous to have a car parked there where he wanted someone to pull over.

"People from Sunnyvale might not pull over very soon," I said.

He shrugged. "Someone will."

"OK. If they don't, you know where I live."

He nodded. "I know."

So I drove home.

That evening at dinner you had your conversation, pseudo-casual, with me.

"Joey seems like a nice boy."

"Yes, he is."

"Young still. Like you."

"The world's before us." I knew what you were saying, and I wasn't about to let you tell me that we were too young to fall in love.

"Yes it is," you nodded. "You haven't seen much yet. But he's got ideas about things."

"He does. So do I."

"I know, I know. But as I said to him, don't shoot yourself in the foot."

"What don't you like about him, Dad?"

"I didn't say I didn't like him."

"Of course you didn't! You said don't shoot myself in the foot!"

You chuckled. "His ideas aren't necessarily going to help him, or the people around him."

"Or his skin is too dark?"

"No! I mean, that might not help him, either, but that's wrong and not what I mean. You know that! No. I mean he comes from this socialist perspective, that everyone has equal rights to everything. We should all share, is his idea, the people who go out and work and save and buy a car should share ownership with a guy bumming a ride. That sounds all grand and maybe Christian even, but it undercuts motivation! You know—if you'd get an A anyway, would you study? Or maybe, if you could go to work or sleep in, and you'd get paid either way, how often would you sleep in? It's what happened to the Soviet Union! People didn't pull their weight, and the whole thing collapsed. It's nothing against Joey, it's just human nature!"

I couldn't say at the time that the US-Soviet Union story wasn't just Capitalism v. Communism, but also Democracy v. Dictatorship, US resource richness v. Soviet resource poverty, and high-level Soviet corruption v. US integrity for the common good, until right around then when your generation came into power and made your argument against idealism stronger. I didn't articulate that I, and Joey, too, would study because the purpose of study wasn't a grade but an understanding and a better world. All I could muster at the time was, "He's not a socialist!"

"I'm sure he wouldn't call himself that," you agreed. "But look what he says and does. He wants a free ride from somebody else. He's getting his tuition paid by somebody else. Those are socialist ideas. I'm not saying he doesn't have life circumstances that promote that kind of thinking."

"He's not lazy, Dad."

"No, well that's a good thing. But he comes from a background that doesn't have the resources you have, and that limits his perspective. It pushes him toward socialism, and it keeps him from broader experiences, things you've had—New York, Boston, Disney World. And broader experiences in his future, too. Most guys with his background will get less and settle for less. For themselves and their children."

I hated you then. Not because you were right but because I couldn't fight against you. I didn't have the knowledge and wisdom and words.

I think that's what happens to people who without knowledge or wisdom or words face opposition. They hate. It's that primitive, inarticulate response, and it's what I felt.

Maybe resistance to that is what drove me into teaching, a desire to steer people from hate, to build understanding. I don't know.

I also don't know whether I would have broken up with Joey without your contribution. But we were never the same. We tried to talk about it that fall.

"Your folks see me as someone else," he said, "someone different from them."

"You are, Joey. You're better than they are," I said. But somewhere I lacked conviction, or maybe even accord. I really did believe that what Joey offered was better than what you did, I'd come around to that. He offered hope for community, for being good. You had truckled down to the despair and drudgery of selfishness, and marketed it to yourself as the best that could be done. But despite all that, still somewhere, in my head or heart or gut, I was stuck with you. I was your daughter whether I wanted to be or not.

That was the curse you laid on me. I couldn't love Joey, at least not in a day-to-day sort of way. I could agree with him, I could wish him well, but I also had to wish him farewell.

Joey smiled at me weakly. Maybe he sort of understood. He probably did, and just swallowed the hurt.

I cried and hated you, and then pretended I hated him when he didn't call or come by, and then again when he did. And gradually I didn't have to do it so often.

But I was not untouched. I went into teaching. I wasn't going to be you whose prime working purpose was to make money. I wanted to make people who could love, and that meant a deeper understanding of who we are. It meant developing knowledge and wisdom and words. It meant fighting the dumbing forces of mass media carrying corporate messages of self as consumer more than as community member.

And of course all my goals were subjugated to child-rearing. A teacher's job is supposedly to teach, but what that really means is a whole lot of warming children to themselves and life, a whole lot of coaching, demanding that work be done and done well, a whole lot of accepting that they are just children, a whole lot of love.

I think that's what's wrong with education today. There isn't enough love in our society.

Anyway, I finished out my undergrad, two more years after Joey's visit to Sunnyvale and continued right at Irvine to earn my teaching credential. I was an English major, after all, with all the world before me.

Teaching. It wasn't so tough in Irvine, except that I was brand new. All the kids came from relatively stable homes, even if there was a divorce, and they mostly had two college-educated parents who had the resources and language to develop their children's familiarity with diverse elements of the world, near and far, concrete and abstract. The kids expected to be treated well, so they trusted you, and they expected to learn and had the words and experience to understand quite a bit. It was easy to think you were good.

Maybe it was helpful to do my student-teaching there; maybe I would have dropped the whole effort if I'd been in San Jose at first. I don't know. If I'd lasted in San Jose, I might have been a stronger teacher when I first started on my own. It would have better prepared me for the challenges. But I've still never taught in the worst sections of San Jose, either, not by a long shot.

I was hired at Prune Orchard Elementary. San Jose was

famous for prunes and apricots long before it was famous for silica. One old grandpa told me about it. His was the last parent-teacher conference of the day, so I had time, and I'd had good things to say about his grandson Javier, so I guess he liked me and wanted to talk. He wasn't just nostalgic, though.

"The kids learn so much more now," he marveled, still sitting in the fourth-grade desk where we'd convened, his barrel body squeezed into the fixed space between the chair and the attached writing surface. "I'm very proud of you, Javier. You'll grow up and be president!" He turned to me. "This school wasn't here when I was a boy. This area was still a real prune orchard back then, not just the name of one. Prunes and apricots, all over. It was very pretty in the spring. Do you know what color the prune blossoms are? Pink and white, acres and acres of them, and they smelled just a little of sweetness, just enough to make you believe in God, and the bees humming very loud, swarming over every tree, the trees buzzed, each one getting louder as you walked to it and then quieter as you walked away. Underneath them the grass and the mustard grew tall as you, blooming like a big yellow lake. And the sky was blue, cool and blue. It was very beautiful. Of course we only passed through in the spring. We'd go to the coast and pick berries and artichokes. It was damp out there. But in the fall we'd be back here, when the fruit was plump and you could eat all you wanted. We didn't get sick on it, either. We must have been used to it. And we didn't have school like you do today! Teachers would come into the Mariani Camp and help us with writing and arithmetic, but that was only for a month or so maybe. In the fall, before we headed south for the oranges. Maybe if we'd had school I'd have been president! Eh, what do you think, Javi? No, you're a smart boy, and you can learn all this stuff. I don't regret my time, but you have a lot more of opportunities."

His daughter, Javi's mother, a heavy young woman with black hair and crimson lipstick, interrupted him. "And we should give

Ms. Self an opportunity to go home. She's been working all day."
She stood and extended her hand. "Thank you, Ms. Self."

But she didn't say "My son really enjoys having you for a
teacher." It was still my second year. The kids didn't hate me, but
I still didn't inspire them much. I still used a lot of teaching
material as it was packaged. That's the thing: it's not that you
don't want teaching material. You need it, age-appropriate text
on whatever you're studying. It's that you've got to, as a teacher,
make the material yours. Mrs. Gard had said it. Otherwise you're
modeling stupidity, just following out someone else's script. I've
seen teachers grade canned tests from a key, and they don't even
know what the questions or answers are, and some of the printed
items, honestly, are really stupid or wrong. I don't know how the
publishers get away with it, where is the state-level oversight
that approves textbooks! But even so, I've used that material,
including the tests, myself. I can forgive myself that flaw, back
then. I was beginning, and the job is so incredibly hard—much
harder than the CEOs of the publishing companies, no matter
that they think they earn as much as seventy teachers every day.
Second year, I was past the crushing daily pain, but the work was
still terribly exhausting, so that sometimes I didn't grade papers
because I was just too tired, falling asleep over them. Sometimes
I still used canned material for the same reason.

But I worked at it, and I got better, and the job hasn't grown
easy, but less impossible.

I love fourth graders. They're the best of both worlds—old
enough to have some academic ability, but young enough to be
eager learners. Some teachers swear by second graders, some
don't want to go younger than high-school juniors. Everyone
who's not in middle school abhors that thought. Think what you
will, for me fourth graders are the best.

I said they're eager learners. That's true, and it's necessary for
anyone to be a successful student. But it's not the full point. I
think kids are eager students until they learn that they're not

good at it. When they're little they're more unselfconscious, so they can more easily be enthusiastic learners. They can risk questions and wonder, they can say "I don't understand" or "What if." When they get older and learn that they're not so bright, because classmates or teachers or parents or tests hammer that understanding into them, they start to quake. They start to second-guess themselves, they worry about how they are perceived socially, so they fear to try, they hide, or they become clowns or drop-outs. Even academically successful kids can struggle with this, and kids who've repeatedly been shown they're wrong shut down. They stop risking and engaging academically. Everyone needs social approval, and if you can't get it by being academic, you get it some other way.

So schools have the job of showing kids that they're not failures or even average. Average isn't motivating; appreciation is. It's like Lake Wobegon, every kid's got to be above average. And that may be arithmetically impossible, but it's not impossible in the real world, because yes, every child, every person, is unique. Our stupid society measures by the narrow ruler of generic academic smarts, but anyone in her, ez, right mind knows that most of a person's happiness and success in life doesn't come from academic intelligence. It comes from human intelligence, the ability and actuality of understanding one another and getting along. It comes from the social wealth and self-discipline of doing good. We can raise the damn academic standards as high as we want, but some people are going to be better at playing ball than writing essays. Some people are going to be better mechanics. Some people are going to be better at handling life's hurts. Some people are going to be better at seeing beauty. And if we can't find a way to value every one and make everyone a success, we'll continue to produce youth who grow into the most imprisoning society in the world.

That's another gift from your generation: the institutional instruction of inadequacy and the resulting maladjusted society.

We administer standardized tests that reward only a minority, usually that minority that gets the academic money-jump before kindergarten. The rest are average or somewhere "below basic." They're stamped "Loser!" We swamp them with advertisements that associate value with possession. "Loser," the dispossessed are stamped again. Teachers and parents and classmates and the kids themselves are part of that same society and absorb its misshapen values. We all stamp the disadvantaged, over and over again, "Losers!"

So we make them failures at the primary path to societal success that we provide, and then we throw them in jail. And the rest of us become desperate over-consumers to avoid being seen as like them, dispossessed, Losers.

And so we are all losers. Thanks for the set-up, Dad.

I'm not saying that we should settle for kids being good only at poker or birdwatching. Few can make a living at those. But if we want kids to succeed in the more specific aims of school, the skills that can fit them for careers, then we need to value their poker and birdwatching. If we only make them wrong they cannot flourish.

And who knows? Maybe card games and birdwatching will be more career-value skills than, say, writing a five-paragraph essay that can be scored by a computer. For some they will surely be more life-value skills, ones that can give pleasure and appreciation. And who wants to turn out successful workers who lack appreciation? That can't be good for any society, and especially for a democracy.

So, teaching. I don't know that Javier's grandfather had a worse education than his grandson will have. The old man has memories of beauty, he had that beauty to fill his life. What will Javier have? A crowded apartment in a neighborhood of pavement and stoplights and cars that spew poison. He's got his family, he'll probably do fine. But the larger world? He doesn't see the yellow lake of blooming mustard or whiff the gentle fragrance of fruit blossoms, or hear each tree get loud and then fade as he walks by its blossom-load of bees. Or Joey talk about the frogs. I'll bet at night Javier just hears car traffic, maybe a booming base as some older kid tries to be somebody.

It's not as beautiful a world as the one you inherited.

Fourteen

I don't think I've wandered from my story, but certainly from my chronology. I broke up with Joey in our junior year. "Broke up." Not like a vase, shattered on the floor. More like a sculpture by Michelangelo, exposed to the elements, eroded away. More like the sphinx, whose nose was bit off by the wind, slowly. We tried to be friends, but you know how that goes, don't you?

He was having second thoughts about his major. Remember, he wanted to understand how money flowed, why some people had it and others didn't. And he wanted to be able to change that flow, so that those who didn't could. I think he was learning that, except in rare cases that could be paraded on TV, those who didn't couldn't. The realities of capitalism and government rigged it all to keep money and power where it was.

And that was before the Supreme Court came along with *Citizens' United*, officially turning money into speech, and democracy, then, into the Rule of Cash.

It was back in the time when the Supreme Court was declaring, legally, properly, and insanely, that the man who had lost the popular vote was the new president of the United States. Heck of a system, eh, Dub?

It was the time when Osama Bin Laden turned Islam into a venue for the disaffected to exercise their social maladjustment. We condemned the attack but kept cranking out the disaffected, and we couldn't imprison them all, so they had to go somewhere. Al Qaeda. Now ISIL. Wherever social ineptitude could find a flag.

And our flag? No, we didn't try to raise the level of our humanity. Our main responses to the 9/11 attack had been to trade our faith in one another for suspicion, and to start a war in Iraq. The suspicion catches a few sad fools and keeps some hearts beating, sure enough; but it is a massive loss of the positive, inclusive American spirit that was. Our belligerence in Iraq killed and kills many more than airport suspicion saves, and has proven misguided, further destabilizing an unstable region that now resurrects "Allah Akbar" as a resounding cry for mayhem instead of a prayer for goodness.

Our national bellicosity was echoed in individual lives. At that time prominent mass shootings began edging up. Three, four, five a year. The deaths of five, six, seven, twelve, thirty-three people. More injured. In schools, in theaters, in army and naval bases, in restaurants, in churches and government buildings. And every few massacres the cry to restrict the weapon of choice, semi-automatic assault guns, was raised and then muted by a congress owned by corporate lobbies. Again, the Democracy of Dollars. Sell mayhem, sell infrastructure, and repeat. Thanks, Dad.

And of course that was the same period when the tide kept rising for the one percent, at the cost of cooked books that did not account for war expenditures or environmental damage or reduced federal oversight of the public's business. Dollars and reality were divorced, just as you had claimed they were in the nineties.

And I, the Child of Money, and Joey, the Child of Manual Labor, couldn't be in love. We drifted distant in the wind you fanned. We eroded. You paid for my study abroad in Paris, and we crumbled apart.

What happened to him? I know he earned his bachelor's in economics, but then what? What sort of job does knowing how money flows offer? He didn't want to work for the corporate world, but what was available then? You have to work where there's money, and Corporate Senior Management is where the money is.

Maybe he did what I did, go into teaching. It's at least work worth doing. I could see him as a high-school teacher. He would try to instill in his students a passion and understanding of money flow and its consequences. Raise a bunch of radicals!

And I can imagine some smaller interest reading this and thinking, *Hmm, we can't have passionate teachers poisoning our youth with understanding and care! And not enough moneyed folks will go into the drudgery of teaching to counterbalance them. So we'll have to neuter them some other way. Replace them with computers. Overload their classrooms. Make test scores uber-important. Poison their pupils with poverty and mind-numbing TV. Keep families pressured into needing two incomes. All easily done! They'll do half of it themselves!*

Yes, the assault on children couldn't have been done much better if it were designed. Evidence, I guess, for Unintelligent Design.

Or evidence of selfishness, or malice.

So anyway, Joey, I expect, is fighting the good fight, somehow, as I hope I am, too.

You gave me a graduation party. It seems now a lot like my wedding reception two years later. Your friends, including Mom, drinking too much. Lots of glitter on lots of gowns on lots of women trying to hide their weight, and lots of coats on lots of men with lots of smug assurance, a few with the lean tautness of bicycling, more with the restrained sag of gym workouts, and at least as many displaying their weight like badges earned from a Crackerjacks box. They all put envelopes on the table for me, so how could I complain?

And you gave me a car, and I was already squared away in the credential program, so there were no surprises, there was no want. We harked back to old times that summer with a kayak trip down the American River. You were as savvy as ever on the water. It was fun, I guess.

But really, I think I'd been poisoned. I was part of your world, the fluff and frivolity and possession, but I didn't have faith in it. So what did anything matter? Everything you did was under-coated with hopelessness, as if playing cards with a friend who has stage-four cancer. And that summer I was just marking time in a pointless world. Why was I staying with you? I should have been volunteering in Africa or at least working as a summer-camp counselor. Bill was interning in L.A. Other classmates, too, were there or in Sacramento or DC, or, if they were in finance or petroleum, they had six-figure jobs. What was I doing? Living with my parents.

I slept in too late. What mattered? I watched TV late. It couldn't interfere with a life that wasn't happening.

Oh, I tried reconnecting with some high-school friends. Debi was working as a receptionist in a dental office. We met at a coffee shop. Isn't that where everyone meets?

"… And I might go back to school to become an office manager," she said, tossing her billow of black hair. "But you're the exciting one. You're going to be a teacher!"

"Yeah, I'm looking forward to it."

"I can't imagine being a teacher! So I won't! But how's your love life, girl?"

I shook my head. "I've seen a few guys." I didn't name Bill. We were together, but only sort of; I was in Sunnyvale, he was in L.A.

"I guess! You're so pretty! You must have to fight the guys off! Now me, you know, I don't have your looks. But there's a new dentist in the office, and we've gone out a couple times. Blond hair, he's pretty nice. And you know, dentistry, that's a good profession. People always have teeth to fix." She smiled a bleached smile.

"So you like him?"

"What's not to like? He'll have a good income, and his parents have money, too. And his breath doesn't stink. So I'm good! But you must meet all kinds of men at college!"

"I dated one guy for a while. He was very considerate, and ambitious."

"Ambitious! Like Fortune 500 CEO ambitious?"

"Not like that at all. Really he wants to alleviate poverty."

"Oh." Debi paused a moment. "Alleviate it, huh? Well, good luck!"

"You can do it some."

"Oh, well maybe then. I really respect that. For me, I can't get past taking care of myself! People should do that, don't you think? Take care of themselves? Did you hear about those two men marrying each other? In Canada, I think. A legal marriage! It kind of gives me the creeps. But I don't have anything against them, gay people, you know. People should take care of themselves, and if they want to do that in Canada it's OK with me. Just don't come to Sunnyvale, know what I mean? But get rid of poverty, girl? How do you do that?"

"Some people say education."

"That won't do it! Look at me, I'm educated!"

"You're pretty wealthy, too!"

"You think so? Maybe I will be."

"Debi, we're way wealthy! You and I are probably in the top one percent of wealth in the whole history of the world!"

She eyed me aslant. "You're jerking me! How could that be?"

"When we study history we study rulers. But the truth is most people aren't rulers. They're farmers, living season to season. Until just recently almost everyone was a farmer!"

"Oh. Well! Lucky for us, I guess!" She smiled vapidly. "Wait," she turned intent, "is that why they're trying to kill us?"

"What?"

"The president said that they, over in Arabia or one of those places, they have Weapons of Mass Destruction that they want to attack us with. I don't understand why. I thought they must just be evil. But you think they don't want to be farmers either?"

"I haven't studied it, Debi. We have very different cultures. Maybe they want *us* to be farmers. Maybe they just want wealth or power, which is a wish of the unthinking. Or maybe they think that we are evil. Or maybe they're just trying to bluster for their own people. I don't know."

"Bluster? What do you mean?"

"Show off. Just like Republicans and Democrats here have to show off what they've done that they think their constituents want."

"Except bluster sounds phony. I'm glad we have a government we can trust!"

I nodded.

"And how could *we* be evil? They're the ones with weapons of mass destruction!"

A woman in a dark business suit quick-stepped by, her heels clacking. She glanced at her watch and rattled her keys lightly as she waited her turn to order. *Something to calm her nerves*, I thought.

"Well, we have far and away the most weapons of mass destruction. And sometimes we're pretty decent with them, and sometimes we're pretty bully with them. I think maybe they really do hate us," I added. "Not in a personal way, but as carriers of a culture they think is harmful or sinful. So they're trying to disrupt us."

At the counter the woman started jangling her keys louder and fidgeting purposefully.

"First with Nine-eleven, and now with Weapons of Mass Destruction," Debi shook her head. "I hate the news."

"Not all of it," I teased.

"Can we get going here?" the key-jangler asked accusatively, loudly.

The barista was a young girl with blonde pixie-cut hair, and she spoke a word to her colleague, an even younger-looking boy with acne-faced nervousness. He nodded, shook his head anxiously, pulled a lever and moved a cup, pulled a second lever and a geyser of steam shot at the girl.

She pulled away crying, *"Oww!!"*

The boy's eyes popped and he quickly raised the lever. The steam stopped and he stepped to the girl. "You should put ice on that, Kayli!" His eyes were round and his jaw hung. He turned and darted to a bin.

The key-jangler rolled her eyes.

"Not now," Kayli cried to the boy, but her eyes were welling wet, I could see even from across the room.

The boy came back with a scoop of ice. "Yes, now! It'll blister if you don't!"

"And I'll be late for a meeting if you do!" the jangler interrupted.

The boy glanced at her but returned his attention to Kayli. He told her, "This isn't even right." He set down the ice scoop, took her arm, and led her to a sink where he turned on the water and felt it. "Here, keep this running on your arm. I'll take care of the customers. Keep it on it cold. Twenty minutes."

"Twenty minutes! I can't do twenty minutes!" she protested.

"Do it." He left her and returned to the service counter.

"Can you make a skinny latte with a double—oh crap!" The jangler looked at her watch for the third time in the last half minute. "Just give me a house blonde. Fast!" She dropped a bill on the counter, took the drink, and clattered away doing her best to look wronged.

Back at the counter the next customer was clearly talking supportively with the boy. The boy shrugged appreciatively. The girl still held her arm under the purring water.

I turned back to Debi. "Sometimes I don't like us much either."

"What do you mean?" Debi asked.

"Who was the incompetent there?" I asked.

"Well, it was an accident. The boy caused it, I think."

"You're right. That was an accident. The failure that wasn't an accident was the woman's. She was a bitch. No one has to be a bitch."

Debi sighed. "I guess. But did you see the suit she was wearing? I liked the collar and bust on it, and I like those form-hugging skirts, too. I'd use a brighter color though."

So. My set swam at the shallow end of the pool. And I couldn't be friends with thoughtfulness, since it was relegated to poverty, and poverty, or having it in your recent background, was an unpardonable sin.

You and Mom tried to help me along in your way. She brought it up. "Jenny, you're so serious all the time. You should have some fun."

I didn't say anything.

She continued, "Do you remember the Waterhouse boy, Milton I think? His parents were at your graduation party."

"Yeah, he was two years ahead of me. Why?"

"His mother was saying that he's around. He just finished school, you know, getting his MBA, and now he's back. He's started working as a junior partner in his father's insurance business."

"Oh."

She looked at me wanting more response, but I didn't give it to her. She resumed in a false-afterthought tone, "Maybe I should invite them over."

I rolled my eyes but didn't say anything. I had nothing against Tony. That's what he went by, not Milton.

So that weekend the Waterhouses came to our house. Their Audi was gold. We all sat in the living room. You poured drinks, scotch and something for the men, wine for the women.

The conversation flowed and ebbed into twosomes. Mom of course had engineered that Tony sat by me.

"Mom said you're working with your dad now," I said.

He nodded. "It's a good fit. I've been exposed to the business, and Dad will bring me along."

"Does your schooling even matter? I mean, selling insurance, how much do you control really?"

"Oh, it matters a lot. You know, Dad's company is his own.

Sure, he's selling products from all the big boys, but he gets to arrange his own deals around theirs. For me, there are marketing and finance pieces that can really make a difference. Right now there are investment products that are soaring through the roof. We can invest our own portfolio there, as well as sell those investments to clients. It ties in with your dad's work. That's how the two of them met, I don't know how many years ago."

"How do those things work?"

"It's complicated. I'm not sure anyone fully understands them, probably a few guys at Lehman Brothers and Goldman Sachs. Basically you package a bunch of mortgages into what's called a derivative. You can control how risky the derivative is because you control which loans go into it. They're lucrative because the riskiest packages, just because they're risky, pay higher. You know, bad risks pay more for their loans. So those are the derivatives that sell the most, because everyone wants the highest return possible." He shrugged. "It's pretty easy money."

"But where does the money come from?"

"From people paying on their loans. And the riskiest borrowers have to pay the highest rates."

"OK. I sort of get it. But who would buy them? And why? And where, even? I don't see them at the pharmacy or grocery store!"

"They're securities, bought through a securities exchange. A stock exchange. And most people don't buy them directly, don't even know they're buying them. They put money into an annuity, for instance. They don't really pay attention to what the annuity manager does; they're busy and they don't want to know. But the annuity manager might buy the derivatives, because he knows they'll up the return he can report, and they up his pay, too. So most people don't even know how they're invested. That's why you go to a professional!"

"Hm." I knew enough to know this stuff made fortunes, and that probably meant it made poverty, too, so I was interested. But revisiting the actual language and machinery of it was thoroughly boring.

Of course I didn't know then how those high-risk derivatives would help crash the entire US economy a couple years later. What I thought about was Joey and his priorities, and Tony's here, and my own. But I smiled at Tony. He wasn't a bad fool. Just a fool.

I was tested again at dinner. You and Mom kept pouring the wine, and I felt it, and then Tony's mother kicked into gear.

"Do you get these door-to-door people, Elsie?" she asked indignantly. "I had another one just today. He wanted to put those, those solar squares on our roof! Some blather about global warming. As if I want those ugly blocks on the roof of my home!"

I was surprised that Tony spoke up. "But, Mom, global warming is a real thing. We're setting new heat records almost every year. And the panels aren't ugly, you're just not used to them."

Mr. Waterhouse leaned aside to you. "For this we pay a king's ransom in tuition."

You laughed.

Mrs. Waterhouse, never at a want for words and now well-greased, continued, "I've never heard such nonsense! As if we have the power to change our climate! As if people in power wouldn't stop it if it were a problem!"

"Unfortunately," Tony returned, "there's a lot of money invested in the infrastructure of global warming. So the people in power don't want to stop it. Heck, they don't even want to see it!"

Mrs. Waterhouse gazed at Mom to complain. "My own son!" Then she returned to Tony. "There's no future in what you're saying, Honey-child."

Mom was tipsy, too, and she offered, "Isn't it the communists trying to undo capitalism again?"

Tony said, "Actually, no. We had a guest speaker in one of my classes, and he said that this was an up-and-coming trend. The point was that, like with everything else, we could make money on it. He was talking about lease plans for solar panels. The company will lease you the panels for less than your monthly power bill. So you buy in because it will save you money, and he makes a profit by selling the energy your panels produce, and selling the clean-energy credits to someone else, a manufacturer maybe."

His mother stared at him. "This doorbell-ringer wanted us to buy the panels. He started talking about how it would save us over the years, not now."

"Right, he's not cutting edge," Tony replied. "I'm surprised you stood at the door that long."

"He wasn't a bad-looking kid."

"Great, Mom. But yeah, the lease plans are just being developed. And they won't work for everyone. The panels have to be able to produce enough energy to offset their lease. And also, the solar lobby can't compete with the oil lobby, now or probably ever. So the legislation that would make the panels competitive isn't there."

Mr. Waterhouse leaned forward. "What legislation would that be?" he asked.

"Oh, how much rooftop producers need to pay for use of powerlines. Local ordinances designating the panels an eyesore. Reducing oil and gas subsidies. I don't know, I haven't studied it."

Mr. Waterhouse persisted, "How do we subsidize oil and gas? I'm a free-enterprise man, not a subsidize man!"

"Like I said, I haven't studied it. But tax structures are always huge. I'm sure Exxon is making billions in tax breaks. And the solar people say that using the air as a free dump for their exhaust is a subsidy."

I remembered Mr. Newell's chicken poop.

Mrs. Waterhouse sloshed forth, "See, now they're going to tax us for exhaling!"

I imagined her breath was taxably toxic right then.

Mr. Waterhouse interrogated, "How can they claim that's a subsidy?"

"They argue that we require everyone to take care of their solid waste, and gas waste should be the same."

"That's crazy," Mr. Waterhouse exclaimed. "Your mother's right, they'll be charging us to breathe!"

"Theoretically that could make sense."

"Who's spewing this nonsense?"

"The usual environmentalists. The term they use is a commons, something publicly owned, and they say it should be protected."

"I'll be damned," said Mr. Waterhouse. He eyed his son warily. "You know quite a bit about this!"

"I'm not preaching it, Dad. It pays to know about it, though."

"Well, as long as it pays. You know, a big chunk of our portfolio is in oil."

"I know. What's good for Chevron is good for us."

Mrs. Waterhouse spoke up again. "Chevron and Schell and Texasco and Beep—," she burped. "All of them. They're the backbone of the country! Drink to them! Oh, fill me up, honey." She extended her glass to Mom, who spilled only a slop or two in pouring.

So that summer was full of waste, with lost mornings and lost friends, and lost clean air and lost care, at home and abroad; and while our familial things seemed fine, the waste continued over the next years with the Great Recession, with lost homes and lost pensions following lost financial integrity, and continuing lost environment with lost honesty and decency. It was a time of the budding and flowering of decades of selfishness, with more fruits yet to come.

So a bunch of bad news, Dad. But still, every few years, despite the moral cesspool we were creating—I say *we*—I'm

Dan P. Greaney

grown and working, and have to accept my responsibility—some good news came along. One was just a couple years ago, remember? It was another shoot-em-up because guns are our right and so is stupidity and ignorance. Remember? Summer morning in Oak Creek, The Land of the Free, and another American sicko had learned the American habit of destruction. So he took his legal gun and killed the A-rabs.

So that was routine destruction, the kind of violence commensurate with the return of the Old West mentality and the ever-present fear of "other." But what was different this time was the survivors' response to the ugliness. They did not cry for vengeance but for sorrow. Their outreach from the ugliness was sadness and forgiveness. They were Americans, not Arabs, and they were Sikhs. And they were more christian than most Christians.

Certainly more than most Americans.

Fifteen

Oh, that may not be true. Just than the Americans in power who were engineering the suffering that afflicted people all over.

For the bad news was mainly on the grand scale, not so much in our local picture. I'm sure Tony and his parents came through the recession just fine, as we did. It's not we who lose, even though we can exclaim on larger dollar losses. It's the people who don't have those extra dollars to lose. It's Joey and his family: they lose their jobs, their homes, their hopes. It's people who don't have savings and real estate and securities portfolios and moneyed connections. It's those others. "Other" is a complex idea; it includes and weighs numerous elements. It might be color or faith, like the A-rabs; it might be music and clothes and age, or the frivolity or frumpiness or deafness that go with age; it might be language, or gender, or all sorts of values and practices. But for your generation, I think it's mostly money. Not even necessarily having money, but reverence for it. As long as money is your ultimate goal, your bottom line, you're in.

And you're definitely in, aren't you, Dad. Maybe not enough to engineer the suffering, but enough to support it and prosper from it. You've been in ever since you left the farm.

Me? I was still learning what I was made of.

But you, as ever, were prosperous, if I grant you your *donnee*, the goal you had selected for yourself. You'd ridden the wave of selling risk in order to profit from bad loans. Now that market had grown even more wide open. You and your sort had financed candidates who would promote the interests of big business, so your reliable Republicans carried the legislation and your dupey Democrats agreed to it, and any pretense of retaining post-Depression protections was destroyed. Now savings banks, investment banks, and insurance companies were all one, and could carry out the business of fleecing clients totally in-house: make the bad loans—you called them "sub-prime"—package them into derivatives, and sell them as investment packages. You were an old hand.

I can picture you in your office instructing a junior colleague.

"Ken, I know you understand the derivatives. Do you know how to make even more on them?"

Young Ken, recently out of college with his business degree, shakes his head and turns his palms up. "No, sir."

"You know the derivatives are going to tank, right? They're chock full of bad loans. So you borrow some from a friend and sell them, let's say for a hundred grand. Then they tank, so you buy them back for, say, fifty grand. See it? You return them to your friend, and you've made a cool fifty grand, for nothing."

"That's pretty clever. Kind of a sure thing, isn't it," Ken says.

"You have to know your product. But that's not too hard, because we make the products."

Ken nods appreciatively. "I knew I was in an industry with smart people!" he says.

"And it gets better," you tell him. "You don't even need a friend to do the short sale if you own them. You can sell the securities to any Charlie, let's say for a hundred grand again. But poor Charlie doesn't have the hundred grand, so you hold the securities for him. He owns them, but hasn't paid you yet, so you have them. You can go ahead with the same short sale: sell them to another dupe for another hundred grand, buy them back at fifty, and then deliver them to Charlie, who has suffered an unfortunate loss."

"You make even more that way," says Ken. "You make a hundred grand from Charlie and fifty grand from the other guy."

"And I get rid of the worthless derivatives. You're a quick study, Ken. So there's something else you should know. You remember Al Gore's invention?"

Ken is puzzled. "Climate change?"

"The internet."

"Oh. OK." Ken is too young to even know the joke. Heck, I only know it because you explained it to me.

"With the internet and an off-shore IP address we become a multinational company. And you know what that means?"

Ken stabs at an answer. "We can market all over the world."

You wave your hand dismissively. "Sure, but we're not Google or Apple or any of those guys to have a big market abroad. But what we do have in common with them is the ability to move money. The Cayman Islands are good. So if we sell securities not from here in Sunnyvale but from the Cayman Islands, we pay no US taxes on it. Just Cayman taxes. And do you know what the Cayman Island corporate tax rate is?"

Ken shakes his head, a little lost.

"Zero. Nothing. Exactly nada."

Ken nods slowly. "That's a big bonus."

"Yes it is. Thirty-five percent bonus."

"But," Ken is processing this ploy, "doesn't that mean the money is in the Cayman Islands then, not here where you can use it?"

"Good thought. But not a problem. The president is giving us a holiday."

Ken looks at you with raised eyebrows.

"We can bring it into the country for just five and a quarter percent."

"That's still a good deal."

"A good deal? It's a great deal! Not that we won't work to improve it! But it's less than a quarter of what working stiffs pay on their taxes! So you see," you add evenly, "it pays to know your product and to time the movement of your money."

"What if you needed the money sooner, though, before the tax holiday?" Ken asks.

"Your teachers must have loved you, Kenny baby! Good question! And the answer is, you're screwed. You've got to be big

220

enough to wait out the swings of politics until you get the holiday."

"So I shouldn't be working for you. I should be working for Citibank or Goldman Sachs, or somebody like that."

"Well, you're right, the big boys have the advantage. Greater capital to ride out the lows, and lobbying advantages, too, setting up rules that 'promote business' as they say, but really only promote their *own* business, *big* business. Yeah, the little guy can get screwed. But we're not that little, Ken, and it's a good time. All the politics and the national mood is in our favor. We just need to be wary, and not overly bullish with our own profile."

I guess the economy was in *my* favor, in a perverted little way. You sold junk to all the Charlies you could sucker, and used their cash to pay my fifth-year tuition.

But then I began to stand at least a little bit on my own. Bill and I were informally engaged, and we moved into an apartment in San Jose, a comfortable one-bedroom, upstairs, with a small garden on the street side of the building. We both had jobs.

"I keep the little monsters kicking and you teach them," Bill joked, referring to his prosthesis engineering and my profession.

We thought we had good jobs, too, but after paying our rent and buying our groceries we had precious little to play with, or to save for a down payment.

We had dinner at your house and I asked, "How did you guys ever save up to buy a house?"

"It was a good time to buy then," you said. "Back then people could afford a home."

"And your father did very well in his work," Mom, tasting her wine, said to me.

"Why is it harder now?"

"The economy moves on," you said. "It's a time when money lies in investment, not labor. My profession has successfully gathered the flow of money; labor is outsourced, and neutered with anti-union legislation." You shrugged complacently.

Bill added, "And technology, don't you think? Technology has reduced labor."

"Oh, yeah. Don't listen to them when they tell you that technology creates jobs. It does create a few, but not nearly as many as it replaces. That's the whole point of technology! It's not, or almost never is, to make a better product. It's to cut labor costs. That's what any business has to look at. I don't think it interferes with your home affordability though."

"We'd like to buy a house," I said.

You scratched at your chin. "You know, I'd wait. The market is pretty inflated right now."

"But now is when we want a house, Dad."

"Sure. But it won't be long before, I think you'll be able to get a much better buy. You know, you don't want to take on extra debt. Debt that could be larger than your assets."

"I thought you always pushed investing. Buying a house is an investment."

"Well, Jenny, for you I'll push prudent investing. Now is not the time to buy. It'll be soon enough. Then you'll probably be able to afford more house, too."

"But we'd be putting money into our own house instead of into rent," I protested.

Bill said, "It's his field, Jenny. It's not like he's trying to tell you how to teach."

"But..."

"We can wait a bit."

I sighed forcefully. But really, I'm a pretty agreeable person. And I knew, even if I didn't like the message, that you probably knew what you were talking about.

Bill schmoozed a change of subject. "Elsie, this is the tenderest steak I've ever eaten!"

"Oh, thank you. It's the cut. Our butcher only gives me the best," she said. "Would you like more wine?"

"Oh, just half a glass, thanks. I've got to drive home."

"Oh, Jenny can drive!" She filled his glass. "I've always liked to cook."

Bill and I cleared the dishes.

"Bill, you sit down!" Mom scolded. "Jenny and I can get those."

"Oh, I'd just as soon help," Bill said.

"Well…" she wavered. "All right. You two can serve the cake then, too." She plopped back into her chair.

We served cake.

When June came we served cake again, or the caterer did. White cake, five layers. Ribbons, banners and balloons, presents on the table, live string band, you self-satisfied, Mom happily drunk, and Niagara Falls waiting.

No home purchased yet, though. The housing market had already crested, but we followed your advice. "There's a lot of movement going on in finance right now. Sit tight," you advised. We sat.

There did seem to be a tension in the national air, but it didn't seem to be in finances. It was in terrorism. Ever since 9/11 there'd been a sense of dis-ease, and taking off our shoes at the airport seemed like a futile charade, and the president's advice to help by shopping more seemed even weirder.

Lacing back up, Bill shook his head. "The terrorists won. Look what they've got us doing. Everyone in the country is taking off his shoes at the airport."

For some reason I didn't object to the process. Maybe it was from working with children; I wanted to protect them. "We have to be safe," I said.

Bill nodded, but didn't agree. He mumbled, "And our heroism is in doing extra shopping."

Bill wasn't a complete oaf, and the honeymoon was beautiful and too brief. Back home we returned to the life we'd already been living. Through the summer I played housewife. When he came home in the evening I had dinner ready, and we ate watching the news.

The death tolls were updated regularly. They continued to climb, despite President Bush's "Mission Accomplished" declaration years earlier. The stories came back about PTSD. "Stay the course," said the president. And what else could he say? His faith was blind.

"He's a bastard," said Bill. "He's in over his head, and he only has one guiding star: God loves Big Business. He may not even understand that it's *Big* Business, not the local guy trying to make ends meet and support his community. It's Big Business that's undercutting the local guy and driving him *out* of business. It's Big Business that's moving money offshore, destroying American jobs and our tax base. It's his senior advisor's bully Halliburton making money on the wars. That's God's gift through him to the world."

"Well, the people voted him in."

"Not the first time."

"Weren't they going to change that rule after the hanging chads?"

"And wasn't technology going to usher in universal prosperity and leisure? It's not just a rule, it's the Constitution. And it's not just Congress, it's the corporations."

"You're in a pricky mood!"

"Well, I've got a prick!"

"We can probably find a better way to use it."

We had talked about having a baby, and I was eager. But I wanted to time things so the birth would be when school let out, so I'd have the summer to be with the baby.

"Isn't there some maternity leave that you could get any time?" Bill asked.

"I could, but it's unpaid, and this would be easier."

It was Halloween when I told him. I got home from work

before him and dressed up in a stork costume. I'd made it of sheets and, for the bill, rolled newspaper wrapped in gray felt. I looked like a Sesame Street reject, or maybe a medieval grim reaper, and when I greeted him at the door he stopped abruptly.

"Everything OK?" he asked.

I nodded my bill up and down.

"OK. Uh, what are you?"

"A kind of bird," I muffled from inside the bill.

"And I'm supposed to guess what kind?"

I nodded.

"OK. Well, I'm glad you had a productive day. Mine was good, too, although uh, not as creative as yours."

I wanted to squawk like a stork, but all I could think of was chicken-cackle, and I didn't imagine that storks sounded like chickens. Instead I said, "Delivery service."

Bill slowly cocked his head sideways. "You're a stork," he whispered, and then shouted, "You're a stork!"

I spread my wings and curtsied confirmation.

He hugged me. "You're sure then?"

"The test was positive."

"Well, what do we do? How does it feel?"

"I don't feel anything, except happy."

"No morning sickness?"

"This is evening. And no. Not even a teensy bit."

"OK, OK. Well, want to celebrate? Let's go out for dinner."

I nodded. "Yes. I have papers to grade, so I don't want to stay out late."

"OK."

So we went out. He had a glass of wine, but I refrained.

"You're so good," he said. "Listen. Are you going to be OK if we're still in the apartment?"

"Oh, you've convinced me. If Dad says wait we should probably trust him."

"You do trust him, don't you? I mean, he knows these things

better than I do."

"Yes, I think he does. I trust him to manage money."

"I can't wait to feel the baby. Kick, you know."

"About now she's the size of that freckle on your arm, and doesn't have anything to kick with yet."

"I know. I'm just imagining. That's all I can do for now, you know."

"Are you jealous? That I have the baby in me and you don't?"

"Jealous? No! That part of it is your job. It is cool, though."

"You are! That's so funny! I'd never thought…"

He swirled his glass of wine, quaffed, and sighed in dramatic, needling relish of the forbidden ambrosia.

"Very funny."

"Hey, you said *she.*"

"I did."

"You don't—"

"Of course not."

"I had to ask."

"Because I'm the expert?"

"Because I'm not!"

"Oo! Can I get that in writing?"

"Regarding this, yes."

Over the next weeks I became more of an expert. It was probably good that I was teaching, because it forced me to focus on other things, too. But I did study how the apartment would work for a newborn.

I asked Bill, "Did I say I trusted Dad to manage money?"

"Yes," he replied.

"I guess I trust him to manage it to make money. But I'm not sure I trust him to manage it to make homes. This is a one-bedroom apartment."

"Yeah, but a newborn doesn't need much space. We'll just make a corner right in the living room."

"I was thinking our room."

"Oh. Well, OK."

"Or we could buy a house."

He nodded without agreeing.

This discussion was going to take more time.

You meantime, as always, were gathering money. The housing market had started to fall, but you said to hold off buying, yes, even with the baby coming. "It's a time when fortunes will be made and lost," you said.

The SEC had been gutted by direct legislation, defunding, and executive practice, so there was no effective government oversight of securities. The FBI had reported that mortgage fraud was pervasive and growing, and centered in collusion among industry insiders. But no one cared. People were riding on people like you, the insiders, to make them a buck. People were counting on the mantra of Freedom of the Market to bring them to the nirvana of wealth, the Golden Calf to bring them to salvation.

For you it was a rerun of the S&L crash. It was all a matter of limiting the government and timing your moves so that you could take profit without taking risk. But you and your Wall Street Purveyors of Penury had become even more powerful and sophisticated than back in the eighties. There was more money in Finance, more of it buying the federal government, and more acceptance of that political sell-out, rueful across the nation, swaggering on Wall Street. Earlier, more of your efforts had gone into swaying elected officials. Now it shaped public opinion and elected officials who were already in your corner. Advertisement dollars, the rise of financial profits as the measure of worth, the higher profile of your mouthpieces—outfits like the Heritage Foundation and Cato Institute, that, with a skin of scholarship but a heart of paid-for bias, were quoted by news outlets, some of which were also owned by collaborating profiteers—who provided arguments supporting lower taxes on the wealthy, reduced oversight of banks, reduced benefits for the impoverished, reduced environmental and labor standards, and, effectively, reduced democracy while the wealthiest controlled more and more.

You told Bill, "You know, the only reason to work is for the fun of it. It's not the way to make money. Investments make money. Investments are working nonstop. While you're sleeping, or watching a ball game or drinking a beer, other people are working around the world, and you are getting a slice of the profits from their work with your investments. That's how it works! And Uncle Sam won't tax you as highly for your income on other people's work, either. Dividends, capital gains—your unearned income, your investment income—only gets taxed at 15%; your day job, you probably get taxed at 28 or 35%."

I objected. "Dad, you've got to start with some money. Like a salary, for instance!"

You demurred with raised shoulders. "I'm not saying don't work. What else are you going to do? But you, you two, have a source of gifts, and gifts are also unearned income, they're tax free, and we're raising the limits on how much can be tax free. And ultimately there will be an inheritance, and if you do it right that'll be tax free. So, work is for fun."

"Dad, my work is worthwhile. And I don't need you to die to make me solvent."

"No, you don't. And I suppose that any work that generates an income is worthwhile."

"Yeah. Like robbing banks," Bill offered.

"Have we had this conversation before?" You frowned.

"I don't think so," Bill replied.

"Hmm. Seemed familiar."

Mom called, "Dennis, stop yakking and pour drinks!"

"Ah," you said, "I am called to worthwhile work!"

In the office you rarely dealt directly with customers then. You sat in the back office directing the packaging and sales goals of your products, and deciding when to buy them yourself.

"Ken." You called him in. "Why are you denying this Jerrod Dinkins a loan?"

"Dinkins?" Ken came in. "Dinkins is a thousand years old and he's got dementia. He's living on social security. There's no way he can pay off the loan; he can't even understand it."

"Ken, most of our clients don't understand what they're buying, so that's no different from anyone else. And remember, we will sell the mortgage. So no matter how badly he defaults, we don't lose."

"I should approve the loan then."

"Absolutely."

"OK. Thanks! Hey, do you still want us exposed on those LTV 20s?"

You grimaced. "They're still cranking out the returns. But...what do you think, Ken? How bullish do you feel?"

Ken scarcely missed a beat. "Freddie Mac is bowing out. But if you're not bullish you're on the sidelines."

You nodded. "All right then."

The campaign heated up and you made your company donations to both parties.

"Both?" Ken asked.

"They're the only two that matter," you replied. "We don't want to support the Greenies!"

"No, but why so much to the Democrats?"

"That? That's almost nothing. Just enough to be on speaking terms."

"Will you actually be on speaking terms?"

"Not me personally. But we do sell products of larger organizations, you know."

Ken nodded.

"Ken, to answer your question, of course we'd rather have Republicans in office, that's why we give them more. Republicans favor small government. I don't need to get as small as Ron Paul; that's throwing the baby out with the bathwater. I'd rather have, say, a Mitt Romney. But it's going to be McCain, and he's a solid small-government, free-enterprise Republican. So he'll further our goals—reduced regulation and low taxation. He's even coming around on the environment, which, no matter how we may feel as individuals, as business entities we can't allow to interfere. This climate-change business would turn the economy upside down."

"And the Democrats are for *just in case*."

"Exactly. You never know who's going to win. And besides, although the Republicans are more in line with our thinking, Democrats are not unswayable. They know that they need money to win elections, and they know who's got the money. You've got to give them a little hope, or they might not cooperate at all."

Ken shook his head. "You're an evil genius!"

"And you are a sycophant." You smiled, accepting his judgment nonetheless.

Even you weren't immune to the Wall Street swank that convinced those who worked in money instead of people that they deserved more money, and all was right with the world.

We entered the time of losses. Mine perhaps was mine alone, but it was far bigger than yours because it was human. Before Christmas I had a period. My little freckle never grew bigger than an apricot.

When I told Bill, he was no worse than he had to be. He just hugged me. He didn't cry though, and although I don't know how he could have been better, I also wondered whether he actually felt some relief, and I was angry at him for that. But I kept all that inside me.

Inside me. I've always had a feeling about, well, feelings. It was easy to hear the line about "letting feelings out" so they didn't fester. That seemed false to me. I pictured feelings more like compost. I don't know where I got that image. But it seemed to me that some feelings were better left to lie quietly until they morphed into something fertile, something rich in earthworms and sow bugs, something that would help good things grow. Otherwise you might just be flinging crap at people. So I kept my sorrow and anger inside, trying to give them time to break down into something fertile.

Of course, some feelings were well ripened and ready to bloom. Like maternal feelings for a baby I never cradled, I never saw, but still loved.

Your compassion, however, had grown shallow as a spreadsheet. Your thoughts were where they'd been: all year you had fretted about agencies backing away from the sub-prime mortgages and securities you hawked. Freddie Mac, Standard & Poor's; but your company, Sunstar, was "standing firm." There were downgrades and bankruptcies around the country, but the government and Wall Street were taking steps to contain them.

So when I told you, you said, "Oh, I'm sorry, Jenny. Things are bad all over." You shook your head. "I don't know."

I bit my lip.

You sighed. "It's good you didn't buy a house, at least."

I stared at you, dead as granite.

"But I'm sure the Fed will lower the prime rate. We'll be OK."

And the granite iced over.

But that's what made you good at what you did, eh, Dad? Even if what you did wasn't good.

Mom at least cried. She hugged me. "I'm so sorry, honey." But then she had to go on about what I already knew, already was feeling for her. "You know, I went through it when your brother died. Of course he was already born, little Stevie. He had the cutest little smile. I'm so sorry, honey." A fresh burst of tears. She poured a glass of wine before I left.

I threw my efforts into my kids at school. I probably was kinder to them and hugged them more than usual. *They* appreciated it. I imagine a dad like you, if he cared at all, would have sued me for hugging them. Or no, he wouldn't have had to care. He'd just have to see that he could screw a dollar out of someone.

That's not true. That wasn't you.

But not far from you, either. At Christmas you sat with Bill, and I heard you talking about what formed your life, telling him that things were all right. "B of A, Citigroup, Morgan Chase, they're all saying they don't need to go forward with their Liquidity Enhancement. Things are settling down, stabilizing."

I sipped my wine, looked in the glass, and drank again. *Stabilizing. Something for the future.* And I grabbed those words, gave them my meaning, and somehow still trusted you.

As did all the country. Not you individually, but the people you trusted.

The New Year came. I poured my emptied love on my students, and their eager faces were all that mattered.

Bill said that you said we could probably start house-hunting that spring. "Then we'll have time to get settled and really be ready for the baby when she comes back."

"Thank you, Bill." He really had been sweet: comes *back*.

He said you'd sold your sub-prime derivatives. "Time to bail, your dad says."

The roadside weeds began to bloom, and mornings I heard a bird sing—a finch, I think, a little red thing on the wire baptizing the world in its accidental love and beauty.

But you were seeing a different world. Bank of America takes over Countrywide, big fish eats little fish. Bush signs the Economic Stimulus Act, tax cut. Morgan Chase, with 30 billion dollars in government support, takes over Bear Stearns, more fish, big money to big fish. The Fed keeps cutting interest rates and increasing access to easy loans.

And suddenly Sunstar, your enterprise, became a little fish

gasping for air. You thought you'd played it right. You'd sold your bad securities. But you were a small fish, and even you, or maybe especially you, given the world of your faith, couldn't know the layers of lies in the securities you still held — mortgages packaged and sold, rated a little on the high side, and sold again, fudged up just a bit more, and again, once more. That was the norm, so normal you had stopped seeing it. Business had traded morality for legality back in the '70s and '80s. Legality was quickly traded for effectiveness, or results, which was code for whatever you could get away with. And now that thuggery was widespread. And you, so thoroughly desensitized to it, were now the guy getting mugged.

You called Ken at his home. You didn't want to tell him face to face.

"Ken, Dennis here."

"Hello, Dennis." A child squalled in the background.

"Ken, I thought we were good, but we had bad securities I didn't know about. I didn't know they were bad. And the real estate has gone south, too, and we can't liquidate now anyway, nothing's got value. So what it amounts to is, I'm sorry, Ken, but there's no job for you to come to anymore. I'm not even sure there'll be a company for you to come to."

Ken was always quick on his feet. "Dennis, get me a check, a paycheck. Write it now, while we're still on the phone, will you? I'll come by and pick it up."

And he heard silence. What were you thinking? *Were you bankrupt? Could you pay him? You could probably pay him, if you did it right away, before your assets were assigned.* You hadn't been taken over yet, and you hadn't declared bankruptcy. You still had money in the bank.

"I don't think I can," you said. "I'm sorry, Ken."

And how I would have loved you if you had been decent. How I would have! What happened to Ken, Dad? And his wife and children? Your child was out of school. Your home was paid for. Your nest egg was many times what you and Mom needed for a very comfortable retirement. What, was your hoarding for me then? Yeah, I'd want money that ruined a family's life, wouldn't I. Thanks, Dad. And you weren't a Depression child, it wasn't some reflexive action. No, it was your home-grown, well-developed selfishness. Just ugly, mean selfishness.

Don't ask me to love you. Don't ask.

I know Mom loved you, whatever there was in you to love. You told her in person, didn't you. Poured her a bowl of wine on a slender stem, one from the pretty set of glasses painted by a serf or a machine with flowers or grapes or some other fruit in eight different patterns, but you didn't know which was her favorite, did you. Probably she still had a favorite then, the one with oranges and blossoms, close up on the tree. She liked the color against the red wine, she said, but there was more, there was memory. Until it didn't matter because they all held wine and the world was hopelessly messed up anyway, oranges and grapes and flowers and bees, all fading. You poured ignorance and served it to her, and asked about her day without listening to her, and said you'd talked with me, yes, I was fine, busy with the start of the school year, and yes, with the economy tanking it was going to be tough for McCain, too bad, it was just bad timing for an adjustment, and after she'd drunk down you filled her glass and told her.

"You know, honey, with the economy the way it is, Sunstar isn't immune. We're going to have our tough times."

"Well, you've seen tough times before, Dennis."

"This one will be the toughest."

"Not tougher than not getting the farm, or seeing your brother lose it."

And you saw, you expected, her ignorance. But you didn't even think how sterile her thought was, that her sense of toughness dealt with money and ownership but not the suicide of her nephew or the death of her baby boy. Those thoughts came out with me, not you. I guess she was a good match for you, or at least a malleable one.

"Elsie, Sunstar might go under."

Her eyes narrowed. She had some understanding. "Are we liable personally?"

"No. But a lot of our assets are invested in the company."

"That wasn't very smart, was it? So. Do I need to go back to work?"

"No, no. I don't think it'll come to that."

"Well, get our personal money back first! Right away!"

You nodded. "I've already begun that. I made transfers this morning. But there are securities I can't liquidate."

She drank deeply. "Well. I guess you've fought the good fight. You can't win every round."

That was pretty nice of her. You smiled grimly, appreciatively.

"You probably have work to do," she said.

You nodded.

"Well, here." She held up her glass. "At least liquidate me, hey?"

So you poured again.

Over the next month Sunstar was dismantled. You successfully poured everything you could liquidate in those first days into your personal accounts. After that your assets were distributed amongst your numerous creditors, who lost anywhere from half to nearly all their investments. Most of them, I imagine, I don't care too much about. They were people like you, they had other investments and properties, and even if they lost three quarters of their wealth they were still better off than most working people in the country. They would have income still, and could write the losses off against it. Maybe they'd vacation in Vegas the next year instead of Hawaii. Poor babies. Or maybe they were like you and didn't vacation at all, not because they couldn't afford it but because everything that wasn't making money tasted like dry toast. You kept your kayaking, I'll give you that. But mostly your tastes had gone stale.

No, I wasn't concerned for most of your losers. But some of them were people like my students' parents. People who worked at low-wage jobs, or two or three of them. People who didn't have a spouse at home drinking wine, because both parents had to work. People who were saving to help their kids go to college in the teetering hope that college would give them a better future. People who loved living more than making money, but understood that money, although not the representation of labor it is reported to be, was the currency to material and career resources for themselves and their children, and so they tried to save it; but people who did not understand that a whole sector of the economy would be built on lies, for which that sector later congratulated itself with bonuses. People who lost their savings because you and a thousand like you lied and ripped them off. My students, who saw the hope of college evaporating in their parents' shell-shocked eyes, and with it their inspiration to try now. You made my kids losers, Dad. You get up on your high horse about fixing education, but then you steal their hope. You and your kind. Clever bastards. Remember your grammar, Dad? The noun is *bastards*. It's the name, connotative, of what you are.

And I'm your daughter. Thank you, Dad!

But at least I'm your daughter and not you. So I can't change where I'm from, but I can choose what direction I go. And amidst all the hell you created there were two signs of hope in spite of you.

One, we elected Obama. It was an effort to say we wanted something better than the money-grubbing selfishness your generation had institutionalized. We wanted the have-nots to be given a place at the table. We wanted to care for our neighborhoods and the global ecosystem. Maybe we even wanted to value the lives and well-being of non-Americans! Imagine that!

I'm not saying Obama has fulfilled those hopes. Your armies of dollars have beat down the rebellion. *Money is power, and we have it. We can abuse the chocolate guy!* So create healthcare reform that honors insurance companies more than healthcare, when everyone involved knows a single-payer plan would deliver better healthcare more smoothly and cheaply. Deny and delay action to minimize climate change. Insist on unhealthy foods in schools and poor neighborhoods, because that's what your clients, Big Business, can mass market. Reinforce the power of money to control government. Twist the truth, screw the little guy, screw the environment, lie about what you plan to do and what you've done. Yeah, you've beat the rebellion down, and Obama was partly to blame. He had the failing of wanting to work with you, and of thinking that you would reach beyond the measure of money to a greater goodness. What a fool.

But him I can love. He is good, and him I can love.

But all that of course, his presidency, rolled out later. Back when he was first elected into the utter ruin you had created, back then I had my second hope.

I missed a period in late September. I didn't say anything, didn't even tell Bill, and he didn't seem to notice that I stopped the occasional glass of wine. Then I missed another. I told Bill, and he smiled and nodded.

"I was wondering," he said.

"Why didn't you say something then?"

"I knew you'd talk when you were ready."

We waited until Thanksgiving to tell you.

"Oh, honey," Mom said. "That's wonderful!"

"I'm real happy for you," you said.

For me. Thanks, Dad. I'm glad you're excited about your grand-child.

So my Thanksgiving, mine and Bill's, was for hope and promise.

But Mom wouldn't remember.

And you, things familial had passed. There'd be little in your world to be thankful for.

Sixteen

Jordan was born on May 31, seven pounds seven ounces, wispy haired and with knowing brown eyes.

"Perfect timing," Bill said. "He'll get a three-day weekend for his birthday."

I was instantly in love. Right from the start he smiled at me, like the happiest frog in the pond, or the cutest angel in heaven. We learned the nursing right off, and never had a problem after. Right when I saw him I knew what I was for. I know that sounds terribly archaic, but I don't mean it to be politically loaded. It's just the way we were.

Bill? I can't say about Bill. The first time he held Jordan he looked stiff and awkward, even though he supported the little head like the nurse told him to. Jordan cried for me, and after some dogged rocking and bouncing, Bill handed him over. That baby didn't always stop crying when I held him, but he usually did, and he did that first time.

"He wants his Mommy," Bill said.

I nodded, my eyes glued to the little beauty I held.

Mom came to the hospital sober as a deacon, and she gushed over her grandbabe, and cuddled him warmly. She offered him to you, but you declined, settling for a little finger-wag in his face.

"Isn't he just the most beautiful baby, Mom?" I asked.

"He is. Do you love him, honey?"

"Mom! Of course I do!"

She nodded. "I had to come around to loving you. You just seemed foreign at first. But you know, it happens."

"It has happened, Mom."

"It doesn't matter if it happens in the first moment or in a while. It's all the same. Like any love, like you and Bill or me and your father. Some of them are instant, some grow. Who's to say what's better?"

"Right, Mom. This one's love at first sight."

"That's sweet. It wasn't for me with you, you know. I think your father took more naturally to you than I did."

"OK." Why was she telling me this now?

"It was different with Stevie. Stevie was my baby." She sighed.

"That's great, Mom. Here, let me see mine." I reached out for Jordan. I wanted him. I wanted him from my stupid mother, who was telling me she hadn't loved me. I didn't want to think about the horror of a dead baby. She handed him to me, and I relaxed.

"There's my sweetie," I cooed.

When we took him home it was to the apartment. We never had bought a house, although you and Bill both told me now was the time. "Buy with blood in the streets," you echoed the old adage, "and there's plenty of blood right now."

We set Jordan up in a corner of our room. Bill had moved his chest of drawers into the living room. I was pleased to have Jordan close.

"I can understand why some moms sleep with their babies," I said. "It's nice. And it would be easier."

"Yeah, but you know what they say, that babies die that way, too," Bill replied.

"I know."

So, little Jordan slept close by where I could hear him breathe if Bill didn't snore too loudly. Not right against me, like I felt inclined, but close by.

I took little Jordan to school on the last day in June. The sub had had my students for two weeks by then, so she had begun to know the kids. But not like I did. The last day, the last week, is always hard, but they were good.

"Yes, you may touch him," I told my fourth graders.

They were so gentle. The girls actually were more timid.

Joshua, obviously practiced with babies, offered his pinky, and Jordan grabbed it. "Hey, he held my pinky!" Joshua reported to the class. That was something better than a principal's award, it seemed.

Deborah asked me quietly, "Did it feel OK?"

"Oh, yes, honey. I suppose it hurt, but that goes away fast, and then, look!"

She looked and beamed, and so did I.

But I didn't stay long. It was, after all, their last day of school, a crazy day.

If the world is a tale of two cities, I was in the best of times. Little Jordan gleamed like the sun, the center of my life, the source of hope and happiness. Oh, he wore me ragged, waking at all hours wanting to be fed or held, but can you fault a baby for that? It is the sweetest want, the want to be with one you love. And if he was my sun, we must have been a double star, for I wanted to be with him no less than he with me. We grew together, and I learned his needs. The cry that asked for diapering, the cry that asked for rocking, the smile that not everyone could see that meant he knew me and was happy. Little Jordan.

It was hard on Bill. He was mature enough to understand, in his brain, that I was exhausted and consumed with caring for Jordan. He even approved of my maternal dedication. But he was not mature enough in his heart. While he could approve he could not, or at least did not, enjoy. That's what I wanted, his rejoicing. But he mostly felt that he was left out.

When Jordan cried for me and could not be consoled by him, Bill felt frustrated and rejected.

"You take him then," he said, holding Jordan with both arms outstretched to me. "I guess he's your baby."

"He is *a* baby," I consoled, taking Jordan and trying to soothe them both. "He's just a little baby."

Jordan cooed at me.

Bill shook his head in exasperation.

"Bill, they say it's often this way. The baby will latch onto one parent or the other, usually the mom at first. And later, when he's older, he'll need you more."

Bill nodded. "I know."

At other times Jordan wasn't crying for me, but Bill didn't learn the difference.

"He needs to be burped, Bill."

"Yeah, I guess. How can you tell?"

"Because he just ate and now he's crying. He always needs to be burped after he eats."

So Bill tried to burp Jordan over his shoulder, and poor Jordan threw up his whole meal down his father's back.

"Bill, you don't burp him that hard!" I lifted the baby and the burp towel, and started wiping his mouth.

"I just tapped him," Bill protested.

I grimaced.

"And now, God!" He looked over his shoulder. His backside, both shirt and pants, was drenched in the creamy froth of throw-up.

"Well it serves you right for burping him so hard! Now he'll be hungry again."

Bill snarled silently and walked stiffly to the bathroom.

Later, after I'd put Jordan down and lain in bed myself, he shuffled in. I had thought about telling him I was sorry for saying it served him right. But I was tired, and when he crawled in I didn't say anything, and neither did he.

Mom pulled out wine glasses. "Here, honey, you can celebrate now!"

I could, but I would only drink one glass, and not very often. "It does go through to the milk, Mom."

"I know, I know. Here's your one drink." She poured the glass full.

I always saw Mom with a glass of wine now. They were inseparable companions. And she looked thinner than ever.

"You've lost weight, Mom."

"Thank you, dear."

I hadn't meant it as a compliment.

"Let me see that little baby," she schmoozed, setting her glass down.

I handed Jordan to her, and she gently bounced him.

You, meanwhile, glad-handed Bill. Your finances had stabilized at a level that did not humble you, and with that you had recovered a genial veneer. You said, "Hello, Bill! How's the prosthesis business these days?"

Bill shook his head. "You know, I'm in R&D. And our funding is drying right up."

"It's a tough time," you commiserated. "Can I get you something?"

You poured mixed drinks, hard stuff for the men. We all sat in the living room, maintaining our gender-separated conversations; but I, now cradling Jordan, listened to yours.

"You going to be all right, Bill?"

Bill raised his shoulders and shook his head. "It's hard to say."

"You've got a responsibility now," you said, nodding toward Jordan.

"I know that. I'll find a way to meet it."

"I'm sure you will."

And you sounded dishonest to me, or at least formulaic. And you didn't offer any help.

Mom's voice floated in, "It's so nice that you have summers off, isn't it."

"Yes. And I'm really taking it off this year. No workshops, no conferences."

"That's nice. Your father never had that."

"Would you have wanted him to, Mom?"

"Yes. Of course I would."

And she sounded honest, or at least genuine.

"Why don't we do things that way, Mom? Everybody just take

more time off. The French do that, don't they?"

"I don't know. But how could it work?"

"We'd just do it. We'd still have enough food. We'd still have enough energy."

"I can't imagine it would work, though."

"Only because we keep pushing ourselves for more. Bill says it's Darwinian, that push. I say we should have the intelligence and discipline to get past it. But it seems we don't."

"I don't know, Jenny. Sometimes it's hard to handle free time."

Your voice wafted across the room, "...so now's the time to buy."

Bill's reply, "I'd like to be in that position."

"Nothing ventured, nothing gained, boy."

"Most gamblers lose, though."

"Not if you're good. Not if you're good."

And I knew Bill was thinking of how you thought your financial success was a reflection of your hard work and cleverness, not recognizing the larger historical currents and readiness to abuse that profited you.

"Jenny," Mom said quietly, "I haven't told your father. I don't want him to worry."

"What would he worry about, Mom?"

"Well, I saw the doctor yesterday, and next week he wants me to have a colonoscopy."

"Does he think there's a problem, Mom? You know, colono-scopies are routine, just to screen for things."

"I know. I've been tired is all."

"So it's just to screen then?"

"Yes. He just wants to rule some things out. You know how they do."

"He wants to rule some things out? What does he want to rule out, Mom? You must have had some other symptoms."

"Well, I had some bleeding. I don't really like to talk about it."

"Mom! You have to tell Dad!"

"I was hoping you could take me to the doctor, honey."

"Mom." I closed my eyes. "It's not just going to the doctor. Do you know what you have to do the night before?"

"I'm not going to do that!"

"Mom, you have to do that, or they can't do the colonoscopy."

Jordan was wet and started to fuss.

His grandmother finished her glass and set it down resolutely. "They'll just have to do the best they can!"

I excused myself to change Jordan. When I came back I had revived my teacher-esque authority.

"Mom. I'll be happy to take you to the doctor. But only if you do the preparation you're supposed to."

"Oh, how will you know?" Mom drank from a fresh glass.

"Dad needs to know."

"You won't tell him!" she worried.

"I can or you can. What day is the procedure?"

She looked forlorn. "Wednesday."

"Do you have the drinks for the night before?"

"Of course not. I have better drinks."

"Go get me your prescription."

"You're not going to tell your father?"

"I'm going to fill your prescription."

She stood slowly, but not with any boozy unsteadiness.

Across the room your voice floated like the wind, "So I don't know what else the government could have done. Otherwise the whole country would have gone belly up. The whole country! It's a death-knell for capitalism, really. What we've learned is that it doesn't work when corporations get too large. Even Alan Greenspan said as much. They become monopolistic. They own the government, to an extent. I don't mind, really. There's nothing so great about capitalism, except that it's been good to me. I've operated in it, so I've tried to do it well. But maybe they'll come up with a better system, some capitalism-democracy hybrid like we had seventy years ago."

"There were steep progressive taxes back then," Bill said.

"Yes, seventy percent and more. That still won't prevent stupidity, though."

"No. But it would share the wealth."

"Which would promote a broader democracy, you think. But that's not the lesson here. It's not socialism that's needed. It's regulation. Free markets over-reach, the gambling instinct is too strong, and so they create the boom-bust cycle."

"Be careful or they'll throw you out of the Heritage Club!"

"I'm not a member of the Heritage Club! It's not pretty, though."

"The Heritage Club?" said Bill.

"That's not what I meant."

Bill said, "You mean regulation, then."

"Yes. The free market is so clean, so elegant." You snorted. "It just doesn't work, I guess."

Mom returned. "Here it is. You can go fill it. But I'm not going to drink it."

"Maybe I can come over and help you."

"Help me drink it? Sure, help yourself. You know, I've heard plenty about that. I don't want it."

"Maybe I can come over."

Driving home in the car that evening I wanted to tell Bill about Mom, but I made the mistake of starting with his discussion. "You and Dad were having quite the conversation. I heard the R word."

Bill grinned. "Regulation? Your dad floored me! He actually thinks we should regulate corporate activity."

I shook my head. "That's a new twist."

"A new twist? It's a whole new map of the world! I thought he was right of Adam Smith, like most of today's capitalists. But don't get too excited. It'll all crumple away."

"You're a cynic!"

"You think I'm wrong?"

I sighed. "Oh, only sometimes."

I listened to the dry hum of the tires.

"I think we have to have hope," I said.

"In what?"

"In people. That we'll be decent."

"I think we have to recognize the truth," he returned, "even if it hurts."

I looked over my shoulder at Jordan snoozing snugly in his car seat, his cheeks reflecting the momentary gleam of a passing car. "But we always have to have hope."

"I'm losing mine," he said.

The tires whirred under us. I don't know why it felt like it should be wet out, that there should be that sound of wheels on wet gravel. It was July in San Jose, when rain was always scarce.

"We can't do that, Bill."

We were quiet, and the tires rolled.

I resumed, "You were talking about your job. You hadn't told me there was a concern."

"Well. There's more than I told your father, too. I think they're going to close down our whole operation here."

"Bill! Why didn't you tell me that?"

"I don't know it yet. I don't even know if they know."

"What will you do?"

"I don't know! I've got to see what's happening, what my choices are. What they decide."

"They!" I said.

"Yeah. The guys like your dad," he spoke angrily. "Finance. Because everything's about money. Not jobs, not people, not even product quality. Just money. I sound like Eisner. He must have been a bastard. But at least he was an honest one! Even at Disneyland, he called it: it's all about money. So don't get upset with me for being honest and cynical."

"You're in a mood!" I said.

"Yep. A cynical, sour, mood. But an honest one."

I suddenly didn't want to talk about Mom with him. I didn't want to talk about anything with him. I wanted to withhold. We rode in silence.

When we arrived at the apartment it felt hot. I put Jordan to bed and opened windows. "I know you don't like the noise, Bill, but it's hot in here."

He didn't say anything.

I went to bed. He said he'd be in later and turned on the TV.

I talked with you. I knew Mom wouldn't tell you about her colonoscopy, so the next day I called. "Dad, did you know Mom has a colonoscopy scheduled next week?"

"No. What's that about?"

"I don't know. But she said she's been tired and she had some rectal bleeding."

"I see. Do you know what that means, Jenny?"

"No. I mean, you can bleed from hemorrhoids, and it's no big deal. But she's tired, and has lost weight, too."

"Are you trying to scare me?"

"Dad! I'm trying to make you aware. She's going to need your support. It may be nothing, but the colonoscopy will help us find out. She should have had one years ago, just as screening."

"I don't like getting into medical things," you said.

"I know, Dad. Do you know how colonoscopies work?"

"Well, they run a tube up your intestines."

"Right. You don't even feel that. The hard part is the night before. Mom has to drink a solution that will clean her out so the doctor can see things with his tube. It's a lot of liquid she has to drink."

"And she'll be sitting on the pot."

"That's right."

"She won't like that."

"That's why you'll have to help her, Dad."

"Well."

I could hear that I needed to control this. "So I will pick up the solution Mom needs to drink. I'll bring it by, probably tomorrow night, and go over it with you. Then you'll have to make sure she drinks it."

I heard what sounded like a pen clicking. "Dad?"

"Yeah, all right. You bring the solution over. I'll see you then, Jenny."

"Right, tomorrow."

And how much did you even feel for her? She seemed dedicated to you, but were you even concerned about her health, or just about the nuisance of trying to get her to drink the prep?

I brought the packet to you the next night. Bill stayed home with Jordan.

"Well, it doesn't *look* so bad," Mom said.

"They say to chill it. Stick it in the freezer for an hour before you start drinking it," I instructed.

"All right, all right."

"So what do I have to do?" you asked.

I wanted to say *You'll figure it out*, but would you? What had you lost with your market crash, or did you just seem to be getting old way too early? Or had you always been narrow, but I'd just never seen you in a difficult situation outside your thin expertise?

"Here are the directions. Just help Mom with the timing of her drinking. You know she won't enjoy it."

"Maybe you should come over," you said to me.

Mom interrupted, "She doesn't need to come over, I don't want her to come over!"

"I'll be a phone call away if you have questions."

"All right. But then you'll take her in the next day? I mean, you're off, and I should be in the office. It's a tricky time right now, and the right moves can mean a lot. Positions are moving now, foreclosures and securities, and I'd be a fool not to attend to them. You know I'm taking a new job in San Francisco. Ken's advice, sort of. I'm going to work with the big boys."

"Right. But I do have a baby, Dad. OK, I'll come over. Mom, I'll take you in on Wednesday."

And so I did. I bundled Jordan into the car before Bill had gone to work, whatever work meant for him, and we picked up Mom. You hadn't called the night before, but I had called you along about nine o'clock, and you said that everything was going right. "She's drinking it and hating it."

So now I asked, "You finish it all, Mom?"

"I'm finished with it, all right!" I was glad to see her feistiness, but she still looked tired. Maybe anyone would at that point.

"Well, they say the rest is easy," I assured her.

The receptionist took my cell number, and Jordan and I sat with Mom in the lobby.

"You know," I said, "if you're going to work in healthcare this might not be bad. I mean, it's clean, and the illnesses you're dealing with aren't usually infectious."

"Who the hell goes into this kind of doctoring, that's what worries me," Mom griped.

I shook my head. "There'll be a nurse with the doctor, Mom." I didn't know that, but I said it anyway. "And as a healthcare job, you know, you wouldn't be on call with this."

Mom snorted. "You can have it!"

A nurse came up to us. "Mrs. Self? I'm Anne-Marie. I'll be getting you ready this morning, so if you can walk with me?" She turned to me as Mom rose. "She'll be all done by nine-thirty, and then a little longer to let the anesthesia wear off, and the doctor will want to talk with you."

"Thank you," I said, and she led Mom down a hall.

I had brought Jordan's stroller, and we drove a few blocks to a park, where we went for a walk. We watched older children play on the jungle gym. It was a new one, with plastic panels that gleamed their greens and yellows in the sun. We sat in a row of matching benches, where a few women were already scattered.

"See, Jordan," I said, holding him on my lap and pointing. "These children are playing on the jungle gym, just like at Hoover Park. Those girls are going down the slide, see her pretty pink dress? I don't know why her mother put her in that to come to the park! And that boy in the red and brown shirt, he's climbing on the web. In a couple years you can play on the bars! That will be fun! Mm, I like the morning sun, don't you?"

At the next bench sat a woman younger than me. She wore a tight sweater, blue leggings, and white sandals with sparkles. Her nails were painted in multiple colors. She called out, "Emma, try not to get dirty!" She sounded like a nag. "Come here," she ordered. "That's enough for today!" She turned to me. "You're lucky, yours isn't into everything yet! But you'll get your turn!"

The girl in pink was coming in.

"It's nice that you can get her to the park, though," I replied.

"Well! I don't know how often we'll do this. We have better things to do than get dirty, don't we, Emma! Come sit now!" she said, indicating a stroller. She again looked at me. "Having her sit keeps her out of trouble."

After she marched away the older woman at the next bench, a grandma, I guessed, moved closer to me. "Isn't that sad," she said. "The child can't get dirty!"

"Yes, and she's kept out of trouble by being put in her stroller. What does her mother want, for the girl to be kept out of preschool troubles or to learn to deal with the world?"

The gray-haired lady smiled sadly. "I grew up here. We used to play all day in the fields. And then Mom would bang on a triangle like you see in the movies to tell us to come in for dinner. We had to figure out plenty, playing our important summer games. I think Joan Baez called them that."

I nodded. I'd only heard the name Joan Baez, but I understood the idea.

"My youngest grandchildren," the woman went on, "are kept in a playpen. Their parents both work, and they want time for themselves, too."

"I guess they at least have each other, the kids," I said.

"Yes," the woman nodded. "And a TV."

I didn't say anything.

"You enjoy your baby, dear. That's the main thing," she said.

"I know," I said. "I will. I do!"

She smiled.

After a good soak in the sun I wished her a good morning and we returned to the doctor's office. We arrived just as a nurse, another one, was walking Mom to some chairs in a side hall.

"Hi, Mom, you look good!" I said, mostly to let the nurse know that I was with the woman she had in tow.

"Well, you were right. That wasn't fun, but it wasn't bad, either."

"You slept, didn't you?" asked the nurse.

"I think so. I don't remember!"

"Well now, if you can sit here a few minutes the relaxant will wear off and the doctor will have a follow-up with you. All right?"

"All right," Mom said, and I nodded.

We sat. These chairs were not so comfortable as the ones in the lobby. They were upholstered in thin, stiff padding. I pictured them as chairs from teachers' desks of fifty years before. Chairs like that would help keep teachers on their feet, but I wouldn't agitate for them.

The doctor came in with his eyes studiously on his clipboard. He was short, slight, and dark complexioned. Mom hadn't said anything against him.

"Mrs. Self." He extended his hand and she shook it. He turned to me. "And your daughter?"

Mom nodded and I said, "Jenny."

He shook my hand. "And grandson then!" he said, indicating

Jordan.

"Yes."

He smiled briefly, the kindly, busy-doctor look. "Mrs. Self, I will be sending the results to your doctor for follow-up. We did find some polyps, which we removed and will biopsy. Here. These are some of the polyps." He pulled a sheet of photos from his clipboard. "The black formations against the pink intestine wall." Mom glanced and turned away, wrinkling her nose. "You may take these," he said to me.

He continued, "We found a larger growth also, right close to the rectum, and that is what I'm more concerned about. How long have you had blood in your stool?"

"Oh, years," Mom said, shaking her head.

"When you get symptoms you should deal with them," he softly scolded. "You said the blood is dark?"

She nodded and said, "Yes. It used to be bright red, but now it's dark."

"OK. Well, I want you to go home and enjoy yourself. Cut back on the alcohol, go for a walk instead. We'll get the results to your doctor and he will be in touch with you."

We stood and he shook our hands. I was trying to read his face, but couldn't tell what he wasn't saying. But of course what was plain was that he wasn't giving us a clean bill of health.

"That wasn't too bad, was it, Jenny."

"Not too bad at all, Mom."

The drinking that night was ours, Bill's and mine. I'd made dinner, but when he got home he right away poured two glasses of wine. We sat at the table.

"To you," he said.

"To us." I could tell I wasn't going to get to talk about Mom right away.

"Yes. To us."

We drank.

"We had a meeting at work today."

"OK." Although it was obvious it wasn't OK. I was still churning with the experience of Mom's colonoscopy, or rather the doctor's review, but that would wait.

"They did it pretty well. They told us right out: they thought they could keep everyone who was willing to relocate."

"We have to move?"

"San Jose is closing. But I can relocate."

"Relocate where."

"Alan talked with me later. He said New Jersey."

"New Jersey?"

"Wilmington."

"Who wants to live in New Jersey?"

"He called it the Garden State."

"Not in Wilmington, I think."

"What else do you think?"

"How can you ask? I don't want to live in New Jersey! I'm not *going* to live in New Jersey!"

"They'd pay for the move."

I set down the wine glass and picked Jordan up from his seat. We kept him at table with us.

"What do babies grow up to be like in New Jersey?" I asked.

"They grow up to be people, like they would anywhere."

"East Coast. Busy, pushy. I like the relax of the West Coast, the...." I thought of Joey.

"Relax like your dad?"

I snapped, "He's an echo of New York-NewJersey-all the New Money, Only Money that you talk about. I don't need to water my baby with it!"

"He's not a plant!"

I resumed, "Do they guarantee a job for the rest of your life?"

"They can't do that, Jenny."

"Will they send you back here in two years?"

"They can't control that kind of thing. It depends how the

company does, how the economy does. I'm sure they would if they could."

"But once he's in school I don't want to be bouncing him all over the country. And if he has a sister I really don't want to be moving her around!"

He didn't say anything.

"Stuck in New Jersey! You go if you want! I'm not going!"

"Jenny, let's think about this. We don't need to decide right now."

"You could look for other work here! Why don't you even think of that?"

Bill looked pained. "There aren't prosthetics companies on every corner. And nobody is growing now." He hesitated and added evenly but viciously, "Your dad reamed the economy too much for that."

I moved the wine glass farther from me. "You haven't looked," I said. *He hasn't looked, hasn't even thought to look. New Jersey!* "And my mom is sick. You haven't asked about her, either."

"What's she got?"

"Remember, Bill? Your wife took her mother in for a colonoscopy this morning? Because her father can't handle it, and then you come home and say let's move to New Jersey? What a family-minded guy you are! *You* go move to New Jersey! Move to *Afghanistan* for all I care!"

"What happened at the colonoscopy?"

I stared at him. "They don't know yet. They've got to do tests."

He nodded. As if I'd told him something.

Maybe I wasn't fair to him, but I was angry. He was so detached, so in his own little bubble, so unaware of *us.* "You want some dinner?" I asked.

"Yes, thanks."

"Serve yourself." I took Jordan to bed with me.

Seventeen

I never apologized to Bill. He never apologized to me. He took me up on my angry lash of an offer. We had a couple cold days, and then he said he had to let Alan know what he was doing.

"So what are you doing?" I asked.

"It's not a time when I can take a chance on a job, Jenny. People are off work all over, and nobody's hiring." He paused, but I wasn't going to help him out. "So I'm thinking I'll go to Jersey, see how it is."

"I hope you like New Jersey."

"I want you to come, too."

I didn't say anything.

"I understand if you don't want to. But maybe later, if it's OK, then you can come out. Or if the economy picks up maybe I can come back here."

"If that's what you want." *You bastard!*

"It won't cost me anything to move, you know."

"If that's how you see it." *And Jordan and I aren't anything!*

"We can Skype."

"That'll be special." *Get out of here!*

He ran his hands down his face. "You should come with me, Jenny."

"No I shouldn't. It won't cost you anything to move."

"They'd pay for both of us."

"*Both* of us! How considerate! There are three of us, Bill! Remember, you have a son? I'll save them the cost, protect your job. You go to New Jersey!" *You go to hell!*

He gave up.

Two days later the moving van arrived, all arranged by the company. He travelled light. The movers were gone in two hours. That evening he flew from San Jose. I didn't even have to take him to the airport. The company sent a shuttle. Gone, just like that.

Oh, we kept in touch. Skype. Like the old ad said, next best thing to being there. But nothing close to it. We kept in touch, until we didn't. Or more truly, we went through the motions of keeping in touch. Bill was smart, but maybe he was never much in touch. I think we're all victims of technology. You get like the hard drives you live with.

I look back on it now and I know I wasn't very good to him. He was in touch, or had been. Maybe I should have gone to New Jersey. Maybe—but I didn't want to, and he didn't work with me. I was worried about Mom, and about you, too, honestly, and, well, I know I didn't treat him right. But I couldn't get my head there at the time. And his heart wasn't there. He was a good employee, and they could pay him more than I could just then. They paid him money, and my love was poor at the time. Love doesn't work that way, direct deposit on the last of the month. He wouldn't have gone if they hadn't moved him. Or maybe I'd have gone if they just gave us more time, time for me to swallow the whole thing. Maybe I would have. But they didn't give us time.

Sometimes they say things are just bad timing. Are you allowed bad timing once you're married? You and Mom weren't what I'd call really close, but in a way you were, too. Certainly timing wasn't a thing that could totally derail you. You were culturally synched. Bill and I didn't have that. Maybe you'd made our generation more free than yours. Or more hasty. What a blessing.

So, Bill. He worked in New Jersey, and of course he met people there, there in the Garden State. He didn't tell me when he started dating. He didn't really date around, actually. He just met another prosthetician, and she and he just hit it off like two little computers sharing their programs and viruses. He came home at Thanksgiving but I think he'd already met her, or at least decided he'd had enough of his wife and child. He brought Jordan a bauble from the airport, and me a flood of empty talk about himself. Then the week before Christmas he told me that he wouldn't be coming home. "Really busy at work," he said, but when I didn't say anything he came straight, "No, it's just, I don't think it's working, Jenny."

I made him file for the divorce, which he did in January. How quickly we slide from the best of times!

By then Mom was bad. Right after her colonoscopy, before Bill left, I had gone online and researched intestinal cancer. It looked like Mom had a colorectal tumor. The prognosis was good if it was caught early, but Mom had had symptoms for years, according to her. And she drank, and she didn't exercise. And you should deal with symptoms when you get them, the doctor had said.

So I wasn't surprised when she saw her doctor and the biopsies showed cancer, the colorectal cancer I'd found online. It was advanced.

"Well I don't want to die!" she said. *As if any of us have an option on that.*

"You should get your affairs in order," the doctor said, directly but not uncompassionately.

"My affairs! My husband is in order, thank you, and this is my daughter and my grandson!" *She knew her affairs better than Bill did.* "And I want to see this boy grow up! So what do I have to do, Doctor? You don't need to tell me my affairs. You need to keep me alive!"

"Your cancer is quite advanced. There is no effective treatment at this stage."

"That can't be the best you can do!"

"Mrs. Self, your cancer has spread extensively. If we had dealt with this sooner we could probably have stopped it surgically. But at this point there are no good options. Chemotherapy may prolong your life, but I can't say it will maintain your quality of life."

"Well, you worry about my life and I'll worry about my quality of life. What do I have to do?"

Mom seemed spirited then, sort of like the self I imagine she was before Stevie died, the self that had flashed forth irregularly for over twenty-five years. But time was no longer her ally.

You, Dad, had always seemed to me so practical and steady, so even-keeled, but when we told you Mom's condition you were uncompassed. "What?" you said. "You have cancer?"

"Yes, I have cancer. The doctor says I have cancer."

"Can the doctor be right?"

"He says I can't do much about it, either."

"That's nonsense! You can always do something about it, about anything!"

"I'm going to do chemotherapy."

"Chemotherapy. Yes, that's the thing. So that will cure you then? And you'll be all better."

"The doctor says no, but the doctor doesn't have much faith. What can the doctor know about me?"

"Right! The doctors can stick their heads in their books and not see, not see what's really going on."

"That's right. And I'm not going to any nursing home, either! I'll be right here!"

"Right!"

Mom turned to me. "So don't just stand there! Pour me a glass!"

And I did. Because why not?

Her first treatment was two weeks later. You wanted me to take her, but I made you. Jordan was in day-care, but I was teaching, and you had to take this responsibility. Besides, the treatment itself was simple. All you had to do was drive her there and back.

I visited that evening. Mom looked gray. But you had poured her a glass, I saw. It was still full.

"Hello, honey," she said spiritlessly. "Never do this."

"Now, Elsie," you comforted her uneasily, "it's just for a while. It's like the market correction, you know—a little pain for a while, but then you come out better. You know the doctor said you'd feel like this."

Mom didn't say anything, didn't raise her eyes.

You continued, talking to me. "And they used to have problems with nausea, but not so much now. New drugs, you know."

I had put Jordan on the floor. He was crawling about like a new caterpillar, slowly, and at the moment inspecting a piece of plastic lint he had managed to pick up in his little fingers.

"Can you keep anything down now, Mom?" I asked her.

She waved her hand dismissively. "No interest. I don't have to until tomorrow."

"I'll come back tomorrow night. Do you have easy foods?"

Mom nodded. "Oatmeal. It's time for oatmeal."

"Dad, let's look in the kitchen. I'll show you what to make for Mom." I picked up Jordan, removing the lint from his lips, and we paraded to the refrigerator, leaving Mom hunched in her chair.

The refrigerator held much as it had throughout my childhood: cans of Coke and Diet Pepsi, a thawing package of some cut of beef, enriched white bread, lettuce getting slimy in the vegetable drawer, sliced meat and cheese in the cheese drawer, peanut butter and jelly, and condiments on the door.

"OK, Dad. Oatmeal for breakfast. Nuke it for what, one minute? Give her some honey, make it taste decent, OK? And then you can make her a ham sandwich for lunch. Be nice, plenty of mayo and mustard. And for dinner. You can nuke potatoes and broil the steak, right? A little salt is all it needs."

You nodded. "I'll make the sandwich before I leave in the morning. We have a meeting at the office…"

"OK, Dad."

Back in the living room I bent to give Mom a hug, and held

Jordan to kiss her scalp, too. "OK, Mom, I'll be back tomorrow after work. Maybe I can help Dad cook."

"OK, honey."

I drove home, Jordan strapped in the back, and the city dry. It was winter, there should be a few storms. When would we have some rain?

She looked much better the next evening. You had successfully prepared her meals, and she had eaten reasonable portions.

"Your father has many talents," she said.

"I know," I confirmed.

That was the pattern we settled into then. Every three weeks Mom went in for her dose of poison. Then the poison gradually faded from her wracked body and she became something like herself. But after a few rounds I could see that her recovery after each treatment came slower and achieved less. I don't think you saw it.

"No, no," you said, "she's recovering. Just like the economy!"

Finance remained your measuring stick and your focus. "You know," you said to me one evening as Mom hunched quietly in the corner, "it's funny I've come around to commercial banking again, right back where I started. But now they're all the same. S&Ls, banks, securities, ratings, I've been in them all, and so have a million other guys, and they're all the same. That was just starting when I started, but now it's nearly complete. I'd thought they might change, really regulate the industry after this last fiasco, but now even those reforms are being beaten down. It's pretty stunning. I don't really know what's best. Bill was a bit of a socialist, wasn't he?"

"Bill is like you, Dad. He's playing by the rules he gets, whether they support decency or not. He's got his liberty."

Mom stirred. "I haven't seen Bill in a while. How's he doing?"

"He's in New Jersey, Mom. He and I are getting a divorce."

"Oh, that's right. I'm sorry, honey."

"It's OK." *No it isn't!* "I've got what matters," I said, looking at Jordan on the carpet.

And you, stupid you, said proudly, "*I've* got what matters! The ear of the most senior management, who have the ear, the hand, of Congress!"

I couldn't quell my irritation. "You just said you don't know what's best, Dad! What good is having their ear if you don't know what's best?"

"Well, I wouldn't say that to them! I know what they can hear!"

"So you have their ear as long as you tell them what they want to hear."

"As long as I tell them how to achieve their goals."

"That's powerful, Dad."

You actually seemed to hear the sarcasm for once. "It sure brought us back from the brink. This last stumble was way worse than the S&L. It could have been worse than the Depression! And it could have hit *us*! Instead, now I'm secure. I remember Ken, my assistant, once saying that he should probably be working for a bigger outfit, one with more clout and staying power, you know. Well, that's what I'm doing now. We're pretty safe. There will always be little nibbles to deal with, little red herrings to toss, but we're in good shape. I even—you know, at Sunstar I carried pretty minimal insurance. Personal insurance, I mean. But the bank offered better, the kind of thing Obama is trying to get the government into. That timing worked out well for us! I'll tell you, your mother's treatments aren't cheap, but we're covered. We're in good shape!"

"That's good, Dad." I was suddenly bored with you. Why had it taken me so long to learn how boring you were? Here was Mom, dying but still living. Here was Jordan, your grandson not yet on two legs, with his dad a million miles away. And here were you, in the same room with us, but you were a million miles away, too. How could Mom love you like she did? You provided her with comfort and status, I suppose. Is that all we're after? How could I ever have loved Bill?

And suddenly I missed Joey. He was the person in my life who had offered more than an income. But now he was gone, I'd let him go, I'd sent him away. You'd wanted him gone. Shame on me.

You turned on the TV, said something about what was on. It didn't matter. It ended conversation. I picked up Jordan, and we kissed Mom goodnight.

There had been a drizzle two mornings before, enough that the pavement looked damp although it did not puddle. Now it was dry again.

I didn't like leaving Jordan at day-care every day, but the director and her staff seemed really good. The place was always clean, there were other children of all pre-school ages, and there were only basic toys like blocks and dolls, with room for imagination, and no swallowable parts. There was a dog, a lumbering old lab, and they didn't have any screen time. Wall sockets were covered and there were no sharp corners. Supervision was close and caring. They had story time and free time and outside time and nap time. It was a good place, and what were my options? I couldn't stay home. Mom was sick. Caring for a baby wasn't in you. So. It was a good place.

Bill, of course, was completely gone now. He sent a monthly check. In that at least, if only, he was reliable.

School continued to be a challenge, but not so exhausting as at first. I had a repertoire now, and more than that I knew better how to manage both the children and their parents. Reviewing student work and providing feedback and grades remained a time-consuming burden, but even that I was learning to accomplish more effectively. Fourth graders continued to be the best age to teach, and I think that will always be true for me.

It is conceivable that having Jordan took some emotional

space and made me a less-attentive teacher. I don't buy it, though. Jordan made me more aware of children, more aware of their childhood, more aware of what I did as a teacher in light of what I hoped he would experience. Parents are bound to have episodes that interfere with their working lives, but all in all I think Jordan made me a better, more sensitive teacher.

In late spring he began to hoist himself up on things, furniture, and stand on wobbly legs; and then he began to walk, those toddly, stumbling steps. I found I sometimes wanted to exclaim about it to Bill, and then his absence, his treachery, would wound me afresh and harden me against him.

I took Jordan to you instead. "Look, he's beginning to walk!"

You nodded. "I'm glad to see that." Your smile flashed and disappeared, a nova come and gone. You had your headset on and were watching a ball game on TV, to which you returned after obligatory acknowledgement.

Mom was better. She smiled brightly and bent to him. "What a big boy you are!" She held his hand and helped him several steps. "You are a traveler, aren't you, Jordan!"

She was two days before her next treatment, so at her best. But she soon settled into her corner chair.

"I'm so tired, Jenny."

"I know, Mom."

She stared at Jordan and smiled wanly, and then her face dropped into sobbing. I bent to her and hugged her. She smelled musty, old.

She was almost embarrassed and both held me and pushed me away. "I just don't know," she said. "I just..."

"It's OK, Mom."

"No. No, it's not OK, honey. I've seen him walk, but I won't see him go to school. I won't put his kindergarten pictures on the refrigerator. I won't, I won't."

I wanted to say *Maybe you will, Mom*, but aside from the leniency of *maybe* I didn't believe it.

She continued, "Your dad doesn't see it. He expects to live forever, and so of course I will too."

"He doesn't think that, Mom."

"He doesn't think it, no. But he doesn't think about it, either. He doesn't deal with it."

"I know. It's a hard thing to deal with."

"That's never an excuse. Never an excuse. Jenny, I don't really want to go in for another treatment. I'm not getting better. I hurt and I'm tired."

I looked at her. There was nothing I could do, was there? I pulled a footstool near her, sat, and held her hands. "Have you talked with Dad about that?"

"He can't talk about it, Jenny."

"Maybe he has to, Mom. Do you want some help?"

She looked at nothing. "No. No."

I held her hands, giving her time to change her mind. But she drew her hands back into her own lap. "Thank you, Jenny. You're a good daughter. Thank you for your little boy, too." Again thin tears welled in her eyes, but they did not pour out.

"OK, Mom. I'd better get that little boy to bed. Goodnight, Mom." I kissed her and then held Jordan up to kiss her, too. "Goodnight, Grandma," I said.

I walked to you and put my hand on your shoulder. You turned smiling and took your headset off. "You leaving then, Jenny? All right, then. Goodnight."

"Goodnight, Dad."

You turned back to your game.

We left and drove home over the dry pavement. If there were blossoms in the spring air, they could only have been an echo of better times. I could not smell them.

A week later you called. "Jenny, your mom's in the hospital."

"What happened, Dad? Is she all right?"

"I got home and she was in her chair, and I couldn't wake

her."

"You called 911?"

"Yes. Then I followed them here to the hospital."

"Is she awake now?"

"The doctor said she's resting. She's all full of tubes. They're giving her medications to ease pain."

That's what they've been doing for months, Dad. Ever since they discovered her cancer too late to deal with it. "I'll come right over."

My stack of student papers would have to wait. I bundled Jordan into the car and drove quickly to the hospital, just fifteen minutes away. There we found our way to Mom's room. She had an oxygen tube but was breathing on her own. An IV went into her left forearm. She had that grayed skin, but I'd seen worse. You were hunched sleeping in a chair at her side.

"Grandma's sleeping," I whispered to Jordan. "Grandpa, too." I held him, standing by the bed.

A nurse about my age entered the room. Her name tag said Janice. "Are you her daughter?" she asked.

"Yes. My dad called, but he didn't know much. What's her status?"

"We're just hydrating her."

"Meaning…?"

"It's too early to know." She hesitated, and then added, "She may not regain consciousness."

I turned back to Mom. There she was, breathing, sleeping in seeming comfort, her skin grayed but still holding faintly the pink of life. On the wall a monitor showed a regular heartbeat.

The nurse wheeled a chair to me. "We never know for sure," she said.

"Thank you." I sat. The nurse left to do her rounds.

I studied Mom for a while, and then said to Jordan in my lap. "See, Jordan, see her chest rise and fall? So gently. That means she is alive, she's breathing. And see Grandpa, too? And if you listen you can him snore a little, just that wheeze. Hear it?"

We listened to Grandpa's breathing.

"They are my Mommy and Daddy. And Grandma's sick now. She might not be able to talk with us anymore. Or listen. You know, Jordan, she wasn't the greatest at it, listening, but she did it in her way. She, I think her life wasn't what it could have been. She was smart and pretty, and she had money all her life. And she started out working for the poor. But that's hard work, and she didn't have the muscle for it. It is a sort of muscle, Jordan. A spiritual muscle. The heart, don't you know? So when you're smart and handsome and rich, keep your heart, too, OK? Grandma had a heart for you, but she didn't have it bigger. It's hard to have it bigger. But we need that now, Jordan. The world is full, and our hearts have to hold us all.

"And Grandpa, too. He'll talk to us. Some. And he used to listen. Did I tell you? He played with me when I was little. He taught me kayaking, as I'll teach you. And he enjoyed it, too, I'm sure he did, as I will. But then, I don't know. Maybe I just got older and we didn't relate the same. He was always into his work. It was like a football game for him—make the right moves, call the right plays, study the playbook, anticipate what the other guy's going to do. And the winner gets the trophy, the money. Maybe getting older he just couldn't be both rich and, and how he used to be. Maybe you can't focus on your game, beating the other businesses, and on your family, too. I don't know. I don't know, little boy."

We sat silently. Jordan fell asleep.

The nurse came in and said gently, "Visiting hours close in ten minutes."

"OK, thank you."

I sat a few moments more, watching Mom breathe. Other than that she did not stir. I rose and put a hand on your shoulder.

"Dad." I rustled your shoulder. "Hey, Dad."

You stirred awake. "Oh, Jenny. Oh." You scanned around at Mom and her bedside. "Oh. Did she wake? Did you talk with her?"

"No, Dad. She's sleeping. Do you know what happened, Dad?"

"No. She was sleeping in her chair, but I couldn't wake her. Here they tested her all up, but they couldn't wake her, either. She's probably very tired from all that chemotherapy. Still, you'd think she'd wake up a little."

"We'll see," I said.

"What do you mean, *We'll see*. What do you mean by that?"

I hesitated, but said, "The nurse said she might not wake up."

"Might not! What does a nurse know!"

"So we'll see."

"As if your mother would not wake up! She prided herself on making my breakfast every morning. To think she wouldn't wake up!"

"It's the end of visiting hours, Dad. Will you walk me out to my car?"

"End of...? Yes, I suppose." He rose. "Good night, Elsie." He didn't touch her. I wondered how many years that had been their pattern.

I kissed her on the forehead and held Jordan to do the same. "I don't know how long I can keep lifting you like that, Jordan!"

Driving home I said to him, "Jordan, it is nice of Grandpa to get a little fuddled with Grandma sick, don't you think? I think so." And it was still dry outside, but my eyes made it all glisten. That made the stoplights look like Christmas for me, but it wasn't.

When I got home from work the next day there was a message on the home phone. "Jenny, your mother's heart stopped there for a while. Good thing they had her in the hospital. She's on a machine now, a respirator. Wanted to let you know."

I called your cell. "Dad, are you at the hospital?" I asked.

"Yes, here with your mother."

"How is she?"

"Oh, fine. She's on the respirator."

"I'll come over. Have you eaten, Dad?"

"I had lunch."

"I'll bring you something."

So I bundled Jordan back into the car. We stopped for fast food on the way to the hospital. Then I had to wish Jordan was older. I packaged him into the backpack and carried the food bag and drink tray.

You welcomed us with a smile. "See, there she is."

Mom looked much the same as she had the night before, except that now another machine was at her bedside and there were more tubes and lines around.

"That's the respirator. Without that we'd have lost her, Jenny!" You sounded more amazed at the machinery than sad at her condition.

I nodded. "Have you talked with the doctor, Dad?"

"No, I got here after work. Well, I left work early, but. No. When she first arrived here, yesterday, I filled out paperwork, and that let them know what to do. To keep her alive."

"I see. So what is her prognosis now?"

You shook your head. "They're still working on it."

"OK. Well I'm going to go talk with a nurse, OK, Dad? Here's a burger and fries, and that one's a Coke for you. I'll be right back."

"All right." He began unpackaging his food.

It took a few minutes before I could track down Mom's nurse, Janice. "What is her prognosis?" I asked.

She shook her head. "I think it's a matter of time," she said. "We don't know. Sometimes patients like your mother come out for a time, really lucid like you'd want, but..." She shook her head again. "I wouldn't say that's probable. In fact it's very unlikely."

"Have you told my father?"

"You know your father," she said. "He has his own opinion

on this. You might be able to help prepare him."

"OK. Thank you." I pursed my lips hard.

So I returned to you and stood by the bedside where now Mom breathed with a machine—was made to breathe with a machine.

"What did the nurse have to say?" you asked.

"Just a minute, Dad."

I held Mom's hand. *Mom, thank you for...for giving me, from yourself. For loving me and Jordan. For...* And what made me cry then was, I'm sure, her love and losing her, but also the smallness of what came to mind about her, about my mom. Yes, she had fed me: the white bread of her time. Yes she had dressed me: always new, always laundered with a softener and machine dried with anti-static. Yes, she had taught me to use deodorant and tampons. But what else? I couldn't remember her laughing with me. She didn't inspire me to study, except as it reflected on her own social splendor. She didn't teach me to garden, even in her roses. She didn't teach me to cook, or love it. She didn't teach me to care for people; she fled from her social-work job! She taught me to value the biggest car, the most exclusive restaurant, the most expensive perfume, the greatest luxury. She taught me to use things, not love them. Becoming me had mostly been a process of rejecting her, or trying to.

So I cried. Jordan, little Jordan began to sob, too. We consoled each other.

"Why are you crying?" you asked. "Why are you crying? She's still here, she's still alive. And we'll keep her alive!"

I fought down my revulsion at your concept of being alive, and said as evenly as I could, "They don't expect her to wake up, Dad."

"They didn't expect her to live this long, either! Come on, where's your fighting spirit, hey?"

I didn't want to attack you for what you weren't equipped to see. "I'd better go, Dad. It'll be time to get Jordan to bed."

"All right, then. All right. We'll keep her going, Jenny, you can count on it."

"Goodnight, Dad."

"Here's your dinner."

"You can have it. Here, give me Jordan's."

I didn't kiss Mom's corpse, or lift Jordan to kiss it. I left.

I forced myself to focus on school. There was no funeral to go to. The hospital moved her body to another room, another floor. You gloated about your insurance, "a Cadillac!" A hearse, I thought.

School ended, and I hugged my happy students into the summer.

We—Jordan and I—visited the hospital in lieu of a cemetery. I imagined Bill saying she should have a granite headboard, Rest in Peace. Peace. The IV tubes fed and watered her, and the heart, however insensible, obliged with its clockwork contractions. Her body still rose and fell as the machine worked her lungs like a bellows. The monitor that showed her brain activity did not rise and fall at all.

Jordan walked, and then talked, "Mumu." But there was no one with whom to share the fun.

Eighteen

The rains did not come that spring, and summer stretched out like salt flats. The gray-brown inversion layer that was our usual summer sky lasted maybe a month longer than when I was a kid. I don't think my students minded or even noticed. It was their normal: the outside was a land of sweat and squinting; there were no plum blossoms, and the soccer fields were turning brown. Inside was cool, with soft-white lights, phosphorated colors, and a pantry and fridge full of sweet refreshment. Just normal. The human mind is flexible, and makes do. The body, however, goes the way of sickness, of Mom's. And the spirit, what does it do— evaporates in the heat? Withers like a flower tricked by climate change? Blooms into sterility in a land where the bees have been paved and poisoned away? I don't think the human spirit is like molds or lichens that can long thrive in rooms or caves or closets.

The fall brought an early and passing rain. The asters along the front of the apartment made an abortive bloom, and then curled up like a dead-man's fist. The liquid ambers that lined the street, each in its square yard of soil, skipped their brilliant red flames of autumn and went straight to crumpled brown. Even less frequently than rainfall, a Republican congressman backed off from climate-change denial, but then said that dealing with it would ruin the economy, so it couldn't be done; or an oil CEO acknowledged that climate change was real and catastrophic but asserted that it was government's responsibility, not free enterprise's; and then the CEO would contribute to deniers' political campaigns. Out in the Central Valley the farmers pumped groundwater that wasn't being replenished, except by the toxic waste from increased oil and gas drilling. But mostly stories of drought were drowned in the floods of partisan bickering and new economic reports that could both agitate and soothe in the same half hour.

And people didn't notice the asters. You certainly didn't.

"Nothing new under the sun." You chuckled. "The media are so easily led, Jenny. It's like *1984*; you read that, didn't you? Always a war, in Iraq or Iran or just in Congress. Always something to keep the people aroused but undirected. Much easier than, who was it? — "

"Orwell."

"Yes. Much easier than Orwell imagined. It's done us all right, though, Jenny. They're even talking about rolling back Dodd-Frank, you know that? Back to the good old days. Old days! It was just a couple years ago!"

"Mommy, sandwich pease?"

Jordan had grown into a bona-fide toddler, cute as a button, a playground puppy and a story-time page-turner. I made him a sandwich, peanut butter on whole wheat. Since we now visited you, alone, every Sunday, I had taken to keeping some decent food at your house. You didn't mind. I had even considered moving in with you. You wouldn't have minded that, either. But I thought better of it. I'd rather pay my own rent and have my own space. Jordan and I still lived in the apartment where I'd moved with Bill.

I held Jordan's sandwich. "What do you say?"

"Mommy's bootiful."

"That's right!" Somebody had to say it. I gave him the sandwich.

You insisted on keeping Mom *alive* as you called it, but even your visits had declined to once a week, Saturday mornings before any games were on TV. You'd had to move her to another facility, where an electric heart stimulus was added to the machinery that forced her body to mimic sleeping; and the bed was motorized and set to flex her legs and abdomen every hour, twelve hours a day; and the IV solution was now chock full of antibiotics to fight the infections in her chronic bedsores. I thought it was almost like a high-temperature cryonics lab, where people paid so they could pretend immortality. I thought you should charge the facility for using her corpse in a Frankenstein experiment. But I didn't say anything. You wanted it, and they made money off you, and snake oil's legal. A business doesn't have to offer actual benefit in order to prosper, does it?

I did not take Jordan to that pseudo-morgue. I didn't know what to tell him. Grandma's sleeping? Hardly. Grandma's dead? Ghoulish, then, keeping her there. I didn't want to give the boy nightmares. Or give them to me, either.

Bill was remarried, gone. He sent his check by automatic recurring deposit, and never asked after Jordan or any of us. I don't know if his little boy even knew what a daddy was.

I tried exchanging Christmas cards with Aunt Agnes, your brother Jake's wife, but it really didn't take. We did it just that first year, and that was it. We were different ages, in different places in the world and in our lives. Jim had been my generation, but that story was done. You didn't keep in touch with Uncle Jake anymore, either.

I called Joey's number once, but it was defunct. I looked for him on Facebook, too, but didn't find him.

Mom would have sent me to Tony, or arranged a meeting. You of course didn't think of such a thing. I wasn't interested anyway.

You continued to work full-time plus at your bank in the City. I don't know what you did, exactly, but you liked it. I expect you were useful in a lot of ways; you'd been around. You must have made them money, because they paid you plenty. Kept Mom's corpse alive, too.

Then you told me that your bank was being bought out by a yet larger one, for I don't remember how many billion dollars. "We should do well, your mother and I," you said.

"I don't think Mom will know the difference," I murmured.

Another year of school ended. I took Jordan to the park, and remembered a different park, where an old lady had bemoaned a child in pink not being allowed to get dirty. With the experience of teaching, and maybe of kayaking, I had felt the same. Now with the experience of more parenting I felt it even stronger. Jordan was old enough to get dirty.

And he was ready! He climbed the kiddy-slide ladder and slid haltingly in his jeans down to the wood chips. I pushed him on the swings, and he screamed with glee. He clambered through concrete tunnels, where he met another boy and they tunneled cautiously by each other. When they peeked out nearby portals they eyed each other, and Jordan smiled bashfully.

The other mom was watching nearby, and I introduced myself to her.

"I'm Jenny, Jordan's mom," I said.

"I'm Angie. My boy's Colin." She had long black hair, sort of half-brushed, and wore a summer blouse and shorts. She looked reassuringly normal.

We sat and watched the boys scrabble around each other.

"Do you come here often?" Angie asked.

"I plan to," I said. "I'm a teacher, so most of the year I can't, except on weekends."

"Lots of times we're the only ones here," she said. "It's nicer with other kids."

"Oh, yeah, much."

The boys romped.

"So you're off for the summer now?" she asked.

I nodded. "Like every job should allow."

"For parents at least. My husband never gets time off."

"What does he do?"

"Silicon Valley. He's in software."

"That can be pretty consuming, I guess?"

She laughed in acknowledgement. "He says seductive. But he's pretty good. He says we make enough, and beyond enough, it's family."

"That seems right to me. And do you get to be home?"

"I do. I worked in retail until Colin came along. Then we decided we'd take the pay cut."

"Is that hard?"

"We'd been living on just his salary all along. Mine was savings toward a down payment." She shrugged. "I think for me it would be harder to keep going to work."

"I like my work, but I understand what you're saying. I don't really have a choice."

Angie didn't say anything, so I finished the thought. "I'm divorced."

She nodded.

Colin toddled up to her, holding a hand out for her inspection.

"What's up?" she asked him.

"Hurt," he said matter-of-factly.

"Oh, you got a splinter." She picked it out. "That was an easy one, wasn't it!" Colin looked at his hand, showed his teeth, and turned back to the tunnels where Jordan was standing watching. They disappeared together.

"Can I give you my cell, Angie, and maybe we can arrange some playdates here?"

"I was thinking the same thing."

We exchanged numbers, and I felt a brightness that surprised me.

Apparently the sale of your bank didn't shape up quite as you had envisioned.

"The stocks are great!" you explained. "Never better! You know, that usually happens for the company being purchased. But it looks like I'm being phased out!"

"Well, Dad, that shouldn't be too bad. It's not like you need the job."

"But what will I do?" you asked.

"Take kayaking back up," I suggested.

You shook your head. "I have no interest in that anymore."

"Well think about it, Dad. What do you want to do?"

"Jenny, you know, you do something for so long, it's what you do. I like my work!"

"You could do things with Jordan now and then."

"Oh. I don't think I'm good at that sort of thing."

I resisted the thought *You pathetic, abhorrent old man!* "Well, you'll have to think about what you want to do."

"I'm sure I could get another job. Even if it was just locally here."

"I'd suppose so. Although it is a tough market."

"I could get a job."

But you kept working in the City through that August. I started back up at school. Jordan and I had met with Angie once or twice a week through the summer, and we continued to meet most Saturdays, when her husband Curtis usually joined us. He was a friendly, soft-spoken man, and I was glad to have Jordan exposed to him.

Going into the last weekend of September it rained. That's a typical time of year for a first fall storm after the string of dry months, but it kept us from our Saturday at the park. Instead Angie called to invite us to a puppet show in the City. We could carpool, she said.

"Oh, that would be crowded," I demurred.

"Nonsense!" she replied. "The kids'll go in back and we have three seats in front! It'll be all day, but we'll be home for dinner."

So we went. They picked Jordan and me up. I latched Jordan's car seat in the back next to Colin's and the adults piled into the front. It all made me feel young and happy.

The rain had let up, but the road was wet, and Curtis drove slowly.

"We won't have time for lunch if you're too slow, Curt," Angie said.

"Better safe than sorry," he replied, and added, "First rain of the year. That's when all the oil from five months of drippings is lifted and the roads are the slickest. There'll be time for lunch."

And there was.

The boys were best buds by then, and sat next to each other in booster seats, and it was all the right kind of warm. Then the puppet show was thoroughly fun, and afterwards the puppeteers gave sock puppets to all the kids and showed them how to make different voices—deep and dangerous, or jivey, or sweet. The boys and all the kids in the auditorium began role-playing with their socks.

On the way home Angie and I talked about puppet shows we could ask the kids to perform, enactments of stories we read to them.

"And they can make the puppets. Paper bags, crayons, maybe some colored paper and help cutting and gluing, some yarn for hair."

"We should do it soon."

"Yes, while the magic's alive in them!"

When they dropped us off I thanked them profusely.

"I'll want to do it again!" Angie said.

"Happy to!" added Curt.

"Say bye-bye!" we told our children.

The next day, October first, I checked my phone right after school. You had called, but not left a message. I dialed you.

"Jenny, they're going to disconnect your mother."

"What?" I asked, shocked.

"The insurance is out. With my job, you know."

"Dad, when did you find out? Why didn't you tell me?"

"Well, I was working with them, all of them, the home and the company and the insurance. But the payment was due today. The home offered to wait until you could get here. Before five, though."

"Just like that! OK, Dad, listen. I'll leave right away. I've got to pick up Jordan, and then we'll be right over. OK?"

"All right, Jenny. I'm over there already."

It's not like she's dying. She's been dead a long time. But still. And for Dad. OK, everything here can wait, it'll have to. Oh, I wanted to look at Jesse's story, I told her I would. She'll understand. OK, I've got to go.

I'd powered down the computer and the whiteboard. The papers on my desk needed to be recorded, but that would wait. I was supposed to meet with Lisa. I texted her—*Sorry, can't meet.*

I grabbed my purse and laptop and locked the door behind me.

"Heading out fast today?" said Craig, the custodian.

"Yeah, I've got to." I kept moving. I liked Craig, but didn't want to stop to explain.

I drove to Jordan's day-care, still under twelve minutes, even missing the two bad lights. *It's good everything's close.* I signed him out and opened the car to the back seat. *Damn, I didn't relatch his car seat after yesterday. That was fun, the puppet show...* I quickly restrapped the seat and buckled him into it, and then drove. It would be ten more minutes to the home.

"Do you remember Grandma, Jordan?"

"She's sick," he said.

"Yes. And usually when people are sick they get better. But Grandma was very sick, and she couldn't get better. So now she's dying."

He spread his arms and threw his head back, "Blaah." I saw him in the rearview. *Where did he get that?*

"But it's sad," I told him.

He looked at me skeptically. "What is it?"

"They go away and never come back."

"Like Daddy?"

"Not really. Daddy's was worse."

And that's when it happened. Life ended. Was it my distraction and hurry? Thinking about Bill, and how he'd left? Was it you, calling me to the death of a dead person whom I loved for no reason except that she was my mother, which only maybe is enough? Was it the roads, slick from oil and rain at last? Or the oil investments you pursued, that lengthened summer and made the autumn rain more slick? Was it the lowlife criminality of the man who hit me, fleeing the police with his contraband? Or the economy you created, that pushed the man to crime to make a living—an economy that made billionaires but not well-being?

All of those, I think. Ultimately an accident, set up by the greed and selfishness that doesn't look beyond today or self. So you do not have an heir for all your fortune, Dad. I am the end, and I despise you.

The report blamed me. The car seat was improperly fastened. I'm sure that's true. The seat flew. The seat you and your generation kept Mom from getting redesigned when you *knew* it was unsafe.

Fuck you, Dad. That's all I have to say. I want to say more. I want to forgive you. I want to thank you for being my father, for raising me.

But I can't. My son is dead. And you know who came to the funeral? His friend Colin, my friend. And you know what, *that* little boy is still alive, and he'll survive your car seats, but you've killed his world. When did you last hear a frog, Dad? When will he?

So there you are. And I know what you'll do about it. Absolutely nothing. You've been practicing ruin your whole life. Why would you change now.

At Roundfire we publish great stories. We lean towards the spiritual and thought-provoking. But whether it's literary or popular, a gentle tale or a pulsating thriller, the connecting theme in all Roundfire fiction titles is that once you pick them up you won't want to put them down.